"I WANT YOU."

Sarah said the words quite simply and knew it wouldn't be the first time Tyler had heard such a remark. And it might not be the last. Still, it didn't matter to Sarah. She repeated the words, tracing his lips with her finger. "I want you, here, now."

The record stopped and the room was suddenly silent. She caught Tyler's intake of breath. Then his lips descended on hers in a long, careful kiss, as though he meant for her to reconsider.

"And I've wanted you from the first moment I saw you at the Merriman flea market, smudged nose and all." Tyler held her and kissed her eyes, her nose, her forehead and then her lips again. "Sarah, beautiful Sarah. You don't even know what you do to me."

She didn't want to think of tomorrow, of his not being there for her. She only knew there was no history, no past, not even any future, just the present. And the present was making love to Tyler...and having him make love to her.

D0669191

ABOUT THE AUTHOR

The Eve Gladstone writing team first visited
Merriman County in *One Hot Summer*—and they
just couldn't leave! This fictitious area of Upper
New York State was a perfect blend of small-town
Americana and the down-home values the authors
nostalgically remember. And from their reluctance
to let go of this upstate paradise and the
unforgettable characters who resided there came
the sequel to *One Hot Summer*, *After All These
Years*. Eve Gladstone and Merriman county fans
will be delighted to know that the third book of
the trilogy—*Wouldn't It Be Lovely*—will be out in
November 1989.

HARLEQUIN SUPERROMANCE
297–ALL'S FAIR
324–ONE HOT SUMMER

HARLEQUIN INTRIGUE
23–A TASTE OF DECEPTION
49–CHECKPOINT
75–OPERATION S.N.A.R.E.

Don't miss any of our special offers. Write to us at the
following address for information on our newest releases.

Harlequin Reader Service
901 Fuhrmann Blvd., P.O. Box 1397, Buffalo, NY 14240
Canadian address: P.O. Box 603,
Fort Erie, Ont. L2A 5X3

Eve Gladstone

AFTER ALL THESE YEARS

Harlequin Books

TORONTO • NEW YORK • LONDON
AMSTERDAM • PARIS • SYDNEY • HAMBURG
STOCKHOLM • ATHENS • TOKYO • MILAN

Published March 1989

First printing January 1989

ISBN 0-373-70349-X

Copyright © 1989 by Joyce Gleit and Herma Werner. All rights reserved.
Except for use in any review, the reproduction or utilization
of this work in whole or in part in any form by any electronic,
mechanical or other means, now known or hereafter invented,
including xerography, photocopying and recording,
or in any information storage or retrieval system, is forbidden without
the permission of the publisher, Harlequin Enterprises Limited,
225 Duncan Mill Road, Don Mills, Ontario, Canada M3B 3K9.

All the characters in this book have no existence outside the
imagination of the author and have no relation whatsoever to
anyone bearing the same name or names. They are not even
distantly inspired by any individual known or unknown to the
author, and all incidents are pure invention.

® are Trademarks registered in the United States Patent and
Trademark Office and in other countries.

Printed in U.S.A.

For Amy Levinson,
Cynthia Bowman
and Terri Collin

CHAPTER ONE

THE TOWN THAT COULDN'T COUNT STRAIGHT
But Celebrated its Tricentennial Anyway

What do you do with 100,000 balloons, 1,000 four-color posters of the Hudson River Valley and a dozen fifty-foot yellow on blue nylon banners? What do you do when you've issued invitations to every fire department within a 500-mile radius to march in a mile-long parade the day of your tricentennial, only to discover you have the right day—a year early?

The town of Ramsey Falls in Merriman County, New York, had just that problem and decided to go through with its celebration anyway.

The article appeared in a back issue of *Country Living*, one of several Tyler Lassiter had brought down to the beach at Malibu that morning. He might have skipped the story about a town that couldn't count straight but for the names involved: Ramsey Falls and Merriman County, New York.

"Of all the places in the world to pop out at me now," he murmured.

"Sorry, Ty, didn't catch what you said." The words were spoken by the blonde roasting at his side on the beach blanket.

"Ramsey Falls, the town that couldn't count straight."

"I won't even bother asking what that means." She sat up, reached for a can of diet soda, downed some and stretched out again.

Ty turned over on his stomach, pressed the magazine flat into the sand and began to laugh.

His blond companion yawned her next question. "What's so funny?"

"A lot of red faces back where my ancestors came from."

"Australia?"

"New York."

"I thought you were from Australia."

"I am, but my venerable ancestors are from Merriman County, and that's upstate New York."

"Where there are a lot of red faces."

"Right," said Tyler. "It seems that Merriman County records are a mess. Because of it, a little town called Ramsey Falls, which is close to the place my forebears came from, mounted its tricentennial celebration a year early."

"What difference does a year make?"

"Precisely what the citizens of Ramsey Falls decided. They celebrated a year early."

"More power to them," said his companion as she reached for the number fifteen suntan oil. "A little extra on my back, please."

Tyler obliged, tossing the magazine aside. His mind, however, wasn't on square meters of tanned, curving flesh, it was on Ramsey Falls and its surrounding countryside.

If Ramsey Falls had fallen victim to the county's bad record keeping, then so would the town of Merriman, and that was where his ancestor Emma Crewes lived around the time of the Civil War. It was from the family estate called Riveredge on the outskirts of Merriman that she set forth on an odyssey that would end in Australia.

He stopped in mid-rub to glance once again at the magazine. He examined the accompanying photograph. Perched decorously on a pile of cardboard files, in a room whose state of dishevelment aptly illustrated the story, was a pretty woman wearing horn-rimmed glasses.

The caption informed Tyler that Sarah Crewes had discovered the mistake concerning the Ramsey Falls tricentennial. How they must have loved Miss Sarah for that one. Light brown hair with golden highlights. He couldn't tell the color of her eyes, but if her skin was anything like the photograph, it was white as porcelain, an inheritance from her Dutch ancestors, no doubt. Long neck, trim figure, good legs. The Crewes line had evidently weathered the centuries quite well.

He wondered what else Miss Sarah's poking around had led her to. The truth about Riveredge, possibly. The truth as Ty Lassiter knew it, anyway.

She had a certain patrician look about her, an air of self-possession, and yet there was a tiny smile on her lips telling the world that what she had done was a gas. Cousin Sarah. It might be interesting to meet the progeny of the Crewes line, after all.

"Hey," said the blonde, "come on, concentrate, Ty, concentrate. The left side, please."

"The left side, love, if that's what you want." Ty put the magazine down, poured some more of the pungent oil on his hands and set obediently to work. Sarah Crewes, he reflected as he eased his palm down the long line of smooth flesh, would be related to Wave Crewes, the current occupant of that old gray mansion high above the Hudson River.

"Mmm, good," said the blonde.

Tyler didn't hear her, however. He was busy reliving his one and only visit to Merriman County, made on his first trip to the States. He had rented a car and driven out to the colonial mansion that was Riveredge, its noble lines still visible despite its weather-beaten, decrepit air.

He had stood on the road opposite, an architect with an ancient dream, mentally stripping the clapboard and repainting it, repairing gutters and the wood-shingled roof and cutting away damp rot.

Given half a chance inside the old mansion, he'd tear though years of wallpaper and paint to discover the original colors. Maybe also come upon the secret of Riveredge under the floorboards or behind the fireplace, a letter or journal that told the truth about the past and set everything straight. Then, when a white-haired gentleman had stepped out of the house and looked across the road at him, Tyler had turned on his heels and left. He had no proof, only hearsay a century old.

He knew the history of the area well enough. It had been fed to him along with his daily ration of oatmeal in the Australian outback. The way Merriman history read it, Tyler Lassiter was related to Sarah Crewes and just about everybody else in Merriman, but in this case history was wrong.

No matter who held the keys to Riveredge, it belonged rightfully to the clan descended on his mother's side, of which he was the last and only representative, and no Crewes blood was mixed in with his. And why, he thought, should any of it matter when more than a hundred years stood between him and the event?

"Ty, I said rub, don't pummel."

"Sorry, love, got carried away."

"I can think of something more interesting to carry us away," she said, reaching back and lightly touching his hand.

"Could you now," he replied a little absentmindedly. No indeed, the old roots established in Merriman County had been dug up, transplanted to Australia and taken hold there, so why think about what had grown in their stead?

"Ty!"

"Right. You've convinced me I'm absolutely no good at the job. I'm resigning and we'll discuss the matter of payment due at a later date." He handed her the bottle of suntan oil just as she turned toward him, her mouth open and her eyes smiling an invitation. "I'm afraid you'll have to finish the job yourself," he said. "I'm booking a flight for the east coast this afternoon."

"OH, SARAH, Tyler Lassiter was looking for you."

Sarah Crews leaned across the reception desk in the lobby of Merriman's town hall and said, "Lovely, and just who is Tyler Lassiter?"

The receptionist promptly handed her a business card. "I was hoping you'd tell me. I never saw a better-looking man. Tall, rugged, tanned, with this absolutely creamy accent, British or something."

"Much to recommend him then." Sarah dug a pair of glasses out of her bag and put them on, but she gleaned little from the card except that Tyler Lassiter seemed to be "Associated" and had offices in Beverly Hills, California. "Any other calls?" she inquired, tucking the card into her bag.

The receptionist made a face, wrinkling her small nose in the process. "The usual sort." She lifted some sheets from a message pad and held them out. "All will-you-call-backs. Incidentally, Mr. Lassiter wanted to know if anyone could look through the files in the basement without permission. I told him you were the archivist in charge. He seemed a little surprised, and when I explained the procedure about filling out forms, etcetera, etcetera, he turned and left."

"Okay, let's not worry about him." Sarah, glancing through her messages, scarcely heard Gert's recital. The unfiled records overflowing the basement of the town hall, as well as several other basements around Merriman, were out of bounds to anyone but Sarah and her part-time assistant. Contemporary records in shiny metal cabinets on the first floor of the town hall were available to anyone filling out proper forms. It was all cut and dried. She had no doubt Mr. Lassiter was part of that long line of applicants wanting to dig for information on ancient land grants. He needed no special treatment.

"Is Alec in by any chance?" she asked.

"Came in just a while ago."

"Thanks, see you later." Sarah walked quickly through the old walnut-paneled lobby with its huge glass chandelier, brightly lit against a gray November day. She headed toward the rear of the building and the town supervisor's office, noting how unusually quiet it was for a Friday morning. Not all of Merriman's business was conducted in the town hall, however. With the enormous growth in the county, several other buildings had been taken over for administration, and only the supervisor's offices, as well as the town council meeting room, still occupied the venerable hall.

The door to Alec Schermmerhorn's office was open, but because she heard voices issuing from it, Sarah sat down on one of the antique wooden benches in his secretary's office to wait her turn. The evening before she'd had a long talk with her cousin Victor Bosworth and wanted to report the outcome to Alec. She had good news and was feeling rather smug when a man's voice burst angrily through the supervisor's open door.

"Alec, they should have hired someone as county archivist from out of state, someone without a vested interest in what's going on around here. Sarah's a Crewes. All she has to do is find something not to her or Victor's liking and pffft, out the window with it, down the drain, into the fire. No one need ever know."

Sarah got quickly to her feet and was about to leave when common sense stopped her. No, might as well march in and defend herself. She'd been aware of resentment in town when she was hired but figured it would be short-lived and that she'd ultimately prove herself to have been the right choice for Merriman County archivist.

"You're talking nonsense, Phil," Alec Schermmerhorn said. "Sarah's as honest as the day is long. What do you think she's going to find that isn't common knowledge? There isn't a square inch of Merriman whose ownership isn't known by people around here."

"And that's the way we want to keep it. We don't need someone with all that power to search and destroy if it suits her."

"Power? Search and destroy? It isn't a government operation against a foreign invader, it's one archivist with a part-time assistant straightening out a century's mess. Besides, as you well know, it's the law," Alec went on patiently. "The governor has signed legislation stating that county records must be cleared up within the next five years. And damn it, from the looks of things, Merriman's problems could stretch out a decade. The good citizens have voted the budget and the job and that's that."

"I don't mind an archivist, Alec. I mind someone nosing around with an interest in the land hereabouts."

Sarah realized who was in Alec's office. Phil Nevins, who owned the stationery store on Main Street. Sarah shook her head slowly. If she dug deep enough, she'd undoubtedly share some kind of personal history with the Nevins clan, as she did with the Schermmerhorns and just about every other old family in the county.

"What are you talking about, Phil?"

Phil's tone was incredulous. "Man, use your imagination. That big monstrosity Wave Crewes owns on the river, for instance."

"You mean Riveredge? Bit of a dump by now, isn't it?"

"Sarah's his niece, she'll come into it one day. Expensive bit of real estate, Alec."

"I don't like you when you go on like this, Phil."

"What if she finds out that Riveredge wasn't Crewes property after all?"

"You know something I don't know?"

"Just speculating, just giving you an example, that's all. Suppose it belongs to somebody else, me or you or your old Aunt Fanny. There's some story loose about that from way back. Listen, Alec, I'm on the town council. They're talking. They're saying there's collusion between you and Sarah. Don't give me that nonsense about her knowing the files better than anybody and that she's a trained archivist."

Sarah heard the sound of a chair scraping back just as she was about to storm into Alec's office to defend herself. No use standing on ceremony. "Phil," Alec replied tautly, "I could punch you out for those words. Suppose you leave now and let me get back to work."

"Only passing on rumor," Phil said. "You don't want to act on it, you'll find yourself shut out of the next election." He came storming out of Alec's office—and found his path blocked by Sarah.

"Nice morning, isn't it, Phil?"

He blanched, then turned red. "Feels like rain, Sarah."

"Is there something you'd like to tell me, Phil? Right to my face?"

He scowled and Sarah curtsied and made room for him to pass. When she walked into the town supervisor's office, she found Alec scowling, as well. He was a small, heavy-set, conservatively dressed man with a fringe of black hair underlining a shiny bald head. "Shouldn't keep your door open like that," she said at once. "All sorts of odd things float out."

"Secretary hasn't come in yet," he mumbled. He rubbed his hand over his bald spot, a habit he used whenever he wanted to score an important point. "Phil's an ass. You heard it all, I suppose."

She smiled. "Shamelessly. I warned you there'd be a backlash when you hired me."

"You're the right one for the job, Sarah."

"He threatened you with an election coming up."

Alec gestured her to a chair. "I don't threaten easily, Sarah. Anyway, you know I'm thinking of retiring."

"I don't want to hear about you retiring, distant, distant, *distant* cousin Alec. And I certainly don't threaten easily. What I'm truly afraid of is the records will reveal Phil's a long lost uncle or something. But that isn't what I came about."

"Whatever it is, Sarah, you and that job belong together like—"

She smiled. "Ham and cheese?"

"On rye with mustard."

"With potato chips and several slices of pickle on the side."

"What did you want to talk about? Feed me some good news to get rid of the sour taste in my mouth left by one Phil Nevins."

"This should do it," Sarah said with a smile. She pulled her chair close to the desk. "Cousin Victor has agreed to my idea and it won't cost the town, or Phil Nevins, a cent."

"Music to my ears. Go on."

In spite of Alec's assurances, when Sarah emerged from the town supervisor's office a quarter of an hour later, she was still smarting over Phil Nevins's words. She was given the job of county archivist because she was the best qualified. The trouble was, she had accepted it for another reason entirely, far more personal than anyone imagined. It had nothing to do with original land grants or family inheritances or who owned Riveredge. It had to do with love and a married man and what might have happened if she had stayed with New York Banking in Manhattan.

As simple as that. Sarah, who was a realist and often thought she had not an ounce of romance in her, left her job because she knew it was wrong to fall in love that way. Escape—and fast—was her prescription, and it was filled by the Merriman County proposal.

The job of archivist was offered to her because she was well qualified for it, having a degree in library science and another in American history. In early summer she had been working on a history of the Crewes family in and around Merriman County when she came across a sensational discovery. Ramsey Falls, a neighboring town in the throes of celebrating its tricentennial, was actually a year younger than assumed. Ramsey Falls became the town that couldn't count straight, but went ahead with the celebration anyway.

It was Sarah who sparked the whole debate about the mess the county records were in. And it was Sarah who had record-keeping experience from her job down state at New York Banking.

Her cousin Victor Bosworth, the wealthy owner of Bosworth Stud and benefactor of many charitable causes in the area, was so pleased with Sarah's return to Merriman that he offered her a pretty little house on his estate, once the blacksmith's shop, with a view of the Hudson River.

The medicine was good; it tasted of autumn harvests and snow in the air and being among people she loved, doing work that intrigued her daily more and more.

The Merriman archives were a monumental mess because the county, which had grown for three centuries in an orderly manner, changed after the Second World War when there was a sudden influx of veterans and their growing families moving up from the city. Old documents and ledgers were placed in cardboard boxes when the files grew too crowded. They were tucked away somewhere in the basement of the county offices, then the jail, and at last overflowed the basement of an old motel purchased by the county for office space. The motel's swimming pool eventually developed a crack and water flooded the corridors and attached basement *and* the cardboard boxes.

For three centuries, memories and friendships were the best sort of filing system. As the population of Merriman grew, so did the files. Impatient clerks sorting through them for documents eased the records further into disarray, and by the time the county supervisor decided something needed to be done, several lawsuits were already in motion that couldn't be solved until Sarah made some progress. Finding information in a hurry was close to impossible and, in any event, extremely costly. An archivist with a computer was a cheap way to solve the problem and a bill was introduced and passed the next time the county board met.

Well, Sarah thought as she headed across the town hall lobby toward the door that led into the basement, Phil Nevins be damned. He was an old gossip and probably had a cousin from out of state he wanted for the job.

The history of the town hall was written from the basement up, and the years peeled away as Sarah descended pine stairs built in the nineteenth century. These yielded to a warren of storage rooms jerry-built sometime in the late eighteenth century into a huge old space defined by enormous stone walls dating back three hundred years. Once she left behind the piney scent of the stairs, she took in the musty odor of old paper, damp and dust.

Sarah's crowded office was located at the front of the basement with a couple of deepset windows just above ground level, where her only view was of a planting of juniper bushes.

"Hi." Her assistant, Reg Casedonte, was sitting at the computer terminal, a huge old ledger covering the table on his right. He had been hired the week before when room was found in the budget for a part-time assistant on a temporary basis. "I just hung up on Mr. Lassiter. He said he'd call back."

"Say what he wanted?"

Reg shook his head no.

"How's the work getting on?" Sarah slipped out of her jacket and sat down at her desk.

A bright, dependable youth, Reg was in his last year at Pack College, where he was enrolled in the social studies program. "Pages are stuck together between M and O," he said.

"Not to worry. I just spoke about the problem to my cousin Victor Bosworth, and our smart town supervisor said it was a good idea. Victor's agreed to be the unofficial consultant on matters such as stuck-together pages. He collects antique manuscripts and has a conservator friend in New York City who'll show us what methods to use. We may have to set up some kind of workroom later on to unstick the pages and preserve them. Anyway, it's all cost-free so certain old town biddies won't have anything to say about it."

"Town biddies?"

"Never mind, Reg. It'll all be straightened out."

"Should I go on entering the stuff?"

"Let's get everything on disk that we can out of each ledger, while we can," Sarah said. "When I have a couple of ledgers entered, I'll call in our unofficial consultant so he'll have plenty to work with. You're making cross-references, aren't you?"

"Right. So far I haven't found any Casedontes, but then my great-grandfather moved here in 1873. Plenty of Creweses, though.

"Great," said Sarah.

"Most interesting," he told Sarah in a puckish voice, continuing to enter information into the program. "Births, year 1809. All the girls seem to be named Sarah or Emma or Amy, and all the boys Ebediah or Waldo or Ezekiel,"

Sarah smiled and reached for her telephone. "I'm descended from a long line of Sarahs. My middle name, incidentally, is Emma."

"Sarah Emma Amy. I hope you have a brother named Ebediah Waldo Ezikiel."

"Only child," Sarah sighed, while dialing the first of her phone messages. "If I had a brother, I wouldn't care if he was named Waldo."

"Being related to everybody in Merriman County isn't bad," Reg said.

"Not everybody, just those who stuck around from the very beginning." The phone was picked up at the other end. "Hello, Mrs. Waldo—I mean Mrs. Walters—Sarah Crewes returning your call." She wasn't related to Mrs. Walters at all, Sarah reflected, as the woman asked her an impossible question for which she had no ready answer. Because she had been given the title of administrator of county records, every citizen in the county thought she now held the secret of their ancestry.

She hung up the receiver and pulled her glasses out of her bag once more. With them came Mr. Lassiter's card. She remembered Gert's description of him. Best-looking man she'd ever seen. Creamy British accent or something. She gazed at the card for a moment, then deposited it in her wastebasket.

When she left at the end of the day, Mr. Lassiter had not called back, nor had Sarah thought more about him.

SATURDAY MORNING at the weekly Merriman Mall Outdoor Antiques Flea Market found Sarah Crewes manning a double-length card table filled with antiques and collectibles.

The sky was bright blue, the autumn air was scented with burning leaves and the mould of centuries, and a crisp wind tossed her soft light brown hair around her face. She wore jeans and a bulky woolen sweater over a turtleneck blouse, which kept the cold at bay.

For sale upon a thick white tablecloth were various items she had collected on foraging trips over the summer and early fall: an assortment of small antiques and collectibles. A shaving mirror, daguerreotypes in fold-up leather frames, a footstool and wooden bookends of carved bears with tiny obsidian eyes. Art deco jewelry and antique irons, pottery and toothpick holders, old camera equipment and advertising cards—a jumble, in other words, of other people's castoffs. Business had been as brisk as the weather, and by the time ten o'clock rolled around, Sarah had returned twice to her borrowed small panel truck to haul out more goods for sale.

There was a lull in the morning traffic at about eleven o'clock. It was always that way, she had noted more than once. Crowds gathered around her stand as though at a fire sale while she rushed to and fro, wrapping, answering questions and making change. Or there was no one, as now. She took advantage of the quiet by pulling out a thermos of coffee and a box of doughnuts.

"Have some?" she asked the dealer whose stand was at her right.

"Thanks, brought a gallon of my own along."

"A doughnut at least," Sarah said, going over to the stand and offering up the box. That was when she spotted the tiny Confederate soldier, musket at the ready, in the midst of an arrangement of toys.

"How much?" she asked, pointing to the soldier.

"This?" A shrug. "Came with a carton of goodies I found in a house auction upstate. Wonderful stuff. The owner had no real idea of the value. Take a close look."

Sarah picked up the soldier and found to her delight that it was hand-carved of wood, with details that were lovingly painted, right down to the blue of his eyes. The carving was in perfect condition, as though created by a grown up, presented to a child and then put away on a shelf never to be played with again. "Nice," she said. "How much?"

"On this?" The dealer shook her head. "I've got forty on it. Dealer's price twenty percent off."

"Mmm," said Sarah, taking another bite of the doughnut and another swig of coffee. She had been thinking of starting a collection of *something*, she wasn't certain what, for Seth Whiting, Jemma Gardner's seven-year-old son. Of course, at the moment he was into dinosaurs, karate and baseball in varying degrees of interest. Sarah liked to have a focal point for her energy, and because she dearly loved young Seth, she wanted to form a collection for him of some kind that would be added to at birthdays and Christmas.

Antique soldiers, she thought, would do perfectly. "That's a bit much, thirty-two dollars," she said at last.

"Hey, give me a break. That soldier is hand-carved, very old, absolutely one of a kind, a steal at thirty-two."

"It's for a little kid."

"I've a cold cold heart, Sarah. I'm not moved at all by puppy dogs or little kids or even fluffy kittens. Tell you what, though. I've been admiring that art deco pin you have, the one with the palm tree on it. How about an even swap?"

"Hmm," said Sarah, picking up the pin. Of marcasite and enamel, it was worth considerably more than thirty-two dollars. But then so was an old, hand-carved toy when you got down to it. She gazed at the pin, at the toy once again, at the pin, and at last nodded in agreement. After all, the pin was part of a collection of art deco jewelry she had purchased in early summer, which had netted her a tidy profit.

"Deal?" said her neighbor.

"Sure, deal. I'm a sucker for puppy dogs, little kids and fluffy kittens." Sarah surrendered the pin and the exchange was duly made.

"Good thing you've got that job keeping the county records, Sarah. You'll never make a living giving away the proceeds from your antiques business."

"Good thing," said Sarah, agreeing readily. "The job is work," she added, "and flea markets are sheer fun." She placed the Confederate soldier on the edge of her table where she could admire it. Jemma had talked about coming by that afternoon with Seth and her new husband, Hunt Gardner. They were in the process of purchasing an old stone house at the edge of Ramsey Falls and were planning an authentic restoration. Hunt, who had spent so many years as a near nomad, had already taken on American history with a vengeance and restoration with a passion. Sarah had even put aside some old tools and kitchen utensils for them: a maul and froe, a dipper and pie crimper.

She smiled at the thought of the Gardners. Imagine Jemma finding so exotic a specimen as Hunt Gardner in tiny Ramsey Falls. And darling Jemma deserved every wonderful inch of him. Divorced with a young son to care for and a full-time job running Whiting Printing and the Ramsey Falls shopping guide, Jemma hadn't been looking for more complications in her life. Hunt had come into town and it was no contest. Something like eyes catching across an uncrowded print shop, as Jemma put it.

Sarah smiled again, then sighed. Five years in New York City and the last and final man she had fished up with was married. She had escaped almost at once. As for the town of Merriman, if she remained buried beneath documents in a basement, the only exotica she'd produce would be bookworms. And as far as flea markets were concerned, windblown hair, a penchant for bargaining and the inevitable smudges of dirt on her nose and chin should discourage even the most hearty suitors.

Besides, she thought, what was she going on about? Marriage was the farthest thing from her mind. Wasn't it? She was independent, she had a past history of falling in love with unsuitable men, and she had no idea why. Still, when the right man presented himself, she hoped she'd know it. But would she? She seemed to go out of her way to choose men who would disappear in a crunch. They tended to be resolute bachelors, rootless types or else married liars. She was beginning to wonder about herself. Did she purposely select a man who'd never ask a commitment from her?

No, she really wanted a relationship that was strong and loving. Sarah reached for her thermos of coffee and her cup. Yes indeed, if romance with a suitable man presented itself, she promised herself she wouldn't be caught napping. She tipped the thermos over but there was no coffee left, and she had no idea when she had consumed the last bit.

"How much?"

She looked up to confront a pair of clear, questioning hazel eyes. "Excuse me?"

"How much?" He was a tall, imposing, sandy-haired man in his mid-thirties, and what he was referring to was the Confederate soldier, which he had picked up. He was wearing jeans, a corduroy jacket and dark turtleneck shirt. His hair was wind tossed, his nose strong and straight, and he had an equally strong, decidedly stubborn chin, softened only by a deep cleft.

"Oh, it's not for sale. Sorry." She smiled apologetically and held out her hand for it.

"I'm puzzled," he said. "The objects on the table *are* for sale, or have we stumbled into a museum display?"

"Both, I suppose." She continued to smile and hold out her hand. He refused to yield the soldier, however, and for a moment his gaze locked purposefully with hers. But there was a faint change in his expression, as though he recognized her and wasn't happy about it. "As a matter of fact," she said, frowning in confusion, "it's the only object *not* for sale."

"I've a famous aversion to the word *not*."

"Okay, I can understand that," Sarah said. "How about this piece *ain't* for sale?"

He laughed but still didn't yield the toy. For a reason Sarah couldn't explain, a slight frisson jumped along her skin. She cursed her pale complexion, which showed every kind of emotion, and knew that a warm flush had risen to her cheeks.

He twisted the figure around and at last discovered a tiny label. "Forty dollars, it says here."

"No," she improvised quickly, "I assure you it's not for sale. I just sold it, I'm holding it to be picked up." She stopped, aware of complications within complications. For the first time she noticed his companion, a very tall, slender and beautiful woman with eyes of a soft violet blue, who seemed faintly familiar.

"Darling, you don't need it," the woman said, deftly removing it from his hand and returning it to Sarah. "He's fixed on the Civil War, you see."

"I'm sorry," Sarah told her, "but this is for a certain little boy who's equally interested in the Civil War, or should soon be, and we couldn't possibly deprive him of it, could we?"

"The Civil War? When he grows up he can have a war all his own, I'm sure," the man said. "Meanwhile, perhaps he ought to be left in all innocence of such things." His accent was unusual, British it seemed, but not quite.

"You have a point of sorts," Sarah conceded, "but the toy is still not for sale. However," she added, "I have an absolutely wonderful mint-condition Yankee sergeant I'd be willing to part with. But not here, at home." She stopped, wondering why her remark sounded so invitational. And anyway, by rights the sergeant should also go to Seth.

"My heart is with the Confederates."

Australian, she thought. Someone who was born in Australia and educated in England. "I'm sorry," she said, "but we're discussing impossibilities."

"Maybe he'd sell it to me at a profit."

"I'd hate to see a seven-year-old engaged in an act of commerce."

The beautiful woman shook her head. "Ty, what in the world's gotten into you? Let's go. We have an appointment, or have you forgotten?"

"Do you have a card?" he asked, still concentrating on Sarah, still watching her closely, as though there were something unsaid between them.

"Yes, yes I do." She picked one from a pile on the table and handed it to him. He began reading the contents out loud, his eyes twinkling as he pronounced each word carefully.

Sarah cursed herself for what had seemed a good idea at the time she ordered the card. And Jemma, who owned Whiting Printing in Ramsey Falls and printed it for her, had agreed.

"Crewes' Collectibles. Antiques, olde and newe." He tucked the card into his breast pocket. "Crewes. That's an important name around here, isn't it?"

"Important?" She was genuinely puzzled. "It's quite old, but I can't say it's important."

He pointed to the soldier. "See if you can buy this little fellow back for me. How about a hundred dollars?"

She was aware of being temporarily dazzled by the clear, cold yet interested look in his eyes, by the cleft in his chin and even by his offer of a hundred dollars, which was extravagant although not entirely out of line. Still, she managed a few words. "I'm sorry, but I really don't think—"

"Ty," said his companion, "she doesn't want to sell it. I've never known you to be so stubborn. Come along."

"Call me," he said to Sarah, "when you're ready to sell. I'm staying at the Merriman Arms." He removed a card from his wallet and handed it to her, then took his companion's arm and they walked quickly away.

Sarah put on her glasses and stared at the card. "Tyler Lassiter. Associated." Offices in Beverly Hills, California. "But I'm Sarah Crewes she called, the wind whipping the words back at her. Damn, he *knew* she was Sarah Crewes.

It was printed on her card in tiny letters under Crewes' Collectibles.

She was suddenly aware of the way she looked, her bulky sweater, her hair in wind-invented knots, the probability of smudges on her pale skin where they didn't belong and undoubtedly stood out a mile. She stared after Lassiter and his companion, noting that the crowd at the flea market parted spontaneously as they headed toward the exit. She angrily picked up the Confederate soldier and dropped the toy into her handbag. Then she pulled it out to stare curiously at it again. Their conversation for some odd reason hadn't been about the toy at all. But if not the toy, then what? And she had sensed a vague hostility that called to mind the conversation she had overheard the day before in the town supervisor's office.

"He wanted the Confederate soldier," the dealer who sold it to her said, coming over to Sarah's table. "That's Tyler Lassiter. Do you know who that was with him?"

"Should I?" Sarah looked down the aisle but they were already out of sight.

"Merriman's own movie star, Maggie Roman. She's the one who redid old Kimberly House. Doesn't she look gorgeous? I mean for somebody her age?"

Sarah realized why the woman had looked familiar. "Maggie Roman, of course. Now why didn't I recognize her?"

"Because they always look different off-screen," the dealer said with a knowing shake of her head. "Older, too. They photograph them through cheesecloth. Do you think there's something between them? I mean Tyler Lassiter and Maggie Roman? She's ages older."

"Who," asked Sarah on a long drawn in breath, "is Tyler Lassiter and how come you know about him?"

"He's an architect for one. Don't you know anything, Sarah?"

"Blame it on my job," she said, aware of something having gotten away from her. "I hardly even know what time of day it is, never mind who Tyler Lassiter might be." There was a time, and not so long ago, when she was a fount of information about the goings-on in her corner of Merriman County.

"He's sort of a well-known architect, but he's the great-great-great-whatever-grandson of Emma Crewes, the one who moved to Australia after the Civil War. Sarah, considering you're knee-deep in Merriman history, you're pretty dense. Listen, as a matter of fact, he was at my table, then he looked over at yours, saw you and saw the soldier. I thought he knew you for a minute."

"No," said Sarah. "Never saw him before in my life."

"Damn, I knew I shouldn't have given that soldier up."

"Emma Crewes." Sarah picked up the Confederate soldier and stared at the tiny figure. She touched the delicately carved musket, then ran her finger along his smooth face, the paint as fresh as the day it was applied.

Emma Crewes. Emma Crewes who lived at Riveredge during the Civil War, Emma who married and moved to Australia. Faraway, long-ago ancestor Emma. And if he were indeed a descendant of Emma, Sarah realized, feeling a shade disappointed, then that made them cousins, she and Tyler Lassiter, however distantly removed.

CHAPTER TWO

"UNCLE WAVE?"

Loaded with groceries, Sarah pushed the door wide and stepped into the darkened entry hall of Riveredge. She kicked the door shut with her heel but not in time to prevent a gust of chill autumn wind from chasing in after her. She shivered. The old mansion was always damp and ill-heated, but this was the first year Waverly Crewes hadn't stockpiled wood by culling fallen trees in the forest, hauling them back and chopping them himself.

She'd have to see about ordering a cord or two for him; simply order it and have it delivered, and that would be that. Most of Riveredge's twenty-five rooms were unused and kept shut in winter, and those left open were heated by oil, supplemented by an efficient wood-burning stove in the library. She'd check with her cousin Victor about exactly how much to order for the winter.

"Uncle Wave? It's Sarah," she called. "Closed up my stand at the flea market early to do your shopping for you." In the kitchen, she decided, which was the warmest room in the house. She hoisted the heavy bags and headed toward the back.

"He's asleep."

The unexpected figure that stepped out into the darkened hall drew a startled cry from Sarah. "Wh-who are you?"

"It's all right, he *is* asleep."

Sarah extricated a hand from the heavy bundles she was carrying and switched on the hall lamp, but she already knew who her uncle's visitor was. A soft light threw the gloomy old hall into a relief of chiaroscuro and confirmed her guess. "You frightened me," she said to Tyler Lassiter.

"I'm sorry, that's the last thing I'd want to do."

"I—I didn't know you knew my uncle." She found herself stammering, wondering why he had the ability to disconcert her so. One of the paper bags began to slip from her grasp.

"Wait a minute," he said, springing into action. "Looks as if you're about to lose your dinner." He immediately relieved her of the bags and deposited them on the hall table. Only now did Sarah understand the significance of the rather expensive car she had spotted in the driveway. Or didn't understand the significance at all, except that it apparently belonged to Tyler Lassiter.

"If my uncle's asleep, then what are you doing here?"

"Obviously rescuing damsels in distress. Have you changed your mind?"

"About what?"

"About our discussion this morning at the flea market," he said. "Hard to believe you've forgotten already."

"I haven't forgotten anything," Sarah told him, and when he gave her a crooked grin, added, "and you still haven't told me why you're here."

"Just leaving. Your young friend willing to part with the statue?"

"It's not a statue, it's a toy, and no, it's safe in his hands."

"Sarah, that you?" It was her great-uncle calling her from the kitchen.

"He isn't asleep, after all," she remarked testily, aware of her belligerence and uncertain why she had adopted such a tone. "Right with you, Uncle Wave."

"Odd," Ty said, "I had the feeling that he'd snoozed off in the middle of a sentence."

"My great-uncle is seventy-five," she said. "That isn't his ticket to senility. No doubt you were boring the pants off him. It's his way of telling you to go home."

"Ah, I understand, you *are* your great-uncle's keeper."

"I'm not, and now if you'll excuse me..." She had to brush past him to reach for the grocery bags.

"Allow me," he said.

For a moment they remained looking at each other, the bags still on the table between them. Once again Sarah was aware of the man wanting to say something, yet perhaps deciding it wasn't the time.

"You wanted to see me," she said at last, "at my office."

"Sarah, haven't had my tea yet." Her great-uncle sounded querulous as usual. She'd have to make up her mind and soon about hiring someone full-time for him whether he liked it or not.

"Co-oming."

"Let me help you," Tyler said, reaching for the heavy bags.

"I can handle them, thank you." Sarah scooped the packages into her arms.

"Well," Ty said, "better serve him his tea. Tell you what. I'll stop by tomorrow morning, at about eleven. We'll talk then."

"I'll be busy at eleven."

"Make it anytime you like."

"Oh," she said impatiently, "then eleven will have to do. I won't be here, though. I don't live at Riveredge."

He tapped his jacket pocket. "At the address on your card, cousin Sarah." He laid some emphasis on the word *cousin* and on that note turned and went over to the hall door.

Without thinking about it, Sarah took in the set of his broad shoulders, his lanky, easy walk, then said spontaneously, "It's not about the soldier at all, is it."

He gave her an enigmatic smile. "Ah, but I think history has everything to do with it."

"Sarah, who's that with you? Lassiter?"

"No." She said the word sharply, aware of Ty Lassiter having heard her as he opened the door. "He just left." The hard autumn wind blew into the hallway once more, and once more Sarah shivered, as though in with it came all manner of difficulties. The door closed and he was gone. She remained very still for a moment, expecting the door to open again. When it didn't, she headed back to the kitchen.

She found Waverly Crewes seated in the big rocking chair near the fireplace, pretending to be asleep, his thin, fine mouth open, a series of delicate snores issuing forth. He wore the heavy wool sweater she had knit for him. A fat, lazy ginger cat on his lap gave her scarcely a glance. The wood-burning stove was going full blast, and the fire in the fireplace hadn't died down. The kitchen was very warm and comfortable and smelled as always of smoke and charcoal. She saw two glasses and a bottle of cognac and surmised that Wave had served it to Tyler Lassiter.

Sarah at once filled the teakettle and set it on the iron stove top. Some water spilled over and a gentle sizzle steamed up, then burned off. She worked quickly and efficiently at stockpiling the glass-fronted walnut cabinets, including tinned food for the cat. It was all accomplished very quietly until she set the table for tea, which she finished with bravado and clatter.

"Hi, Uncle Wave," she announced, "come along, let's have tea. I found scones in Merriman and they look outrageously tasty."

The cat jumped off her uncle's lap and dashed out of the room.

"It's about time." Wave Crewes got slowly to his feet and came over to the table. A tall, straight man who was excessively thin, he had eyes of an uncommon shade of blue bordering on azure, the Crewes eyes, echoed in Sarah's, although hers were shaded by long, dark lashes. "Don't know what I'd do without you," he said, giving a kiss to his great-niece's cheek. "I hate being dependent. They took away my license to drive—"

"Because you suffer from night blindness and smashed that lovely old Dodge into a tree," she said patiently, repeating the litany that occurred between them each time she came with groceries. She sat down and poured him a cup of tea. "What was Tyler Lassiter doing here?"

"Left, did he?"

"Did he bore you so much that you pretended to fall asleep?"

"Nice fellow," he said, ignoring her question. "You know I enjoy attractive young people. Said his great-great-great-grandmother was Emma Crewes. Anyway, man's an architect and is interested in old houses."

"How interested?"

"Asked if he could look around, asked how come it's fallen into disrepair. I explained it got old at about the same rate I did and that we're in the same condition." Wave laughed, his hand shaking as he directed the tea cup to his lips.

"And he believed you."

Her uncle put the cup down with a clatter, then reached over and placed his hand on hers. "I'm not sick, Sarah, and

I'm not senile. Maybe I'm not as energetic as I was, but that's reasonable. A man reaches seventy-five, has a few arthritic pains and the whole world thinks he's a doddering idiot. I let Riveredge go when the wife died. Took the stuffing out of me, you know that. I see the condition it's in. I'm also not blind." He waved his hand around to indicate the state of the dark paneled kitchen with its ancient cherry-wood pieces and old-fashioned fixtures. "About time I got my act together and began making some repairs. Chopping wood, too. Autumn sort of snuck up on me in more ways than one. No, it's about time I began to think of the house again."

Sarah, who felt the interior of Riveredge needed nothing so much as a painting, fresh wallpaper and a good sanding of its pine floors, and who loved the house dearly, said, "I'm glad to hear it, Uncle Wave. You plan on doing all the work yourself?"

He shrugged as though it mattered little when the work would begin or when it would end.

"Ideas without money won't come to fruition," Sarah said. "Sell some land, even a teensy bit along the river. It's worth a fortune."

"Sarah." The last was said in an imperious voice.

"Okay, okay." She backed away. "I know how you feel. I brought you your grocery order. The food's already stacked in the cabinets. I threw out the old potatoes with sprouted eyes and replaced them with new ones. Now *use* them. You need the potassium."

"How much do I owe you?"

"Nothing." Which was the truth, since Victor had generously volunteered to pay the weekly food bill for his impoverished relative, provided Sarah kept quiet about the fact. Bosworth Stud and Riveredge sat side by side along the river, with the stud farm part of Ramsey Falls and River-edge belonging to the larger township of Merriman.

It was Wave who wasn't speaking to Victor, not the other way around. He never explained why, and any attempt to elicit the reason drew nothing but stony silence. Real or imagined, Waverly Crewes wanted nothing to do with Victor Bosworth. "Victor knows why," he'd say darkly when Sarah questioned him. Victor Bosworth claimed he had no idea why Wave Crewes was angry with him and, in fact, shrugged the matter off. If his great-uncle needed help paying his bills, Victor was prepared to help him, whether he knew it or not.

"I pay my bills, Sarah. This is the third time this month you've refused to take a penny." Wave had been an engineer before retiring but high real estate taxes and the cost of living were eroding his pension. "I'll send you a check as soon as I get everything straightened out," he told her.

If it was a game they played with each visit, Sarah was certain her uncle had every intention of paying his bills sooner or later. "Look, I know what taxes are doing to you, and I know what the cost of living is, and I know the size of your pension and social security. You can pay me by telling me more about Tyler Lassiter."

"Lassiter? He wasn't talking, I was."

"Really? He's a good listener, then."

"Good questioner. Oh, he wants something all right," her great-uncle said, "but I haven't figured out what."

Sarah was silent. She had the odd feeling that Tyler Lassiter had come to town to stir up the air. But why, and for what purpose, she had no idea. "What kind of questions?"

"How old the house is. Wanted to know if there was a deed extant."

"Really? What did you tell him?"

"The original deed, lost in the annals of time or the mess in town hall. Keep an eye out for it, Sarah. I told him the house hasn't changed hands and was always willed to the first male heir, and until you, Sarah, it came down in the male Crewes line. That sort of thing. I can't remember everything I told him."

"How long was he here?"

Her great-uncle shrugged. "Beats me. He said he was an architect, wanted to look around, so I took him on a tour. Said he was sentimental because of Emma Crewes."

"And you believed him?"

Wave looked at her, his eyes bright and canny. "He's a bit of an Australian charmer, though I saw nothing of the Crewes in him. But as far as I'm concerned, if he says he's related, he's related."

"At what point did you decide to go to sleep so he'd leave?"

Wave laughed and shook his head. "I decided I'd talked enough for one day."

"Before you pull that on me," Sarah said, "we have to discuss something else. The matter of live-in help."

He cut her off at once with a wave of his hand. "Don't need it, don't want it, can't afford it and anyway don't want anyone living here turning over the dust."

"But *why*, Uncle Wave? You need help?"

"I can throw a frozen bone into the microwave by myself and open up a can of cat food for Ginger. As for dusting, all I do is open the front door and the back door and let it rip."

"Uncle Wave," Sarah said, laughing, "I'm sure that's precisely what happens."

"Tell you what," he said suddenly. "I'm willing to compromise on something. It's what Lassiter said."

"Really? You mean he has the power to make you compromise? I must thank him."

"He said what I already know, Sarah, that Riveredge is a public monument in a way, but one that descends through a family line. That I don't own it, the generations do. I'm merely the caretaker. And so will you be when you inherit. That's why I think the place ought to come back to life, because it doesn't belong to me, it doesn't belong to you. We're caretakers for history."

It was Sarah's turn to reach out to Waverly Crewes, to lay her hand softly upon his arm. "I like history and I like my funny antiques, Uncle Wave. I have no cravings for real estate. In a way my father was destroyed by owning too much, wanting too much, and my mother, too, you know that. Riveredge is yours and I hope you live a thousand years to enjoy it."

"It's always been in the Crewes family, Sarah."

"I really don't want to talk about it now. I expect you to live to be a hundred and fifty."

He gave a pleased snort. "Not likely."

"You will." She stood and began to collect the tea things. "You're ornery enough to beat the devil."

"You're a funny girl, Sarah."

"Woman," she corrected. "I'm thirty years old. That makes me unarguably a woman, not the little girl who used to go running along the lawn dragging an old rag doll with her." She bent over and kissed her uncle's white head. "I don't want you to be alone here any longer, Uncle Wave. You need help and you need companionship."

He grinned. "Thinking of a woman for me?"

She picked up her jacket. It was turning into a long day and she was expected at Victor's house for dinner. "A woman, Uncle Wave? If that's what it takes to get your juices flowing, absolutely."

"CERULEAN," Ty Lassiter announced, coming through the door to the old-fashioned drawing room of Kimberly Hall where Maggie Roman waited for him.

"Ty, what are you talking about? You're the most amazing man for speaking in, in—"

"Mysterious tongues?"

"Cerulean what?"

"Eyes." He was thinking of Sarah Crewes.

"Mine are extremely blue, but they certainly aren't cerulean," Maggie said. "More of a violet cast." Indeed, she was beautifully dressed in a long gown of violet, which emphasized the color of her eyes.

"Right, absolutely right," Ty agreed, giving her an affectionate kiss on the cheek.

"Well, come along, we're late enough as it is," she informed him, reaching for her bag and wrap, which had been thrown over a chair. "Where in the world have you been? Steve said to say hello and goodbye," she added, referring to her son, who was attending Pack College in Ramsey Falls.

"Not coming with us?"

"Oh, he thinks evenings with his mother are impossibly boring. I'm delighted you're going to meet Victor Bosworth at last," she told him. "You know, he's the most remarkable gentleman."

"The owner of Bosworth Stud," Tyler remarked. "I've been wanting to see the place."

"One of the largest Thoroughbred farms in the country," Maggie noted.

Ty smiled. Trust Maggie to have the man's credentials at her fingertips. "Part of the Crewes family, isn't he?"

"I think the expression is the Crewes family is part of Bosworth."

"Stand corrected." He helped her into her wrap, which was made of satin-lined wool, Maggie's latest charity project requiring that she give up wearing furs.

"He's a bachelor, never been married," Maggie said as she settled in the car. "Don't you absolutely adore Kimberly Hall, Ty? I'm thrilled I decided to move back. Roots and all. I mean, of course, I wasn't born at Kimberly Hall. I grew up on a dairy farm, but I knew Kimberly as a child and it thrills me to think I could own it at last."

As they headed down the circular driveway, Ty glanced back at the tall narrow building with its fanciful turrets and porches edged with Victorian tracery. Like many of the beautiful mansions in that part of the Hudson Valley, Kimberly Hall had fallen into disrepair, and it was Maggie who had rescued it a decade before and brought the building lovingly back to life.

Ty and Maggie had begun a friendship in California when he was hired to remodel a beach house for her. Maggie had been born in Merriman and perhaps that was why their friendship flourished, although the Australian and she had very little in common except perhaps for an interest in Maggie Roman.

She was, in spite of her self-involvement, of a very simple, generous and kind nature whose penchant for marrying inappropriate men had taken her into and out of four marriages. Ty had helped Maggie through her last divorce and the subsequent sale of the house he had built for her in Malibu, which she never lived in. There was a point, just after she received her divorce, when whey might have become lovers. They decided against it, knowing that for them friendship would be finer and more lasting.

There were several cars parked in the driveway of Bosworth Stud. The mansion was a large white Colonial with,

Tyler guessed, one-story wings added sometime in the nineteenth century.

"I wonder who else is here," Maggie said cheerfully. "The local honchos, I suppose. I've had Kimberly Hall for years, you know, but until now never stayed around long enough to meet my neighbors. Anyway, it was Victor Bosworth who had the inspiration. I received a phone call from him and an invitation to dinner. It turned out he wanted me to volunteer to work with the Pack College drama department. I was thrilled over the idea. Imagine me a college professor. I only made it through college to please my father, but that was a million years ago. All I ever wanted to be was an actress. Well, never mind, you know my history better than I do, don't you, darling?" She reached across and touched Ty's hand softly. "Anyway, that's how it started with Victor. He and Celie Decatur are mad about the idea of enlarging the drama department and building a separate small theater. Isn't it fantastic? They've even set about forming a board of trustees. It'll take ages, of course."

"Well," Ty said admiringly, "you haven't let any grass grow under your feet."

"Should I?"

"No, my Maggie, I wouldn't if I were you."

"Hollywood's not the same as it was." Left unsaid was the lack of interesting work for actresses her age. She'd always land feet solid on the ground, Ty thought. The world of Merriman would do her good.

She let Ty help her out of the car and took his arm as they headed toward the front door.

"I heard it's *très moderne* inside," she said. "Victor's not a man to be kept napping."

He wouldn't, Ty thought, with Maggie Roman as his guest. They were ushered into a large light-filled drawing room in which half a dozen people were already seated, including, he saw with surprise, Sarah Crewes. The room was not decorated in a contemporary style but was an authentic art deco creation, which drew a smile of admiration from Ty and breathless prose from Maggie Roman.

"Really, Victor, art deco, how scrumptious," she said to the man who came forward to greet her. "You know when I did *Starcrossed* the entire setting was deco. I wanted to take it home with me. Of course," she added with a laugh, "a devil of a lot of it was paste and plywood. And this is the man I told you about, Ty Lassiter."

Victor Bosworth, in his mid-forties, was of medium height. He wore a gray suit of expensive fabric, which nonetheless was faintly rumpled. It was that rumpled, carelessly aristocratic air, in fact, that made Ty think he and Victor Bosworth might get along and quite well.

Victor thrust his hand out, his gray eyes peering curiously at Ty through thin-rimmed spectacles. "The room was imported in the thirties by my father from a Paris apartment he admired. Paneling, paintings, furniture, lamps, the works. I'm afraid the Colonial shape of the house is merely a shell. Bosworths have always had a penchant for moving with the times." He shook Ty's hand vigorously. "An architect," he said, as though Ty had accomplished something not usually allowed mere mortals. "You know, architecture's a special interest of mine."

"An obsession of mine," Ty told him with a smile.

"Then we're going to get along splendidly. Come and meet my other guests."

Sitting in a round plush chair the color of frosted plum was Sarah Crewes, legs tucked under her so that her voluminous black velvet skirt covered her like a blanket. Her blouse was white and lacy with a high collar that emphasized her long neck. As when they first met at the flea market earlier that day, Ty was struck by the clear cerulean of her eyes and her pale beautiful complexion. As then, he thought of breeding, a thoroughbred whose tracings led in a single line to the first extraordinary forebear.

"We've met," she said dryly to Victor when he tried to introduce them. "This is the third time in one very long, very busy day. In fact, I'm trying to work out how we might manage to avoid meeting." She held her hand up. "How are you, Cousin Ty?"

"Cousin?" Victor looked nonplussed. "Did I miss something?"

"You'll have to ask your guest, Victor."

Ty took her hand and held it while he spoke, feeling its satiny texture. "My mother's ancestors came from Merriman. We have Crewes in common."

Victor beamed at him. "Well," he said. "Well well well. Sarah did mention something, come to think of it. We'll have to have a long chat. You know I've written a history of Ramsey Falls that crosses and crisscrosses the town line into Merriman—"

"Victor," Sarah said, smiling and shaking her head as if to deflect a lecture most people would find boring. "Your guests, they're waiting."

Victor gave her a fond smile in return. Ty understood at once that Victor Bosworth indulged Sarah Crewes and that no one else would dare chide him publicly or even privately.

Ty, in quick succession, met Celie Decatur, an attractive blonde in her late thirties who published a newspaper in Ramsey Falls, then Jemma and Hunt Gardner, two people he realized instinctively he'd like to know better, and Merriman's town supervisor and his wife. He took special note of the man's name, Alec Schermmerhorn, and decided that sometime during the evening he'd bring the conversation around to the mess the town's records were in and how he might gain access to them to research his family history.

As he settled with a glass of Scotch in hand on the couch opposite Sarah Crewes, Ty noted that Maggie had managed to crowd Victor Bosworth onto a small settee across the room. Clever Maggie. Ty suspected, however, that if she had designs on Victor it would do well to make friends with his young cousin.

"We were just going to play a game," Sarah told him. "Care to join? It's the way we while away our Saturday nights, at least until Victor serves dinner, which is always fashionably, starvingly late."

"Charades?" Ty asked, lifting an eyebrow. "That should be Maggie's bag."

"No, something we call Finesse."

"The trivial pursuing of something or other?"

"No," she said, shaking her head and smiling. "It's twenty questions only different. We made it up."

"Sarah made it up," Celie said with an indulgent smile "Let's give credit where it's due."

Sarah ignored her remark, saying to Ty, "How good are you at questioning?"

"My line of work has made me rather adept at getting to the heart of the matter."

"And just what kind of architect are you, Mr. Lassiter?" inquired Jemma.

"The name is Ty," he said, turning and smiling at her.

"Post modern?" her husband Hunt asked.

"*Sui generis* would be more like it," Ty replied "Under my skillful questioning, you tell me what your requirements are, and I tailor the building to those needs."

"You're a man without prejudice, then, a man without a point of view," Sarah said.

"I'm neither a borrower nor a lender of styles."

"Ah." She leaned back and reached for her glass of wine. She held it up. "Here's to unique man, here's to honest man, here's to the man who'll give you what you want, whether you know it or not." She took a sip, her eyes holding his with a merry, mischievous glint.

"You're from Australia, aren't you?" Jemma asked, addressing Ty.

"Late of Australia, via Oxford, then California, where I have an office, and a few other places where I might have picked up the local accent."

"And what brings you to these parts?"

"Oh, visiting his old relatives," Sarah threw in.

Victor called across the room, "Sarah, let the man answer for himself."

But it was Celie Decatur who spoke up instead. "You know Central Towers in Manhattan, the building that brought back elegant graceful spires to the skyline?"

Sarah looked at him in genuine surprise. "You?"

"Lassiter Associates," he said. "I'm part of a very talented team. Is this Finesse? Twenty questions?"

"Sarah's a cynic," Alec Schermmerhorn informed him. "She went from a corner office high in a Manhattan skyscraper to the basement of our town hall and considers it an absolute move up in the world."

"Go ahead, pick on me as if I weren't even here," Sarah remarked. "And I rather enjoy the view of juniper bushes outside my basement window. You'd be surprised how slowly they grow."

"One of the ways Sarah held us up when we offered her the job," Alec said, "was cleaning the windows. We hated wiping off all that antique grime. Killed the year's maintenance budget."

"You're lucky you have Sarah," Jemma told the town supervisor.

"I'm impressed with Central Towers," Sarah said quickly to Ty, evidently anxious to turn the discussion away from herself and in another direction. Her smile had turned diffident. It was clear to Ty that she was fond of her friends and that she accepted their gentle chiding as nothing more than teasing of the most loving kind. She was in her element here—he understood that—yet he wondered what happened to make her leave a Manhattan skyscraper for a dingy basement in Merriman. And he was certain it would have had nothing to do with money but with something personal.

"Speaking of luck, we had plenty of it with Central Towers," he told her. "We had a client who felt the New York skyline had lost a lot of its beauty, a lot of its vigor with all those flat-topped buildings. We added a graceful spire and then made tracks for the West Coast and hoped for the best."

"Win any prizes for your building?" Sarah asked.

"Architects who don't self-promote never win prizes," he told her.

"And you don't believe in self-promotion."

"I believe in doing what I'm paid to do the best way I can." He said the last with an edge of annoyance to his voice. He wasn't a man to talk about himself and he had the feeling that Sarah was still smarting over finding him at Riveredge. There wasn't anything Wave Crewes could have told her, because there was nothing to tell.

"Shall we get on to Finesse?" she asked.

"By all means."

"Count me out," said Maggie Roman.

"And me, " Victor added.

Ty noted that his glance went to Celie Decatur, who turned to Sarah and said, "I'm in."

"Hunt? Jemma?"

"I'm out, too," said the wife of the town supervisor. She had picked up a magazine and was leafing through it.

"Alec?" Sarah glanced at her boss. "Okay, six is fine. We'll let you off easy this time, Ty, by making you the man behind the word. Think of something, anything, and keep it to yourself."

"One word?"

"It can be a recipe for making French bread if that suits you." She smiled, her eyes twinkling with something resembling a challenge.

Cerulean blue eyes. He smiled. There was no contest.

"Got it then?" she asked.

"Wish I had."

"I don't know what that means, cousin, but I'll take your word for it. Now, we play this game fast and furious. One go around and if we can't figure the answer, the game is yours. Here are the rules. Each of us gets to ask you three questions, each series based on the questions before and your answers. After we've all had our turn, we powwow, come up with the solution—"

"Or not," he commented.

"Well, you're on your honor to say whether we've guessed it right."

"I'm an honorable man."

"That, of course, is a definite Crewes trait, cousin Tyler."

"However," he said, "if you like, I'll write it down on a piece of paper and hand it over to Victor for safekeeping."

"We trust Victor's guests implicitly, don't we?" she said with a nod to their host.

"It's the name of the game," Victor answered with a smile at Maggie Roman. He got up and went over to a rosewood cabinet, which he opened to reveal a stereo player. "Anybody mind a bit of background music?" He put a tape on and fiddled with the sound and at last a soft Viennese waltz filled the room.

"Ah, a waltz," Maggie said. "I grew very fond of them when we filmed *Sir Strauss* in Vienna. That was, oh, a dozen years ago." She put her hand to her head. "Please, please, I don't even want to discuss how time flies."

"The game of Finesse begins with three basic questions asked by us all," explained Sarah. "You can answer yes, no, or you're barking up the wrong tree." She had uncurled herself from the chair and stood in her stocking feet. "One. Animal, vegetable or mineral?"

"Animal."

"Two. Past, future or the here and now?"

"Definitely here and now."

"Three. Is it a human being or not?"

"It?"

Sarah looked curiously at him. "Okay, we're into deep semantics here. Are we discussing humans or animal animals?"

"Clever," he said, bending his head in acknowledgment. "Still, I'm not certain we're discussing anything within those categories."

"You win, you win by a semantic landslide. Human or animal, damn it."

Jemma laughed. "Sarah, you take these games too seriously in the best of times. Don't mind her, Ty, she'll draw every ounce of blood from you if she can."

"Okay, now you know I play mean," Sarah said, sitting down and once again drawing her legs up under her.

"Fire away," Ty invited with a smile. He was beginning to enjoy himself. "I think I can defend my territory. Human rather than animal is my answer to question number three. I'm not certain which tree you're barking up."

"Okay. At this point we can each ask you our individual three questions. Who's first?"

There was a moment's silence, then Hunt spoke up. "One: is this human famous? I don't mean the famous for fifteen minutes kind, I mean the famous they'll know him or her in Hong Kong, for instance?"

"That kind of famous," Ty said, "no."

"Two. But there's something about this human we should all know."

"Hunt, darling, that's not a question," Jemma said.

"Question mark," Hunt added, giving her a fond yet exasperated smile.

"Yes to question two," Ty said. *Sarah's cerulean eyes*, he wondered. Did they know her so well that her luminous eyes ceased to fascinate?

"Something about this human we should all know." Hunt looked around the room, then suddenly smiled. "Question three. Is the here and now you referred to the here and now of this room?"

Man after my own heart, Ty thought. "Yes to question three. Give the chap a round of applause."

"We'll save the applause till later," Celie said. "My question one. Are we talking about a human being in this room?"

"No." Cerulean blue eyes, Ty reflected, separate and apart, just bits and pieces of the whole. In themselves decidedly not a human being. They still had a long way to go.

"I don't get it," Celie said.

"Is that question two?" Ty remarked.

"In this room, human, but not one of us. Two, is it made up of human cells, I mean, not a statue?" She looked across the room at a small deco bronze statue of a woman being pulled along by two Afghan hounds.

"Yes," Ty said.

"Not one of us but made up of cells. Listen," Celie said, leaning forward and looking hard at Ty. "I'm not talking prison cells."

"Neither am I," he said with a good-natured laugh.

"Is it flesh color?"

"No."

"Ah-hah," Celie exclaimed, leaning back and giving Jemma a self-satisfied smile.

"Okay, I'll plunge," Jemma said. "Is the color red?"

"No."

"Yellow?"

"Jemma," Sarah threw in hastily, "the color spectrum is pretty big. Sure you want to keep on?"

"I'm not sure of anything. It's made up of human cells, though. It's here in this room. Question three. Ty, are we talking about part of the human anatomy?"

He gave her an admiring glance. "So it is."

"A human animal, a feature and it has a color, not red or yellow," Alec said. He stood up and paced the area in front of the couch. "Question one: is it one of the primary colors or a mixture?"

"No to primary colors, yes to mixture."

Alec turned to Sarah. "I have two questions left, you have three, and after that either we come up with the exact color and the exact feature or we're out. Question two. Is this thing above the waist?"

"Yes."

"Color above the waist, a mixture that could mean flesh—"

"Not flesh," Sarah said. "He already threw that out."

"Or pink as in lips, or brown, black or blond as in hair. Or eyes. Question three. Is it a facial feature?"

"Yes to facial feature," Ty said, amazed at how quickly they had homed in. Cerulean blue. Not there yet.

"We're old hands at this," Sarah told him. "It's team-work, not individual bravado, that makes us call the game Finesse. Facial feature lets out hair. I think. Question one, is it hair?"

"Ouch," Alec said. "I think you should have talked that one out, Sarah. Hair isn't a facial feature."

"Eyebrows," Hunt said. "Mustache. Eyelashes."

"No one here has a mustache," Jemma said.

"I'm thinking of growing one," Hunt threw in.

"Over my dead body," Jemma remarked with a smile.

"No, it's not hair," Ty said.

"Eyes, ears, nose or mouth," Sarah went on. "Which means blue eyes, or green like Jemma's. Or," she added, "hazel," looking at Ty. "Otherwise we're considering ears or a nose, but they're flesh color, or a mouth."

"A mouth is red," Jemma interposed.

"Is there a time limit to questions?" Ty asked quietly.

"Okay, point well taken. Question two. Is it the most interesting feature on the face?"

Ty was surprised to find her glancing at Maggie, who was still engaged in a quiet conversation with Victor. Maggie's eyes which bordered decidedly on the violet.

He smiled. "Yes."

"Question three," she said, now watching him carefully. "Are we discussing eye color?"

"Yes."

"You realize you just threw away your last question, Sarah," Alec told her. "You're usually a lot more calculating than that."

"Maybe I know instinctively what the answer is," she said.

Ty was acutely aware of the moment and the way she held her head. He was convinced that the lady had just lost her advantage. The music swelled. "Tales from the Vienna

Woods." The atmosphere in the room, which might have been parochial and stuffy, was warm and friendly. The word *cozy* came to mind, hardly a word in Ty's vocabulary. He didn't even blanch at the idea, but instead a fleeting feeling came over him of having waited for this moment for a long time.

Glancing at the others, he surprised a gentle smile on Hunt Gardner's lips and noted Jemma's knitted brow. They were thinking about him, he felt it, and knew as easily that Sarah was part of what they were thinking.

Celie Decatur and Alec Schermmerhorn were whispering together on the huge overstuffed couch. He caught the word *eyes* and was brought back to reality. A group of friends were aligned against him in a game they had played often before, and yet he knew he'd beat them at it. If they had locked in on the beauty of Sarah's eyes, of their long, sloe shape and the jeweled tone of the irises, they would still have to find the word that best described that luminous shade of blue.

"Powwow time," Sarah said.

Ty stood up. "I presume at the moment I'm a man without a country."

"Precisely."

He went over to the settee and joined Maggie and Victor. Sarah was huddled with the others and over the strains of the music he heard an occasional giggle.

"Finished with the game?" Maggie asked.

"I've been given the bum's rush."

"Sarah's an old coraller," said Victor. "Get half a dozen people together and she has them playing games."

"Anybody ever try to find out why?" Ty asked.

"She was an only child living in the country with a doll, assorted dogs and horses and a governess to keep her company," Victor replied. "I mark that down to her military ways. I remember seeing her on any number of occasions with a couple of animals, including a miniature pony, and of course her governess and a doll or two lined up, giving them marching orders.''

Ty laughed but Maggie put in a question about the large estate.

"Sold long ago to pay off debts," Victor said, "and a rather remarkable house torn down to make way for progress. Pity."

"Pity for progress or pity for the remarkable house," Ty said.

"I'm a great believer in progress," Victor said in a solemn tone. "In fact, I'm an admirer of contemporary art, architecture, you name it. However, I equally agree that what's old should be preserved."

Ty heard Sarah laugh, heard Jemma say, "My eyes aren't green in this light. He wouldn't know, tell them, Hunt." Then, seconds later, he heard the word *violet* spoken in a very determined manner by Sarah. He had to suppress a smile. That's what came of leadership. She'd think it was Maggie and never guess it was about herself, and she'd lead the willing lemmings straight over a cliff.

Celie said, "No, violet includes red, and red's out."

"Violet's bluer than red," Sarah remarked stubbornly.

"Violet," Maggie murmured, looking at Victor.

Ty heard Sarah call him, "Come on, Ty, we have it."

When he came back, he found Hunt Gardner smiling at him. A slight shake of his head told Ty that Sarah had it all wrong and that Hunt knew exactly what Ty had in mind.

"Incidentally," Ty said, giving Hunt a nod that in a sense brought them together in collusion, "as loser, what am I supposed to lose besides my self-esteem?"

"That's quite enough," Sarah replied.

"I think we all ought to name our price," Celie put in. "I, for one, will insist upon an interview for my paper. West Coast architect visits ancestor's beginnings, that sort of thing."

"Agreed," Ty said.

Alec Schermmerhorn shook his head. "I'll pass on that one. I've a sore temptation to ask him to donate his services in rebuilding our blighted waterfront district."

"Ask him," Sarah said, turning her eyes on Ty in a challenge.

Ty threw up his hands. "I've got a dozen projects on my agenda, and I'm due back in California—" He left the sentence unfinished. He wanted to talk to Alec; he wanted to gain access to the files in the basement of the town hall, and he often donated his services to worthy causes.

"Only joking," Alec threw in. "I lost my pride when I took on the job of town supervisor. I'll beg with a tin cup in hand when I have to."

"Tell you what," Ty said. "I'll come by your office next week. Talk won't cost either of us anything."

"Pass on the Gardners," Hunt said quickly. He gazed at his wife. "Our plate is full to overflowing and we take no prisoners. As for loss of self-esteem, Sarah, the game isn't over until it's over."

"Hunt," Sarah said, "I hate it when you're reasonable."

He laughed. "Go ahead, tell him what the consensus is."

"Violet-blue eyes," she said with a smile of triumph on her face. He noted that she carefully avoided taking in Maggie Roman while she said it.

Maggie, however, caught the reference at once. "I'm sorry," she called, "did I miss something?"

"Nothing," Ty said. "Nothing at all." He glanced quickly at Hunt and then turned to Sarah. The whole game

had been a private challenge between them. She was way off
the mark but he was going to lie rather than tell her the true
answer. "You win, of course," he said. "That's it, violet-
blue eyes. You never did name your prize."

"No," she said, watching him. "I haven't, cousin Ty, but
I'll think of one."

CHAPTER THREE

"DELICIOUS. FANTASTIC. *Très tendre*," Maggie Roman said of the Coquille St. Jacques, the faintest reminder of which was all that remained on her plate. She leaned toward Victor, who sat at her left, and touched his arm lightly. "Don't tell me the recipe's a family secret, I won't hear of it."

"I'll ask my cook to make a copy for you," Victor said in a soft, faintly embarrassed voice.

"Wonderful. Isn't that wonderful, Ty," she said, calling down the table in her throaty voice.

She was auditioning for a part, Ty thought affectionately. Her best role in a long time, mistress of Bosworth Stud. "Terrific," he said, and clearly heard Sarah, sitting opposite, exhale a little puff of breath.

Maggie gave Victor a klieg-light smile. Ty knew the scenario by heart. She saw something she wanted, would tightly focus on it and, without a doubt, make it happen. Poor Victor, he thought, the hapless beggar didn't stand a chance.

Ty might have smiled over the idea but then caught Sarah's intense expression as she took in the scene. He saw her glance across at Celie Decatur, who was seated at Ty's left, and noticed for the first time that Celie hadn't touched her food. Uh-uh, he thought with sudden understanding, Maggie might be wandering into a mine field. He'd have to warn her to take it easy. Maggie was far too used to stepping out into the sunshine as if she owned the territory. It was going to surprise her to find that someone might have a claim on exactly the same spot.

"Coquille St. Jacques," Jemma Gardner remarked. "Yummy. Victor, I'm going to insist on the recipe, also."

"Tell you what," said Celie, her voice a little bright and brittle. "We'll print it in the Sunday edition of the *Times Herald.*"

Dinner was being served on the glass-enclosed patio. Large pots of brilliantly colored fall mums were placed around the slate floor, and bright autumn leaves in vases left a delicate scent in the air. From where he sat, Ty could see the windows of a distant barn lit against the night. Far away in the black rise of mountains, lights twinkled through an occasional break in the trees. It was the soft and rolling countryside that appealed to him, the change of seasons and especially autumn, which he thought was never more beautiful than in Ramsey Falls, New York.

The dinner plates were removed and a delicate dessert served: a flan, which Maggie fussed over. With coffee poured, Ty leaned back in his chair and quietly observed Sarah speaking in a low voice with Hunt Gardner. A small lock of hair fell into her eye and with an impatient gesture she brushed it away, only to have it delicately fall forward once more.

Around him voices engaged in local gossip: a coming horse auction, the Gardners' new house, the rising price of land and the mess the county's records were in. The words rolled off him. He felt disengaged, but pleasantly so, as though he had stepped into someone else's dream. He had come to Merriman with one purpose in mind, had tripped over Sarah Crewes and found himself fascinated by his pretty little cousin who wasn't.

"Hunt darling, call the baby-sitter, will you?" Jemma said, just as Ty's coffee cup was filled a second time.

Hunt Gardner checked his watch, then excused himself.

His leaving signaled everyone to rise from the table. Victor suggested they have after-dinner drinks in the library, which turned out to be a large comfortable room full of books and modern paintings.

Over Cointreau and cognac there was more talk about horses, which Maggie seemed extraordinarily interested in.

"I heard you have a stud worth the moon," she said to Victor. She sat on the arm of a well-worn leather chair while Victor poked at the logs in the fireplace.

Sarah had taken a seat on the library ladder and cradled an untouched glass of Cointreau in her lap. "Wouldn't it be Loverly," she said.

"Well, yes, it would, I suppose," Maggie said, arching her eyebrows in confusion.

"The name of the horse," Victor told her, turning and giving her an engaging smile, as though to remind Maggie that his young cousin liked nothing better than word games.

"Ah," she said, "of course."

Ty came to her rescue. "And just what do you call this stud to his face, Victor? Wouldn't or Loverly?"

"Hey you, mostly," Sarah replied.

"Not true," Victor said, putting the poker away and standing with his back to the fire. "Woody, as a matter of fact."

"I'd absolutely adore to see him," Maggie said.

"He's asleep," Sarah put in quickly, throwing another glance at Celie, but since Celie seemed intent upon examining the spine of every book in the library, it was a look she didn't catch.

"They sleep standing up," Maggie said.

Ty tried only once to deflect her. "Maggie," he began, but she pretended not to hear him. Still, he couldn't abandon the woman to her own devices. He knew she was perfectly capable of pressing the point until everyone gave in from exhaustion. He put his glass down and went over to her, but she was smiling at Victor.

"A peek, that's all. Of course I ride like a dream. Had to for *Cowboy West*."

"*Cowboy West*," Jemma said enthusiastically. "Seth is watching the reruns. Oh, of course, how wonderful! That's you, Maggie, running the saloon." She stopped short when Hunt grinned at her, shaking his head. "Right, I mean," she began, and let the rest of the thought fade away.

It was Victor, in fact, who gave in. "Come on, I'd be delighted to show you Wouldn't it be Loverly." He smiled graciously at his guests. "Anyone else?"

"Sorry, Victor, I have to take the baby-sitter home." Hunt held out his hand, which Victor shook warmly. Then Jemma came over to Ty and spontaneously kissed his cheek.

"Come take a look at the house we're renovating," she said. "I'd love to show it off."

"I will," Ty said, and meant it as he shook Hunt's hand.

As though by common agreement, everyone moved out of the library to the front door, chatting as coats were put on and fingers stuffed into gloves.

There were comfortable farewells as the Gardners and Schermmerhorns took their leave.

"Darling, coming along to see what's his name, the horse?" Maggie asked Ty. In her eyes he read a clear warning to stay behind. She slipped into the wrap that Victor held for her.

"I'll wait for you here," Ty said. He didn't want to waste his time with Maggie and her latest moth and believed that Victor Bosworth could fend for himself. There was no doubt in Ty's mind that the owner of Wouldn't it be Loverly could handle one Maggie Roman, as well. She might be a volatile package of goods, but chances were he'd emerge unscathed. Ty remained at the open front door and watched as they headed toward the main barn. He could see straight through to the stalls, where a lone figure stood. A match was struck, which lingered for a moment as the flame touched a cigarette then went out.

The sky above was a sheet of black through which a million tiny holes were punched, letting bits of sparkle through. Almost like home, Ty thought, that clear deep sky and the stars. Not California, where a persevering smog made the dark just a memory. When he thought of home he thought of Australia.

For a moment he had a rush of nostalgia for the vast empty land where he grew up and the lone house in the middle of an almost forgotten boyhood where the sky and its mass of stars kissed the edges of the earth.

He closed the door quietly and turned back. He was alone in the hallway and wondered where Sarah and Celie had gone off to. He headed for the library and his drink. He'd wait for Maggie there.

"You stop her before she gets out of the starting gate, Celie." Ty pulled up short at the sound of Sarah's voice coming from the library. "You listen to me, now. Don't suddenly get all mushy, it's not like you."

"I don't blame her, I blame him, the fool."

"Celie, he's not a fool, just a little starstruck."

"Let's not discuss it. I'm going home. Coming?"

"No," Sarah said. "Think I'll stick around and hear what my illustrious cousin has to say."

Ty came quickly into the room and caught Sarah's look of surprise. "Maggie always did like horses," he said.

"Good night, Ty." Celie thrust her hand out and gave him a keen look. "Remember, you owe me an interview."

"Don't mind one at all. How about lunch next week?"

"Call me at the paper," she said. "Come visit us and see how small-town gossip gets blown up into front-page news."

"Was that directed at me?" Sarah asked.

"Well, you might be making a mountain out of a molehill," Celie said.

"Possibly." Their conversation seemed to be pointedly for Ty's benefit. "You'd have to be blind not to notice that certain molehills gather moss and then, pouf, you've Everest."

"You're incorrigible." Celie exchanged a light kiss with Sarah. "Say good-night to Victor for me, will you?"

"Right, I'll call you."

Ty went over to his glass and picked it up, examining its golden light against the flame in the fireplace. There was a long silence as the front door closed behind Celie. Sarah had taken to circling the room, picking up glasses and putting them on a tray, then poking at the fireplace. In the distance he heard an engine start and heard a car move out of the driveway. He waited another moment, then said, "We seem to have the place to ourselves."

"Victor should be right back. With your friend."

"He can take as long as he wants," Ty remarked. "I'm perfectly happy."

"Really?" She stopped her pacing to confront him. "You *are* the most remarkable man."

He raised his glass. "The last person who told me that was my mother, and that was when I won a scholarship to university."

"I mean, you let *her* put on that performance with my cousin. Horses, *Cowboy West*...good Lord, haven't you any character?"

"A minute ago I was a remarkable man and now I'm devoid of character. You want to know what the hell's going on between Maggie and me," he added with a smile, "just come out and ask it. How come I arrived at the house with her and how come I've let her take over Victor as if she were Napoleon and he were Moscow."

"I'm thinking of Victor."

"Not of me? Pity."

"I don't want to see my cousin hurt."

"And you think a fling with Maggie Roman is bad news. For Victor, that is."

"You're the most contrary human being," Sarah said hotly. "You know exactly what I mean and you're making me go round in circles."

"Victor strikes me as the kind of man who can take care of himself."

"And you don't care?"

"Why should I?"

"Well, I mean you and Maggie arrived together tonight—"

"We aren't joined at the hip. I'm going to answer your question because I think I detect enough self-interest in it to answer."

She stopped, faced him and said, "You're rather insufferable."

"I'm insufferable?" He shook his head. "Lady, you've just been hinting at the most personal, private relationship two people can have, and I'm insufferable. Get me a dictionary. There must be another meaning to the word."

"Forget it," she said, storming out of the room and tossing a good-night back at him over her shoulder. Ty found her in the front hall pulling on her jacket.

"Come on," he said, "I'll walk you to your car."

"I live on the property," she told him. "The old blacksmith's house."

"Your favorite song being The Anvil's Chorus."

She laughed in a forgiving way and held out her hand. "Goodbye, Tyler. Sorry for my outburst. I've a real reason for being angry."

"I know you have," he said quietly. "I'll walk you home."

She pulled the door open and looked up at the sky. "No moon tonight. You'll need a flashlight to get back. The way is dark and mysterious."

"With a blacksmith's cottage at the end," he remarked.

"In the good old days properties like this were really self-sustaining. The buildings are made of fieldstone and stood the test of time pretty well. When Victor decided to go from dairy farming to raising horses, he left a lovely forest standing above the river with the cottage as a jewel. It's about a quarter mile distant." She pulled a flashlight from her pocket and shone it along the ground. "You can come along if you want to," she said, walking rapidly ahead of him for a few steps and then waiting as he came toward her.

She lifted the flashlight and caught him in its glare. "Just why are you here? In Merriman, I mean. Visiting Uncle Wave and nosying down at town hall?"

"You get your dander up pretty easily." He reached over and turned the flashlight down so that its beam traced the path ahead of them. "All I want to do is clear up some old outback folklore, that's all."

"Come to think of it, so would I. Trouble is, the files are a mess and we've placed a moratorium on allowing people to handle them." The beam cast its shadow on the ground as they went slowly down the path, the gravel crunching underfoot.

"You can make an exception of a long lost relation, can't you?"

"I could if I wanted to lose my job. Are you in a hurry to get back to Beverly Hills?" Without waiting for an answer, she added, "And why have you come now, anyway?"

"Been a mighty busy man."

"I guess we'll have to make up for lost time," she said after a moment. "Maybe we can gather together a cousins' clan and introduce you to your kinfolk."

"You do that and I'll head for the hills."

As the path they took led them past the main barn, Ty heard the distant easy sound of Maggie's laughter. He glanced quickly at Sarah and in the light cast from the window of the barn caught her frowning.

"Maggie's all right," he said quietly. "She had a good heart and wouldn't hurt a fly."

"Really? Have you ever seen a horsefly? They fight back."

He laughed. He had no idea why he might be defending Maggie. He almost made up his mind to take the woman aside and tell her to lay off when Sarah strode rapidly away from him.

"Wait a minute," he said, going after her. He took her elbow and spun her around. "If there's anything I hate it's an unfinished argument. Stand still and we'll talk."

"I can talk and walk at the same time."

"I'd like to look at your face when I talk to you so just quiet down." He added in a more gentle tone, "I want you to know this, and I would've told you even if you hadn't asked."

"Really—"

"There's nothing between Maggie and me except friendship. There never has been. We've never been lovers and neither of us wants it. She's much more sensitive than she seems. She hurts easily, and all that stagey stuff is just a cover for her lack of confidence."

"Oh, spare me. Famous movie actress just a bundle of insecurity. How often I've read that story. She's been married four times and I'm supposed to feel sorry for her when she comes on to my cousin like a tramp steamer bellying into port. For your information, Victor and Celie are what the Hollywood gossip columnists call an item."

He reached out and gripped her shoulders. "Sarah, you can't control other people's lives. They're consenting adults and they don't need us around telling them what to do. Let them iron it out, whatever you think it is."

"Victor's rather vulnerable in many ways," she began.

"If Celie's the one that Victor wants, then that's just what will happen," Ty said patiently. "But if it's Maggie, then all your jumping through hoops won't help Celie one bit."

"Kismet, the stars, fortune cookies." Sarah threw the words at him. "Don't tell me you believe in fate."

He waited a moment before answering, then brushed her hair from her face. "Maybe that's what I do believe in, fate."

"You believe in a good line," she said, then added with a little uncertain sigh, "Look, I've got a busy day ahead of me tomorrow. I have to get home." She turned away from him, but when he took her arm, she raised no objection.

"You're right about me," he remarked. "I certainly hope I can change the things I want changed."

The blacksmith's cottage was a low plump building set in behind a clump of carefully pruned bushes, just off what was once the main road but was now a graveled path. A copper lighting fixture in the shape of a horse's head rested on a ledge above the door, giving off an amber glow.

"The road swerved along the river and eventually led to the falls, but all that changed," Sarah said. "Now this quiet little spot is reverting to nature."

The path to the house was lit by a row of flickering lanterns, which cast the twisted shapes of branches on the ground. Sarah unlocked the front door and pushed it open. A light was shining in a small foyer furnished with a table and mirror. Ty caught a glimpse of himself in the mirror.

Sarah handed him the flashlight. "Thanks for walking me home."

"Incidentally," he said, smiling at her and knowing she meant it and that the door would close firmly behind her, "the word was *cerulean*."

She gave him a quizzical look. "I beg your pardon."

"I never meant *violet*. As in violet eyes. I meant *cerulean*."

"Ty, I still don't know what you're talking about."

"Don't you?"

"Cerulean. That's a kind of very clear blue with green in it."

"I won that little game, you know, Finesse. Finessed the lot of you," he added, remembering that only Hunt Gardner wasn't fooled but had wisely kept his silence.

"Cerulean eyes? But who? You lied in other words about the violet, Maggie's eyes. I'm confused."

"Come on." He brushed past her into the foyer, and when she turned, her eyes wide with surprise, Ty put his hands on her shoulders and directed her toward her reflection in the mirror. "Take a good look."

"I am. I see a tall sandy-haired man who's standing a little too close. And who cleverly stepped into my house without being asked."

He laughed but didn't step back. He almost felt he couldn't, that he didn't want to release her from his grasp. He even knew his touch was making her uncomfortable, yet drew some satisfaction from her not pulling away. He breathed in the faint scent of some flowery perfume that clung to her hair. Then their eyes met through the mirror and Ty realized that the blue had deepened in the lamplight. She took in a light breath, then, as if she were holding back words, bit her lower lip.

"Azure, cerulean," he said, "take your pick."

"Why did you lie when you could have won our little game?"

"You were so sure of yourself, Sarah, I hated to burst your bubble." He released her and went quickly out the door. He turned and saluted her just before closing it behind him. Sarah was watching him through the mirror, her expression serious and uncertain.

"THAT JUNIPER BUSH is turning brown," Reg Casedonte said, peering through the window of the basement office he shared with Sarah. "The tips. It needs fertilizer."

Sarah came over and stared out the window. The midday sun brushed the thick low-lying bush and slanted into the room. It felt warm and good although outside the air was nippy. "They put in expensive plants and expect nature to do the rest, only no one counts on smoke and exhaust fumes," she said. "I'd hate to see the poor thing die. I've grown rather fond of it."

"Maybe we should apply a little fertilizer and clip the brown off. That's what my mom does."

"I'll spring for the fertilizer," Sarah offered. "And I've got a pair of clippers at home. Reg, if you get a chance—"

"I'll do it in exchange for a favor," he said with a sudden boyish grin on his friendly face.

"You swindler." Sarah feigned exasperation. "I think that bush is perfectly all right. You painted it just to get my attention. You absolutely, positively can't have an advance on that rather meager salary we're paying you. It'll create a budget crisis."

"Nah, it's my great-aunt Nellie. She's coming back to Ramsey Falls today."

Sarah gave a pleased smile. "Nellie! For good? How wonderful, I've always adored her."

"She needs some help moving her stuff down from Albany. I've got the loan of a big panel truck—"

"This afternoon," Sarah said, "right?"

"Yeah, right. I figured I could make up the time," he went on enthusiastically, "by working an additional hour a day all week."

"Do you mean she's actually retiring? Do you mean the governor is letting her go after all?" Ten years previously Nellie Casedonte had officially retired from her job as head of the education department in the state capitol. The governor had asked her to stay on in an advisory capacity that ultimately stretched out a decade.

Reg waved a hand to encompass the crowded files in their basement office. "Aunt Nellie knew more than anybody else alive about what was going on in her department. Except now it's all on computers, just the same as we're doing here. She figured it was time to get out, but according to what my mom says, she's having second thoughts."

"You mean she's afraid of becoming bored."

"Yeah, something like that."

"Is she coming to live with you?"

Reg nodded. "She doesn't want to, but Mom figured she could stay with us until she decides what she really wants to do with her life."

"Well, there's plenty of volunteer work around Merriman," Sarah said. "And in the field of education, adult and otherwise. That's Hunt Gardner's territory. Maybe they could get together."

"Mom wants her to have a big fat rest for a while."

"Nellie? Rest?" Sarah shook her head. "The last time I saw your great-aunt was at the tri-bicentennial dance. She was full of energy and dancing up a storm."

Reg gave her a look of astonishment, as though he and Sarah had been discussing two different people. "Dancing up a storm? My great-aunt? I mean, she's seventy-*two*."

"Oh, yes, seventy-two, ancient history. Dancing and looking lovely not allowed. Reg, by all means, scoot up to Albany before she turns seventy-three and forgets how to walk. Oh, just a sec," she added. "There's something I'd like you to do."

He saluted smartly. "Yes, chief."

"It may take a little time. I'm searching for a carton that might have Riveredge scribbled on it. I noticed in the basement of the old country club that there are a number of boxes with their contents scribbled on the outside in crayon. I gather that someone made an attempt some years ago to divide the files into something resembling order. When you get a chance, maybe in the next couple of days, I'd appreciate your going over there for me and checking them out. If you find any reference at all to Riveredge, haul the box back here."

Reg drew his eyebrows together at her recital. "Riveredge. That's your uncle's place, isn't it?"

"Yes." She thought of Phil Nevins and his remark about her protecting her family, but Phil wasn't quite right. The Riveredge property had been divided and redivided and Waverly held on to only a small portion of the original land grant. Thousands of acres had been sold under the Crewes name and a lot of Merriman homes had been built on the land. If Tyler Lassiter had come to town to shake things up, she wanted to know exactly where everything stood.

"Oh, by the way," Reg said. He apparently thought no more about the errand she had asked of him. "I've been going through that metal box we found near the boiler room. The one with the rusty lock? It's got old medical records in it and stuff."

"Oh, yes," Sarah said, remembering. She had pasted a note on the box indicating the dates of the material it contained, going back to the turn of the century. The lock was what interested her at the moment. With a little polishing, she could sell it at the flea market, where it might fetch a few dollars. Sarah wanted to establish a fund to house important historic documents in glass-enclosed humidity-controlled cases. The old basement had plenty of antique artifacts, which, if sold, could add to the fund. The trouble was, of course, that someone was bound to come along and suggest a museum for everything about the county's past, including pencil shavings.

"I found an old newspaper clipping that was attached to a death certificate," Reg said. "I guess he was a cousin of yours, a private. I think his name was something like Emanuel. The article said he was recovering from war wounds, but I guess he didn't."

"Private Emanuel Waverly Crewes died of wounds *encountered* in the Spanish American war," Sarah told him.

"I guess you know everything about your ancestors," Reg remarked.

"Not everything. Yet. Look, Reg, if your great-aunt is waiting for you..."

"Yeah, right," he said, gathering up his canvas shoulder pack, his denim jacket and his earphones. At the door he turned to her. "I think Aunt Nellie is really neat."

"Give her my love, tell her I'll call her as soon as she's settled in."

Once he was gone Sarah sat back in her chair and relaxed, glad to be alone for the rest of the afternoon. The weekend had been busy, crazy; Saturday as long a day as she

had ever lived. On Sunday she had gone back to the flea
market. It had turned freezing, the sky clouding over, and
when at last she packed up and escaped home, it was with a
sense of disappointment that had nothing to do with the
selling of memorabilia.

It all had to do with Tyler Lassiter. She knew he wouldn't
keep their eleven-o'clock appointment since she'd seen him
the night before, but somehow she'd expected him to turn
up at the flea market, although from the first, intuition told
her that his charming smile, his self-confidence spelled
trouble. She hadn't any doubt at all he was after something
specific.

But what? He had talked about an ancient bit of lore he'd
learned in the outback. It would have to do with their common ancestors, Emma Crewes and the man she married. It
had all been cut and dried, hadn't it? She sighed and looked
at the file-laden office. Endless cartons filled with documents on the towns and townships both big and minuscule
that made up Merriman County. A job to last a decade, and
Tyler Lassiter figured he'd be able to pounce on the information he wanted at once. Would he?

"You're in there somewhere, damn it," she said aloud.
"But what, where? If I found you, would I even know it?"
She sighed. She'd have to organize her thoughts, plan a
searching campaign if Reg didn't come back with a carton
marked Riveredge and find what she was looking for before Tyler with his easy charm could talk Alec into gaining
access to the files.

Tit for tat. Alec had a passion about revitalizing the
waterfront. If Tyler were desperate for information, there
was no doubt he'd make a deal with the town supervisor.

No, ridiculous, it couldn't be. What in the world was she
thinking of, assigning nefarious deeds to a man she didn't
even know. Anyway, Sarah admitted to herself, her feeling

of unease had nothing to do with Crewes history. It had to do with the man himself and her reaction to him.

When he came into Victor's house with Maggie Roman, Sarah's first thought was, he's taken. She'd been almost relieved. But then she *would* be. She wanted no more complications in her life than she already had.

What was there about the man that made her want to back him into a corner, to emerge from her silly little game of Finesse in triumph? And cerulean eyes! She had looked long and hard at her eyes Sunday in the bright morning light. They were blue, as blue as they had always been, the Crewes eyes, her father's eyes, Uncle Wave's eyes. Cerulean, indeed.

Her thoughts were interrupted by the sound of her telephone ringing. When she picked it up she found Celie at the other end.

"Hello, Sarah, what are you doing?"

Sarah flushed. "Staring into mindless space. How are you?"

"My usual cheerful self. I'm calling for two reasons. One concerns the archives department. It's about time we did an update on the mixed-up records of Merriman County. Can I send over a reporter?"

"Hey, that sounds impressive. You're talking about your part-time freshman reporter, Adriana Scott. Sure, I'd love to see her if all you want is a story about logistics, statistics and stasis."

Celie laughed. "Okay, I'll give you a couple of weeks."

"You do sound pretty cheerful," Sarah said. "But the truth is I feel there's a certain forced sound to it. Have you, um, oh hell, you know how direct I am. What about Victor? Have you talked with him since Saturday?"

"Sarah, my love, back away. Victor and I aren't teenagers who keep in touch every few hours. He has his life and I have mine and that's all there is to it."

"You're right," Sarah said. "I know I might be out of line, but I really—"

"Mean well and I love you for it. We'll have lunch and talk about just how out of line you are. We could go to Haddie's here in Ramsey Falls. She has a new luncheon menu, Hungarian specialties."

"Goulash, great. I think I've actually had too much native American home cooking for the moment." She and Celie would continue to wind around the subject of Victor unless she had a talk with her cousin. She made a mental note to corner him even if it weren't any of her business.

"Anyway, I called you for another reason," Celie went on. "I've been going through the classified ads for Sunday's edition and I found something you might be interested in."

"Antiques."

"Precisely. A private house sale. The ad says the old Franklin orchard is for sale. He's clearing out the contents of his house and in the lot being offered are various old diaries and documents."

"The Franklin orchard? Jed Franklin's place? It borders on Riveredge. I wonder why he's giving the place up."

"Something about going out west to live with his son. The diaries he's offering could yield some good local information. No reason why you shouldn't take a look at them. If they're worth something, perhaps the town might spring for the cost."

"More old papers? I don't have the energy to even think about it." But in spite of her objections, Sarah felt the familiar rise of excitement that happened whenever she heard of an old cache being offered for sale to the public. She would always look, search, dig into the past, her past, theCrewes past, the past of this corner of the world that she loved so much.

"I'm a little worried about who might buy the place." Celie said. "My husband and I used to go there for apples. Mr. Franklin has some very old trees with unusual varieties. Well, who ever said progress was a good thing."

"Not I. Celie, thanks a million for the tip. It's great to have friends in important places. But," she added, "isn't that a little like cheating? Your telling me ahead about the sale?"

"I'm sure he's anxious to sell. He doesn't have to open the door to you, Sarah. If you buy him out I'll gladly take the ad out of the paper and return Mr. Franklin's money to him. Will that salve your conscience?"

"If I decide to go, I'll call ahead. Lunch Wednesday sound good?"

"Sorry," Celie said, "but that's the day Tyler Lassiter is taking me out for lunch."

"Ah, the interview, of course."

"Do I detect a note of curiosity in your voice? Totally unforced, that is?"

"Goodbye," Sarah said hurriedly, "and thanks for the scoop."

When she replaced the receiver, Sarah sat for a few minutes with her hands locked behind her head. If Tyler was anxious to make friends, he was going about it in all the right places. She reached for the telephone and asked information for the number of the Franklin house. Mr. Franklin was in when she dialed and agreed to show her documents before the announced sale.

She decided to run over after office hours and dutifully picked up the manila folder that Reg had put on her desk earlier that day.

The telephone rang again, and after she dealt with that call, another came in. All the while she sifted through the stained envelopes that the folder contained, one after the other, trying to make meanings out of the faint red-colored script that still clung tenaciously to the paper.

The second call disposed of, Sarah gingerly picked an old envelope out of the folder. She could make out the name Decatur, perhaps a relation of Celie's late husband. She stared at it unmoving. Celie and Ty Lassiter having lunch together. She realized she'd felt a certain amount of envy over the idea, as though with his confession that he and Maggie weren't and never had been lovers, Tyler had become her property for his time in Merriman.

"You look as if you're in a trance."

Sarah jumped, startled at the intrusion, but she knew without even looking up that Tyler was there, digging into her thoughts as he would no doubt like to dig into the Merriman County files.

CHAPTER FOUR

"SORRY," Tyler Lassiter said. "I didn't mean to alarm you." He gave her a crooked grin and leaned against the doorjamb, his fists in his pockets. He seemed to bring in with him something fresh and wonderful of the outdoors. He was casually dressed in khakis and a heavy Irish knit sweater. His hair was ruffled as though by the wind, a lock drawn carelessly over his forehead.

But in spite of the unexpected joy Sarah experienced at seeing him, her alarm signals had begun to go off wildly in all directions, as though he'd stormed the citadel and was about to make off with the files.

"Wh-what are you doing here?" she stuttered at last. "How'd you get past Gert at the front desk?"

"Lead cinch."

"Really? Usually she's like a tiger out there protecting her cubs."

"I told her you were expecting me." His grin broadened. "Weren't you?"

"I was not."

"Funny, I could've sworn—"

"Did I miss something?" she said hotly. "I don't remember making a date with you."

He raised his hands, as if he were at fault, it couldn't be helped, there he was. Sarah shook her head slowly, almost imperceptibly. She couldn't stay angry; he could charm Medusa.

"The truth is," he said, "I tried to get you at noon and spoke with someone named Reg and told him to tell you I was on my way over."

Sarah nodded. "That explains it. If you catch him with those earphones on, then you're out of luck."

"That kind of music."

"That kind of music. With the salary we're paying him I can't tell him to knock off listening to rock while he's working. Now," she added in a burst of efficiency, "just how can I help you?"

"It seems that I haven't any choice in the matter." He grabbed a chair, sat down and faced her across her desk. "If I expect to go through the public record, you're the person to see."

"You've known that all along, Ty."

He laughed, sat back and locked his hands behind his head. "True, but you can't blame me for trying to pull a few strings."

"Such as?"

His eyes took in the chaos of the office, and without answering her question, he remarked casually, "All the history of Merriman County in this tight little place?"

"Not quite." She looked around and her hand went automatically to the folder she had just been examining. Ty caught the gesture and she felt herself coloring slightly. It was as though he'd caught her out in some act of piracy when it was no such thing. "I believe we have a problem," she began. "I'm in sole charge of the county records. You're interested in finding out about your very very great-grandmother Emma Crewes, and I'm not about to let you invade this domain, or any other, not at the present time."

He said nothing, continuing to watch her with a slight smile on his face.

"Look, Ty, as every newspaper and magazine in the country reported during the bi, tri, whatever centennial, we have a delicate predicament here in Merriman County. Our records are scattered all over the place, they're a mess, they're in no discernible order, some are water damaged, some are stuck together and need experts to pry them apart. Your distant grandma Emma may not come to light for the next decade. You're not the only one in town anxious to go into his personal history and I can't make any exceptions to my strict rule."

"Much as I sympathize with your plight, lady archivist," he said, "I still want access to the records."

She shook her head slowly and for a moment their gaze held.

"They're in the public domain, I trust," he said. "I can get a court order, you know."

"Can you? We're a tight little community here. It might take years to process your request through the system."

He smiled once again. "There's nothing I like better than a tough fight."

"Have you the time? I thought you were just passing through on the way to Beverly Hills."

He laughed suddenly, the moment of tension broken. "Finessed by one Sarah Crewes. For the time being. Come on," he said, "let me buy you lunch. If there's anything I hate it's an argument on an empty stomach."

"As a matter of fact I'm brown-bagging it, but you can share my lunch. Tuna fish, a couple of carrot sticks and fresh coffee."

"Deal," he told her.

"I have the oddest feeling that minor skirmish ended too quickly and too peacefully," she observed. "I don't quite trust the terms of the treaty, come to think of it."

"Hey, I know how to withdraw when bested, that's all."

"For the time being, you mean."

"For the time being."

Once again she gazed at him for a long moment. Neither turned away. With a sudden little thrill that danced lightly through her body, Sarah thought how easily she could fall in love with Tyler Lassiter and what a fool she'd be to try.

"It's a beautiful day outside," he told her. "Why don't we take that brown bag, those healthy little carrot sticks and that fresh coffee and have a picnic somewhere?"

Her first inclination was to refuse, but when she looked past him out the window, she found the juniper bush awash with sunlight. She couldn't see the sky but knew it would be a clear dazzling blue, a typical autumn sky. "Done. I've an errand I want to run anyway, and we can take care of that while we're at it." They'd go out in the direction of the Franklin house and see what the owner had for sale. It wasn't playing hookey at all, it was legitimately doing an archivist's work.

"I'll drive," Sarah said as they made their way past a quizzical Gert at the reception desk. "Gert, I'm going out for a while. Could you take my messages, please?"

"Okay, when will you be back?" Gert reserved her smile for Ty, who winked at her, bringing a bright blush to her cheeks.

"Can't say. I'm on my way to examine a boxful of old papers somebody has for sale."

"More papers, ouch!"

When they were in Sarah's car, she turned to Ty. "I caught that wink back there. Thought you'd like to know Gert's as loyal as the day is long."

"What's that supposed to mean?"

"It means don't try it."

Ty clicked his tongue. "You have a suspicious nature, Sarah. Aussies are known for their scrupulous honesty and above-board methods in all dealings."

"I'll bear that in mind," she said, engaging the engine and moving out of the parking lot onto the main road. She was quiet for a while as she maneuvered through the busy traffic that always clogged the center of town.

Ten miles north of town Sarah drew up in a small grove of trees that sheltered a couple of picnic tables just off the main road. "Thought we could have our picnic here," she said. The day, which had started out gray, had a brash, dogged chilliness to it, the kind of weather Sarah liked and was dressed for in a quilted denim jacket, wool sweater, skirt and boots.

They waded noisily through a thick carpet of fallen leaves to get to the picnic table. "I like this part of Merriman," she told him once the brown bag had been opened and its contents split between them. "A mix of dairy farms, apple orchards and vineyards. And plenty of land still left for forests, especially along the mountain route." She poured a steaming cup of coffee for Tyler out of the thermos.

"You travel ten miles from where I grew up in Australia and you end up in exactly the same place," Tyler said.

Sarah stared at him in astonishment. "I'm not sure I understand."

"The outback, flat, vast, unpopulated. My parents owned a sheep ranch and I spent my youth gazing at the horizon, imagining something tremendous and exciting just beyond it. The trouble is," he said, laughing, "when you get there—"

"Beyond the horizon, you mean."

He nodded. "When you get there, there's no there, there."

"Gertrude Stein said that, didn't she?" Sarah remarked.

"She must have been talking about the outback then. Hundreds of miles of nothing. I used to imagine that the rare cloud formations I'd see on the horizon were cities just suddenly built overnight."

"What was it like to live in such an empty place?"

"Lonely."

"Oh well, loneliness isn't endemic to Australia. I've been lonely in the middle of New York City." She stopped short, aware of his raised eyebrow's and the curious tilt of his head. She could have kicked herself for such a revelatory remark and wondered what had even made her say it.

"It's a different kind of loneliness where I came from," he said. "There's no one around for hundreds of miles. You'd give your soul to be lost in a crowd." He wasn't looking at her but past her to something that hovered out of sight. "The sky stretches from one end of the universe to the other." His voice was so soft she had to lean forward to hear him. "So many stars the heavens resemble a vast polka dot curtain encircling the earth."

"Do you want to go back? Do you ever go back?"

"Do I want to live there again? No. Do I go back? Yes, to see my parents, but they sold the ranch and live in Sydney now. Do I feel nostalgic? For clear unsullied skies, always, until I hit your neck of the woods. Same clarity, softened at the edges." He picked up his half of the tuna fish sandwich and bit into it.

A sudden gust of wind riffled through the leaves. The sky had begun to cloud over and there was a rush of chilled air and a longing quality Sarah associated with fall. A feeling of the long white winter to come, of red noses and snowball fights and Christmas plans and skiing. "I like this, too," he said. "Want to talk about your kind of loneliness?"

"Yours is far more interesting," she replied. "How and when did you escape?"

"My family sent me to England to go to school. I wanted to be an architect early on."

"Those cloud cities."

He gave her an admiring smile. "You hit the nail on the head. I wanted to build cluster housing, skyscrapers, I wanted to bunch people together so they literally had to touch in passing. For the most part I've worked in cities, New York, London, Rome, wherever the crowds are."

"So you'd never be alone again."

He shook his head. "Oh, I'd be hit every now and then with a desire for space and quiet and plenty of it. I'd hie me off to Australia or someplace equally remote." He stopped all at once and reached for his coffee. "I'm talking too damn much about myself," he remarked gruffly.

"But that's what one does in society. If you don't want to talk, there's always that vast empty desert."

"Ah," he said, "but you're not in that desert, you're here and I want to know how in hell you were ever lonely in the middle of Manhattan."

Sarah screwed the top back on the thermos and then wrapped up the empty sandwich bags. She didn't quite know how to answer, but it seemed important to her that Ty believed she had her life under control. That, in fact, if she were alone, it was by design.

"I wonder if we were in Manhattan at the same time," Ty mused. "That was four, five years ago."

"If we were, our paths wouldn't have crossed. I was buried in a bank vault and you had your head in the sky."

"Do you always take jobs that have you squirreling away in some basement?"

His question was asked not unkindly, yet Sarah bridled. "Actually it was on the twenty-seventh floor of a skyscraper. I'm an archivist by trade. Squirreling is the name of the game. It's what we do, work in museums or libraries or vaults or the basements of town halls. We spend our time poring over arcane stuff, records, documents, moldy old papers. We always have our fingers sifting through files, pushing something in or taking something out. We tap things into computers and hope they won't get lost. Windows and wide views of the park aren't part of our work. In fact the outside world is a hindrance, not a help."

"Is it your trade by design?"

"Of course," she said. "You don't think I just fell into it on my way somewhere else."

"Come on," he said, reaching for the thermos and paper bag, "let's see those documents that are waiting for you. Archivists must archive, I suppose, if they're to get through the day."

"OH WAIT, WAIT." Sarah pulled up short in front of an antique shop in the center of a small one-street town. "You never know." She turned to him, eyes glistening. "You can wait here, I won't be a minute."

Since it was the third shop he had followed her into on the way to her destination, Ty smiled and dutifully stepped out of the car. "Won't be a minute? Amazing how time flies when you're having fun."

"I'm sorry," she said, walking rapidly into the store, a crowded cocoon of old and curious artifacts that held little meaning for Ty. Sarah went rapidly around the shop after greeting the owner, who was waiting on a customer. "Hi, Mrs. Reardon."

"Sarah, how's everything?"

"Fi-ine. Whatcha got that's absolutely fantastic?"

"Some embossed leather traveling frames."

"Nobody's buying them, Mrs. Reardon. I'm up to here with them." She peered down at a case of jewelry, then began to pick her way through the pieces, aware of Ty standing close.

"What in hell are you looking for?" he asked. She felt his breath whisper against her hair. "You're like one of those bowerbirds that are pretty fussy about what goes into a nest."

"Fussy?" She turned suddenly and bumped into him, and felt his steadying hand on her arm. "I didn't know bowerbirds were fussy."

He laughed and for a moment pulled her close. "Well, if they aren't, they should be. What are you looking for?"

"I don't know." For a moment they stood there, faces close, hers serious, his puzzled. "I don't know," she said again, and pulled away to resume her restless search through the jewelry box. He reached past her to pick up a garish ruby-red necklace and placed it around her neck. "There. Queen of the Hops."

He placed a quick kiss on her forehead and with a soft gesture pushed her hair back. "No, not you. Let's see, your pearls." He removed the necklace, thrust it back in the box and began to go through the collection, now apparently interested.

Sarah brushed past him, feeling the imprint of his lips upon her skin and knowing that if she let him look at her a moment longer he would see the rise of color to her cheeks. She went quickly over to a table that held a number of small tin boxes with advertising slogans on them. "Something new," she called across to him without looking up. "I mean something old that intrigues me and is the right price for resale."

"I understand perfectly." He sifted his hands through the jewelry again and then abandoned it. She found him following close on her heels once again, as though trying to learn what was propelling her, but she couldn't tell him if she wanted to.

"It's the bug," she admitted. "The collecting bug. The finding of a treasure."

"Just the finding of a treasure?"

"What's wrong with that?"

"This is the third shop I've trailed you through, Sarah. I have the distinct impression you're looking for something and you don't know what."

"I don't," she said with a triumphant smile. "That's the secret of antique hunting. You don't know what you're looking for until you find it."

He shook his head. "And you, my bowerbird, don't know what I'm talking about, do you?"

An unexpected little curl of fear crawled along her skin and disappeared without a trace. "No," she said in a quiet voice and turned away. She felt, without knowing exactly why, that he was stepping on territory that was strictly hers. She began moving restlessly around the shop once again, stopping only when she discovered a marble bookend in the form of a polar bear pushing half a giant snowball. "Mrs. Reardon, where's the other half of this bookend?"

"Broken, can you beat that? And I've only myself to blame. I can let you have it for ten dollars, eight dealer's price. If I had the other half I could sell the set for a hundred."

"Well," Sarah said with a satisfied smile on her face, "somebody will want half a snowball sooner or later. Ty, look how beautifully he's carved."

"He?" Tyler asked, examining the carving.

"He," she said firmly, carrying the bookend in triumph to the counter, where she concluded the sale.

She made yet another brief tour of the store before marching out with her prize.

"Take that to the flea market with you?" Ty asked.

"Right. It's kind of round robin. You sell something, and you need to replace it. You've made a profit so you sink the original investment plus the profit into something else. You never catch up."

"But you also never take the profit and run."

"Where would be the fun in that?"

He laughed and in the cold wrapped his arms around her. "That the only fun you're having?"

She raised her hands spontaneously and drew them about his neck, still holding the polar bear bookend. The air felt good, the crispness almost tart. "You're a funny sort of character," she said, the remark almost surprising her. "On the one hand you build skyscrapers and pool houses for Hollywood ladies, and on the other, you're trailing archivists around the countryside. I feel as if something's missing here and I'm not sure what."

He lifted her chin and placed his lips against hers for a long moment, then quickly released her. "Maybe that's what's missing."

Sarah put her hand to her lips and stared at him, knowing she had wanted the kiss, had wanted it perhaps from the first moment they met. "Why'd you do that?" She moved away from him.

"You asked for it. Anyway, we're kissin' cousins, aren't we?"

She laughed, but nervously. She had a feeling she couldn't quite trust him, that he had something up his sleeve, that, if she weren't careful, he'd charm her into acquiescing to whatever it was he wanted.

"Let's go," she said, heading for the car. "It's still business hours and we're on county time."

"After clearing out three antique shops, you're telling me about county time?"

Sarah laughed as she slid into the driver's seat. "The county'll get its money's worth, believe me."

It was Ty's turn to order the car stopped when they were back in the countryside passing a large apple orchard that encompassed hundreds of acres on both sides of the road.

"Okay, driver, pull up right over there."

"What for?" Sarah asked, giving him a worried glance.

"Apples."

"Haven't you ever seen an orchard before?"

"Come on, pull up, I feel an urge coming on to steal an apple."

"You're kidding. Let's go, we're late as it is."

"I'm not kidding, Sarah, pull over, indulge me."

"But—"

"But me no buts."

"We don't do that sort thing here," she said stiffly. "We don't steal Farmer Brown's apples just for a gag."

"You paragon of virtue, you," he teased with an unbelieving smile.

"Okay, it's your head, not mine." Sarah drew over to the side of the road and came to an abrupt halt. "Go on, steal your apple. It tastes better that way, I know."

Ty stepped out of the car but leaned back in. "One little apple, Sarah. It's a man's duty, you know."

"I hope the farmer sees you and fills you full of buckshot."

He laughed and went down the steep embankment and scrambled up the other side into the orchard. Most of the trees had already been picked clean of autumn apples, but she could see a few that were still laden. Winters, no doubt. She watched as he took his time selecting the apple and carefully twisting it off. Deep into the orchard she saw five or six deer under a tree, munching at windfalls. One stood on her hind legs and tested an apple still pendent on a tree.

Without any effort, Sarah's eyes slipped back to Ty. He was reaching for an apple high on a branch. Was he always like that, she wondered, trying for something just beyond his grasp? As he pulled the branch down, she focused on the graceful line of muscles that strained against his pants, on the tilt of his head, the strong chin, the intense concentration discernible even at that distance.

She followed his movements with a mix of apprehension and something else she couldn't quite name. She was afraid he posed a threat, a danger, but knew with a certainty that it wouldn't come in the expected way. She kept her eyes on him until he turned and began making his way back to the car, holding the apple as though it were an extraordinary prize. She took a deep breath and swallowed hard. Dangerous perhaps, but fascinating. And such a little boy.

When Ty came back into the car, he brought in a chill scent of the outdoors. "Take a bite," he told her.

"Uh-uh."

"Stolen merchandise."

"Uh-huh. We're respecters of private property around here. You don't pick my geraniums and I won't pick your apples."

He bit into the apple, making a loud crunching noise. "Fantastic. Winey, crisp, with a good memory." He grinned at her. "Take a bite. Live dangerously."

She reluctantly took the apple he handed her and bit into the spot his teeth had gouged out. "Macoun, I think," she said, chewing around her words. It was a tart apple with a distinct McIntosh flavor. She solemnly handed it back and started the car. "Don't tell me stealing apples is part of your boyhood memories. Somehow I won't be able to believe it."

"The English countryside," he told her. "I had my share of it in university. Rites of manhood, all that sort of thing."

"Sure, Lassiter."

"As for you, my pretty cousin, you believe in living the uptight, forthright life in which there are no secrets and you'd never lie to save your soul. And decidedly never stop on the side of the road to case your neighbor's orchard."

"I go by one rule, Ty. If you don't lie, cheat or steal, even apples, you won't be stuck with the consequences."

"You must live a pretty uneventful life under the circumstances." He finished the last of the apple, opened the window and tossed the core to the side of the road.

"And I don't litter, either," she said.

"That's sending organic material right where it belongs."

Sarah laughed and shook her head. "I can say one thing about you and me, Ty. We find plenty to argue about."

"Those are the minor problems. The major ones, I suspect, can take care of themselves."

"Such as . . ."

He waited a long moment before answering, then said, "Such as your lips tasting better than that apple."

The wheel slipped under her grasp and it took her several seconds to right it. "And that's something else you're not supposed to steal," she told him.

"No, I suppose not. Pilfering of kisses requires careful planning, long-range goals, that sort of thing."

"There's the juncture of Marlboro coming up," she said hastily, glad of the diversion. She made the turn, then turned once again a quarter mile down into a narrow two-lane road snaking between another large apple orchard.

"Ah," Ty remarked, spying the large stone Dutch Colonial up ahead. "Wonderful architecture. Nothing like it in California. There it's all Spanish influence or 'Gee, look how much money I make.' "

There were bright red curtains in the farmhouse window and a thin spiral of smoke out of one of the chimneys. On the left was a large barn, and near that a smokehouse and chicken coop. A dun-colored swayback horse grazed behind a fence. When Sarah pulled the car up and stilled the engine, the animal trotted to the gate and looked out at her as though waiting for a handout. She stepped from the car and discovered a bin of apples near the barn. She picked up two deep red Romes and handed them to the horse, petting him as he daintily accepted the fruit, lips curled around his teeth.

"Been here before?" Ty asked her.

"Oh, when I was a kid and came apple picking with Waverly."

He glanced at the bin of apples and smiled.

"Let's go," Sarah said. "But before we speak to Mr. Franklin, a word of caution. No oohing and aahing allowed, for instance. When buying anything, we play it cool. Remember, I'm an old hand at bargaining, and the price rises directly in proportion to your show of interest."

"Subterfuge at all costs," he agreed. "I bow to your superior knowledge of the fine art of game playing." He followed her to the house. "I'm here to learn and I'm grateful I've a master to teach me the techniques of dissembling."

"I'll decide how I feel about that remark later." Sarah led the way to a bright red front door. It opened just as she was about to knock.

The man who stood there was tall and gray-haired. His eyes were a pale blue set in a weather-beaten face. He looked at her sharply and said without preliminaries, "You the one who called about that passel of old papers?"

"I'm Sarah Crewes. Remember me, Mr. Franklin? And this is Ty Lassiter."

Franklin nodded. "You're Waverly Crewes's niece."

Sarah gave him a surprised smile. "His great-niece. Mr. Lassiter is also a relation."

"Distant," said Ty, putting out his hand and shaking Franklin's.

"Well, come in then." Franklin stood aside and let them into a big, warm, old-fashioned farmhouse kitchen with a cast-iron stove and pine floors. It smelled of apples and spices. Sarah glanced at the huge pot bubbling on the stove and thought he was probably making applesauce.

"Celie Decatur said you grow some rare varieties of apples," Sarah remarked.

"This should be my last year doing it," Franklin replied in a truculent voice. "I'm giving up the place and going to live with my son in Santa Fe."

"Nice town, Santa Fe," Ty commented.

"Maybe so, maybe not. Back this way," he said, and led them to a rear bedroom that was being used for storage. "Always liked collecting the bits of history about this place. This was my daughter's room. Married now, living in France."

There was an old four-poster bed covered with a flowered tablecloth upon which Franklin had placed cartons filled with household goods. Bookshelves were stuffed with old books and small collectibles. Sarah longed to examine them but she had come to the Franklin house for one purpose only and that was to examine whatever old documents he had to offer.

"Wife spent all her spare time browsing in flea markets," Franklin explained with an apologetic air. "She died last May, and I just got around to sorting things out."

He bent down and hauled a large cardboard box from under the bed. "Selling everything now and giving up the place. Going to live with my son in Santa Fe."

"I'm sorry about your wife," Sarah said quietly. "I guess Santa Fe is going to be a big change."

"A change I can't say I'm anxious to make," Franklin told her. "The fact is I can't run the place by myself. Daughter isn't about to come back and watch apples grow. Son runs an art gallery in Santa Fe. Art gallery." He shook his head as though he would never cease being puzzled over the fact. "Don't know where he got that from. Neither the wife nor I knew a damn thing about art."

"Beautiful city, Santa Fe," Ty said. "Plenty of sun and it has a big art colony."

"If that's where you want to be," Franklin replied. "No change of seasons, what kind of life is that?" He rummaged around in the carton and then removed a faded green velvet-covered book. "This is my home," he went on. "Always thought I'd die here just like my wife. Now I've got to leave her, too."

"You'll take your memories with you," Sarah said.

He stiffened slightly and then abruptly handed the velvet-covered book to Sarah. "Well, you didn't come to hear my problems. Here's one of the diaries. Go ahead, look through the carton. Pack of old deeds down at the bottom."

"All pertaining to the property?" Ty asked.

"The deeds for the house? No, I'm afraid not. I'll have to hold on to those until I sell the place. Imagine the new owners would want them. No, the wife picked these up some damn house sale or other. Well," he said, smiling at them. "Take your time. I've got to feed my animals."

"Thanks, Mr. Franklin."

"You'll be doing me a favor," he said, as he went slowly out of the room.

Ty took the diary out of Sarah's hands and flipped through the pages. Then he handed it back. "There you have it in a glance. Continuity, old deeds, birth, marriage, death, and is there life after Santa Fe?"

"He strikes me as being a sturdy, resourceful curmudgeon. Maybe Santa Fe could use him." Sarah sat down on a chair and began checking through the contents of the box. Then she picked up the diary and opened it.

"The intense concentration," Ty said after a moment.

Sarah glanced up to find him grinning at her. "Listen to this." She began reading from the diary. "'March 4, 1864. Margaret had a letter from Tom today.'" She paused for a moment, squinting at the pale slanted script and wondering what the writer looked like. "'The letter took two months to reach her, so only God knows if he is still on this earth. I, myself, will never get over the loss of my beloved Jeremy. No one will ever take his place.'" Sarah gazed over at Ty and found his expression one of intense seriousness. She gave him a wobbly smile and returned to the faded page. "'There are several soldiers recovering from wounds at the hospital in Herkimer County. Confederate soldiers, too, imagine! Today I made up my mind to call on them even though it's some distance away. They must be so lonely so very far from home. Confederates or Yankees, they are wounded and suffering.'"

Sarah did not look at Ty, feeling the ghost of a tear in the corner of her eye. She turned hastily to the first page of the diary. "I really think that's what fascinates me most of all. You trace your finger over a signature that's more than a century old and you've made contact with the past. Look," she said, holding up the book so that Ty could see the handwriting. "It belonged to Addie Schermmerhorn Ranger."

"Ancestor to Alec Schermmerhorn?"

"Could be," Sarah said, "although it's a common name in these parts."

"Eighteen sixty-four. I wonder if Addie knew my ancestor Emma."

"Our ancestor," Sarah corrected. She replaced the diary. "I think I'll put in a bid for these diaries. And whatever else is here." She dug into the carton and pulled out a marriage certificate dating from the nineteen twenties, then a deed for a house in Ramsey Falls. There were also a dozen or so rolled-up documents tied with ribbon. "I wonder what Mr. Franklin wants for the works." She checked her watch. "While we're waiting for him, do you suppose he'd mind if I looked at the other stuff he has for sale?"

"I've a feeling," Ty said, "he'd pay you to truck it all away." He took the chair she had vacated, picked the diary from the carton again and began to page through it.

Sarah went over to the bookshelf and examined some of the old toys sitting on it. "Look at this," she said, referring to a hand-carved horse pulling a wagon.

"Mmm." Ty turned a page.

"Okay, don't look. No Confederate soldiers around here, anyway."

He laughed, but she was already diverted by the sight of a charming dollhouse sitting on an old school desk. Sarah bent to peer through a cellophane window. "I should think architects would be interested in houses of all sizes and varieties. I'd judge this as turn-of-the-century Edwardian." The furniture was still intact and the rooms were peopled with tiny celluloid figures. There was that slight expected tightening of her chest as she stared in at the miniature scene. Somewhere in the back of her mind was the memory of a similar dollhouse. It was always like this, this sense of déjà vu in a place she'd never been in before, this sudden transportation to another achingly familiar time and place.

"What was that you were saying about architecture?" Ty asked.

"Was I saying something?" She wandered away from the dollhouse and picked up a piece of torn lace with a delicate rose embroidered in the corner. She let it slip through her fingers. Whose dollhouse was it? Whose bit of lace?

She heard the rustle of a page as Ty examined the diary. But for that sound, the room was close and quiet, a museum of a room. She looked about with a quick searching glance, filled with the same expectancy as always that she'd find something special, some positive aspect of memory, hers or someone else's. Then she saw it, the doll, curled into a small blue basket. With trembling fingers, Sarah reached for it and exhaled a little sigh she'd been scarcely aware of holding.

"I had a doll like this when I was young." She held it up and examined it carefully. The face was grimy; there was a fingerprint of dirt on the tiny nose and one eye was washed away. Its red hair was matted and unruly.

She smoothed her fingers down the lace-trimmed dress. A bit of the lace had pulled away from the hem. Then with a gesture that came straight from her childhood, Sarah peeked under the hem, knowing just what she would find: long lacy underpants full of holes with a bit of ribbon holding them up.

"I called her Ferdy," Sarah said to Ty. She turned, clutching the limp toy, to find him gazing curiously at her. "I can't remember what happened to her."

"Probably in doll heaven romping with a regiment of tin soldiers I once owned."

Sarah stuck her tongue out at him. "Trust you to prick my nostalgia balloon."

He closed the journal and stood, shaking his head. "Is that what you've been looking for so avidly all afternoon?" he said, gesturing toward the doll. "Ferdy? And when and if you find her, what will it mean?"

His words washed over her, cool and analytical, making her feel a fool. "I said she *looked* like a doll I once owned, that's all. I attach no importance to it, Ty, no importance whatsoever."

He was a long time answering, his eyes holding hers. "If you say so, Sarah, I believe you."

CHAPTER FIVE

"FOUND SOMETHING you wanted?"

Sarah turned, startled. Mr. Franklin had come back into the room bearing two steaming mugs of apple cider. "Here, figured you might like some of the real thing. Nice and hot."

"Ah," Ty said with a satisfied smile as he accepted one of the mugs, "that's what smelled so great when we came into the kitchen."

Like the memories that seemed to drift about her in the small cluttered room, the taste of the cider took Sarah a long way back to a time she couldn't quite name. "Delicious. The same recipe we use at home, cloves, cinnamon, but something else I can't quite name."

"Lemon and orange peel for a little bit of bite," Franklin told her. "Incidentally, tucked a gallon of cider into the car for you folks when you leave."

"You did?" Sarah gave him a pleased smile.

"Used to sell it in town, but now every supermarket carries some brand or other and it's enough for me to see this year's apple crop picked."

"Lemon and orange peel," Sarah told Ty wistfully. "That's it, that's it, I'm sure. It draws me all the way back to when I was a little girl at Christmas."

"The doll, too?" he asked, pointing to the toy she held on to so tightly.

"Yes," she said, although his remark made her feel suddenly sheepish. "That, too."

"Daughter's," Franklin told her. "Wrote me and said to sell everything, not to worry about her being sentimental."

"I'd like to make an offer on the carton," Sarah said, "but I'll have to speak with the town supervisor first."

"Need a hundred dollars for the carton and everything in it," Franklin replied in an unexpectedly businesslike tone. "I know there are plenty of collectors out there who'd pay it."

"It's a fair price," Sarah told him. She heard a sharp breath and turned to Ty.

His look was faintly mocking, and when Franklin excused himself to get his ledger, Ty said, "So that's how an old pro bargains. Glad I came along for the lesson."

"Glad you did, too," she remarked cheerfully. "Now you know there's a time and place for everything, including not bargaining."

"Soft hearts and big business don't go together."

"This isn't big business, this is getting the town archives in order."

"Got to write everything down or I forget it," Franklin said, coming back into the room.

"Mr. Franklin, could I use your phone?" Sarah asked. "I'll have to check with the town supervisor first about spending the money. Budget," she added apologetically. She put the doll back where she had found it.

"Sure thing, young lady. It's in the kitchen near the window."

She had no luck locating Alec Schermmerhorn, however, neither at his office nor at his home. She didn't bother to leave a message with his secretary, deciding to take the carton, anyway, pay for it herself and worry later about who was going to pick up the final bill. "I couldn't find Mr. Schermmerhorn, but it doesn't matter," she told Franklin, "since I'll pay for them myself."

Ty, standing at the window with his back to the room, did not turn around at Sarah's entrance.

"Don't worry, Mr. Lassiter has already paid for them," Franklin remarked.

Sarah frowned but managed to cover her annoyance with a laugh. "Oh really, how nice, but since they're for our town records, I'd like to make out the check."

Ty faced her, shaking his head. "Sorry, Sarah, you're a little late."

"You mean you couldn't have waited five minutes." Her voice was low and even and directed at Ty. She didn't like being snookered, and especially by him.

"Addie fascinates me. Besides, if she knew Emma, I want to read about it. Incidentally," he added, "the diary makes great bedtime reading."

"A book on manners will do you a lot more good," she snapped.

"Take it easy, Sarah. The whole works become a gift to the county as soon as I get my fill of Addie and her family and friends."

Sarah forced a smile. "Let's go." She turned to Mr. Franklin, who had listened to their conversation with a rather puzzled look on his face, "I'll call you tomorrow, Mr. Franklin. I'd like to come by again and perhaps purchase a few things for myself." She glanced around but couldn't remember where she had put the little doll.

"There's not much I'm going to take with me to Santa Fe," he said, extending a hand to her, "so you're welcome anytime. Say hello to Waverly for me."

"Yes, certainly, I'll be glad to."

Once she and Ty were back in the car, however, Sarah wasn't nearly so polite. "That was despicable," she told Ty hotly. "You knew I wanted that carton. How could you?"

"Easily. I made him a better offer. And besides, I told him you'd get them in the end, anyway."

She gritted her teeth. "Oh, don't talk to me. Do you know what would happen if you ran a booth at the flea market?"

"Certainly. I'd turn a profit."

"You'd be ostracized, that's what."

"It's happened once or twice before," he told her dryly. "Anyway, what's one thing to do with another? I thought you wanted the papers for your archives. Where do flea markets come in?"

"The issue is you and how you stole them out from under my nose."

"Stole them for a hundred twenty-five dollars. I told him the carton was underpriced at a penny less."

"A hundred twenty-five dollars! Too bad this wasn't Sotheby's. Maybe Mr. Franklin could've auctioned them off for a million, ten million, a hundred million dollars. I mean, they're *so* valuable."

Ty gave a good-humored laugh. "I think there's a streak of craziness in the Crewes line. You drag me along and then—"

"Drag you? I didn't drag you. You came along of your own free will. What are you doing in Merriman anyway? Why are you following me around?"

"Following you? Sarah, beautiful, paranoid Sarah, think back. You invited me to lunch, half a tuna fish sandwich and a carrot stick being the bargaining chips. I think it was the carrot stick that convinced me to come along. I'm a sucker for bait like carrot sticks. Then, having enticed me, you dragged me into a dozen antique shops. Following upon that little caper, you offered to be stake-out while I stole an apple for you at the risk of my life. Then, before I'd had a chance to recover from that serious adventure, what with its portents of buckshot, I was made the shill when you bargained with the poor fellow, who's about to lose his orchard to Simon Legree, and you're blaming me for wanting to give the man peace of mind.''

Sarah angrily turned the key in the ignition. "You're such a phony. And you've a genius for twisting things around to make you look good. And not answering questions when they're put to you fair and square.''

She spun the car around on the dirt driveway, leaving a trail of dust as she headed out for the main road.

"Don't worry about the carton and its contents," Ty said. "It will all go to the Merriman County archives—"

"When you die."

"A little before that, believe me. All I want to do is read the diaries—"

"Before bed."

"And go through the documents."

"Why?" she asked sharply.

"I said, great bedtime reading, the adventures of Addie Schermmerhorn Ranger, beloved of the late Jeremy Ranger."

Bedtime reading like hell, Sarah thought, exceeding the speed limit once she hit the highway and not even noticing it. The nerve, the twenty-four karat nerve of him, planning on snatching the carton out from under her while she in all innocence trusted him. She was a fool, too, allowing herself to waddle in nostalgia and dollhouses while he hatched his nefarious plan.

"I can't tell whether that's you burning or the tires," Ty remarked, pointing to the speedometer.

"Both," she admitted reluctantly.

She lightened her foot on the accelerator and automatically glanced at the rearview mirror. No sheriff's car, yet.

"Want me to take over?"

"No thanks. Put you behind the wheel and I'll probably end up in a ditch wondering how I got there. What do you expect to find in that carton, anyway? And if you find it, how am I going to know? Are you going to keep it, whatever it is? Never tell me, just hand over the useless stuff to the county archives?"

"My reasons for being in Merriman haven't changed, Sarah, not from the day I arrived. Emma Forrester Crewes. I'm looking for a bit of history about the lady."

"And it's so important, learning about her?"

He waited a moment before answering. "Isn't it to you?"

"Oh, maybe," she said, calming down. After all, they shared Emma Crewes and in a way she was as curious about Emma as Ty was.

"Sarah."

"Yes?"

He reached out and drew his fingers along her hair. "I came for Emma and discovered the scenery. From where I sit, the scenery looks pretty good to me." He ran his fingers along her neck and rested them there. "I wasn't trying to finesse you out of the contents of that carton. Just figured I'd see them before you hid them away for the next decade."

She held her breath for a long moment. All the anger drained away with his touch and his easy, soothing logic. "What school did you attend in Australia?"

"Why do you ask?"

"You must have specialized in smooth talk."

He laughed and pulled his hand away. "You're an eminently touchable lady. You can't blame me for failing to resist the irresistible."

"You mean there's something you've failed at? Hard for me to believe. There's an inn called the Pigeons Roost about a mile down the road," she added quickly, before he had time to answer. "I'd like to buy you a drink, make up for the parsimonious lunch."

"You're on."

The Pigeons Roost was a small restaurant about a mile in from the highway. "Serves the best seafood and poultry dishes for miles around," Sarah told him.

"In that case," Ty said, "you can buy me a drink, but I'm going to buy you dinner."

The dining room was a small intimate room with a bay window overlooking a back garden filled with ornamental evergreens and a pond that held a solitary mallard in it. The sun had already disappeared, and the early-evening light cast the garden in soft-edged shadows. The room was softly lit with old-fashioned sconces and candles in silver holders on each table. Once they were seated Sarah realized she had brought Ty to the most romantic restaurant in the county.

It was only after their drinks were served that Ty spoke up, his question direct and surprising her. "Exactly what is it you're looking for, Sarah?" When she frowned, he added, "I mean, your time here isn't budgeted like mine. I have a week, maybe two, to find what I want. Why all that racing around antique shops, all that pacing, all that suppressed energy bent on finding . . . what?"

She bridled. "I'm afraid I don't know what you mean."

"Searching," he said. "Picking, searching, rummaging around in other people's history. Bowerbird except you're not feathering your own nest."

"I like old things. Does everything have to have a reason beyond its own reason for being?"

He looked down at his glass of Scotch for a moment, holding it between his palms as though trying to steady it. "I saw the way you looked at that doll back at Franklin's. You were mesmerized, you were lost in the past, you were a delighted little girl again."

Sarah picked up her glass of wine and sipped quickly at it. "You were watching me." Her voice held reproach.

He reached out and placed his hand over hers. "Tell me about the little girl who loved a red-haired doll in a lace dress."

"The little girl grew up and—" She heard her voice crack and couldn't go on. It wasn't fair. She didn't want him asking questions, didn't want anyone seeking that part of her she thought well hidden. It hurt to remember. Her mother had given her a doll on her eighth birthday and Sarah had promptly named her Ferdy. Damn, she'd call Franklin in the morning and ask him to hold the doll for her even if it weren't the real thing.

"Sarah!"

His voice was a soft command drawing her back. She regarded him, almost startled. "My past is uninteresting. I've forgotten most of it," she said in a dull voice.

"I have the impression you grew up on a stud farm. Hardly strikes me as uninteresting."

"Believe me. My parents raised horses. They didn't make a go of it." She realized she was stating the facts in a terse manner as though she were reading off the headlines of her life. "When I was orphaned I went to live with Victor, who treated me like delicate china. He hadn't a notion how to deal with me, so he hired a governess whose express purpose in life was to see I had a lousy time of it. As for Victor, my darling cousin was born old with a deep sense of responsibility to himself, to the fortune he inherited, to the people of Merriman County and ultimately to his young orphaned cousin, namely me. He was never, bless him, a barrel of laughs. And," she added as an afterthought, "Maggie Roman is decidedly inappropriate for him."

"You let Victor handle her. He's a student of good breeding stock."

"Breeding stock! Maggie Roman! Well, I never!"

Ty laughed. "Sarah speechless. Amazing."

"What do you know about me?" she asked, annoyed. "I mean truly about me."

"Nothing, and I'd like to know everything. Who's the man in your life for instance?"

"Who's the woman in yours?"

He looked at her shrewdly. "Are we playing games again?"

"Point taken, ball into your court. There's no man in my life at the moment."

"But there was."

"Oh, when I worked in Manhattan there was someone. Married." She gave an exasperated sigh aimed mainly at herself. "I mean it was nothing, just possibility. We worked together."

"He was interested," Ty said quietly.

"Yes."

"I don't blame him one bit."

"I felt myself falling in love and ran away, back here. The job in Merriman opened up at the right time. It's funny," she added with a touch of uncertainty, "when I'm away from home, I don't miss the place, but whenever any kind of disaster comes along, even if it's only a washed-up love affair, it's where I head."

"Still think about him?"

"Yes."

He picked up his glass and watched her over the rim. "And you'd go back if he called."

"No, I wouldn't. He has a wife, a child, another life. Maybe I fell in love with him because we were together eight hours a day. Maybe love was in the air, I don't know. Why am I telling you all this?"

"Because you want me to know."

Yes, it was true, she wanted him to know. With the most extraordinary sense of calm she realized that Tyler Lassiter was a man to love. That if in fact she fell in love with him, she could never run away; that loving him would inform her whole life. Take care, she warned herself. Her heart was not for sale to a man who had come to Merriman on a mysterious errand that she knew instinctively might wreak hurricanes of damage in his path.

"What are you thinking about?" he asked.

"You."

"Ah, then we're making progress."

"You haven't a wife, a child, another life in California? Or Australia?"

"Will it help if I do?"

Sarah laughed. What had he caught on to? "Nope, I've no place to run as I'm home already."

"You can stay put then. There's nothing to worry about." Ty, who was sitting opposite her, had a view of the entrance to the restaurant. Sarah was surprised by a sudden look of recognition on his face. Then she heard a feminine trill of laughter behind her. "I'll be damned," he said.

She caught his eye and turned around. Maggie Roman had come into the restaurant and was threading her way through the tables to reach them. Behind her was Sarah's cousin Victor. "Oh Lord," Sarah said.

"Take it easy, Sarah." Ty reached out and put his hand over hers briefly before getting to his feet.

"Don't worry, I won't make a scene," she promised. "Scenes are Maggie's specialty, aren't they?"

"Darlings," Maggie cried, swooping down on them, "I don't believe this, how amazing! What in hell are you doing here, hiding away in plain sight?"

"Waiting for you," Ty said, kissing her cheek and then shaking Victor's hand.

"Oh, darling, you weren't. How'd you know? I mean this has been so spontaneous. We were just out driving and suddenly I was famished."

"Sarah." Looking faintly discomposed, Victor bent over his cousin and directed a misplaced kiss on her hair. "Have you eaten?"

"Just stopped by for a drink," Sarah told him hastily, her mind racing, trying to sort out her emotions.

"Oh darlings, do stay," Maggie said, giving her an imploring smile. "It'll be so much fun."

"Sorry, pet." Ty reached for Sarah's hand. "Sarah promised to make dinner for me. Something about tuna casserole."

Maggie gave them a bright smile, the idea of tuna casseroles compared to the gourmet fare offered by the Pigeons Roost leaving her speechless for a moment. Then she said, "Ty darling, I'll want you to come over to the college and visit my drama class, remember, you promised."

"And I always keep my promises, Maggie. Try the Pigeon Pot Pie."

"Not really."

"Sarah, stop by for dinner tomorrow night," Victor said. His words were terse, the command of a father to a child, but the look on his face struck Sarah as being slightly constrained, as though he wasn't quite certain what had happened to him. She repressed a smile. He'd want to know about Ty. It looked as though the Bosworth-Crewes line had something to worry about, she thought, reluctantly letting Ty lead her out of the restaurant.

"I wanted to stay," she told him once they were out of earshot. "And I don't like being hauled out by my lapel, either."

"Your cousin wanted you out of there, or couldn't you guess?"

"I think I know him better than you," she said coldly.

"Sarah, you can't stop them from doing what you know they're going to do, if they haven't already done it, that is." Ty took her elbow and propelled her through the parking lot toward her car.

"Who says I can't?"

"Common sense, and it's none of your business."

"You're making it yours, aren't you? Maybe you'd like to see Maggie off your neck and around Victor's for good."

"That hurt. Give me your key."

"I'll drive," she said, opening her car door. "And you can forget about tuna casserole."

"With pleasure."

"We'll have a hamburger. There's a diner I rather like just outside of Merriman. And I don't want to hear one more word about Maggie or Victor, not a word."

Ty laughed. "Let's go eat."

It was nearly nine when Sarah drove Ty back to his hotel in Merriman. She drew into a parking space to the right of the entrance. It was dark outside but for the soft glow of an old-fashioned street lamp, one of several that had recently been installed as part of the town's half-hearted attempts at restoration.

"Oh, by the way, I've a little gift for you." Ty reached into the back to the carton he had placed there, opened it and pulled something out. "Here we go." He handed her the doll with the matted hair and smudged nose. "For you, young Sarah, so you'll stop searching and realize you really are home."

"Ty, no, I, no, I couldn't." Nevertheless Sarah took the doll in her hand, feeling her throat constrict. Was it really the beloved Ferdy of her childhood? It had happened before, discovering dolls and deciding they had once been hers, only to sell them a short time later at a flea market, knowing they weren't.

"I saw the look on your face back there at the Franklin house," Ty said, "and decided it was a look I wanted to see again." He raised her chin. "Go on. Little girl delight, nostalgia, all the nice stuff."

Was it the doll? The one she called Ferdy? But Mr. Franklin had referred to it as being his daughter's.

"The look," Ty repeated, searching her eyes. "That was the whole idea." He took her face between his hands. "Did I do something I shouldn't have?"

"Oh, Ty, no," she said, and still grasping the doll, she spontaneously drew her arms around his neck. "No." She was aware of the night quiet outside the car, the golden lamplight and the unexpected joy of his gift. "I'm deeply touched by your generosity." He smiled, and a soft breath struck her lips. She pressed her cheek against his, feeling the rough edge of his skin.

"Beautiful Sarah," he said. "I must keep on the lookout for raggy dolls if this is my reward." Then he moved and took possession of her mouth, letting the kiss deepen for a moment before pulling back. He reached for the door handle and after a slight hesitation stepped out. Sarah watched as he retrieved the carton of documents. The doll lay on the seat he had vacated. She could feel the imprint of his lips upon hers, and when he slammed the back door of the car shut, she was ready to turn the key in the ignition. She was tired, so tired, overwhelmed by a flood of emotions that was seeping into every corner of her carefully ordered life.

Ty looked through the window and called, "Apple cider's on the floor in the back. Don't forget, half of it's mine."

She laughed, although she knew the sound was shaky. "Goodbye, Ty."

"You mean good-night."

"Yes," she said, releasing the brake, "maybe that's what I mean."

THE MERRIMAN ARMS had undergone recent renovation, which had retained most of its century-old charm but did away with its equally old inconveniences. The grand circular stairway of burnished walnut was unaltered, for instance, while a bank of elevators was hidden discreetly behind it.

The more delicate antique pieces in a lobby that predated the Revolutionary War were protected by silk cording as in a museum, yet other pieces, equally valuable, were in daily use by the hotel's guests. Pictures by the Hudson River school of artists dotted the walls along with primitive stiff-necked portraits of the owner's ancestors. And in cold weather the great stone fireplace was always burning with great chunky logs.

Ty liked stepping into the lobby, liked the scent of the wood-burning fire and even liked his old-fashioned antique-filled room on the fourth floor. It overlooked a tranquil, carefully pruned colonial garden that formed a square courtyard at the rear of the hotel. The Merriman Arms, in fact, was unlike the tall modern hotels he usually stayed at, but then again he seldom fished up in backwater towns. Ty, in fact, kicked around a lot and knew he'd never settle down in distant, tranquil Australia. As for the cities he knew well—London, Los Angeles, New York—he liked their pace but hadn't made permanent commitments to any one of them. The Pacific Palisades house he occupied was rented; he never gave a thought to buying or building his own. He wondered why this corner of the universe was so comforting, why it was holding him in its power.

He had been around Merriman for a week and the only thing that took some getting used to was the large primitive painting over his bed. It seemed to illustrate the story of an Indian maiden and her lover near a waterfall. Ramsey Falls, no doubt, with the water painted as though it were about to spill out of the picture and over his bed.

He had stepped out of the shower the next morning and was absentmindedly examining the painting when the telephone rang. It was Maggie. "Darling, why did you run away last evening? Tuna casserole, really. I hate it when you're obvious and I think Victor was annoyed. Well, we make a fine pair, don't we? You with Sarah, I with Victor." She laughed in a throaty, self-satisfied way. "You know she has some money, too, not quite in Victor's range, of course."

"No, I didn't know."

"You've heard her story, at least."

"I suppose you're about to tell me." He leaned back against his pillow, arm behind his head. Maggie would tell him, and damn it, he wanted to know, not about Sarah's bank account but about the mechanism that was driving her so.

"Long story. The money is actually from her fraternal grandfather, who outlived both his son and daughter-in-law. Also from the sale of the small stud farm her mother owned. Turned out to be *très* valuable after all."

"Learn all this from Victor?"

"Good heavens, no. General gossip, and pretty old stuff. You're talking to someone who was born here."

"Maggie," Ty said, "get to the point." He reached over to his night table and absently picked up the velvet-covered diary he'd been reading the night before.

"Her parents owned an extravagantly valuable stud farm some twenty or so years ago, but unfortunately they invested in a stud that didn't, you know, *produce*." She laughed. "Low sperm count, I guess you'd say. The whole thing really busted them flat. I remember that story. Happened just before I left Merriman for New York. Then I heard later that her father was in the Air Force Reserves and they called him up. He was killed in Vietnam." She waited for a moment, as though her recital called for a dramatic pause. "Her mother sold off the larger place to pay their debts, bought a smaller piece of property but never really made a go of raising Thoroughbred horses. Then she died. Victor took in Sarah and brought her up. She was maybe eight, ten at the time. Can you imagine? Victor was just a youngster himself but he knew what he had to do. Isn't he splendid? Isn't he wonderful?"

And that's what it was all about, Ty thought, idly opening the book and gazing at the faint brown spidery handwriting of Mrs. Addie Schermmerhorn Ranger. His friend Maggie had called to crow about Victor Bosworth.

Maggie's voice droned on. "Serious, knows so much, knowledgeable, intensely shy, I've never known anyone like him. I'm in the most awful danger of falling in love. And after all, he's not even handsome. And so good. So good, so generous-hearted. Oh, darling, be an angel and agree with me."

"Maggie, we're not in Hollywood, and Bosworth isn't one of your leading men. Why don't you just tread water on this one for a while?"

"He's ripe, he's never been *married*. Did you hear what I said? Never. And he's not, you know . . . I mean he's in his late forties and you'd wonder, but—"

"Spare me the details," Ty said, suddenly wanting to hang up. He'd been an unwilling confidante to Maggie long enough. For a while she had amused him, this child-woman who had depended upon him through too many crises of the heart.

"Ty, what's gotten into you? Morning grouches?"

"You might say that." He was remembering the finish of her last marriage. He had received a telephone call at midnight and rushed out to find her standing at the edge of a cliff overlooking the Pacific, threatening to jump. She had been appropriately dressed in something white and filmy.

"He's fascinated with me. His life has been without, you know, glamour," Maggie went on hurriedly.

"He'd be crazy not to fall for you," Ty told her in a patient manner he didn't feel. "However, a little caution on your part would be the wisest route to take. Victor Bosworth can't possibly live the kind of life you lead. One of you is bound to get hurt. Can you bear a few more knocks?"

"This is different, Ty, I know it," Maggie insisted. "I think I've finally found the man I've always dreamed of. Imagine, right back here at home. I knew about him as a kid, of course, but does a kitten look at a king?"

"Obviously."

She laughed. "We're planning a weekend in Manhattan, isn't that wonderful? He maintains a room at the Plaza Hotel. So elegant. Now, tell me about you and Sarah."

"Goodbye, Maggie. I'm late for an appointment." He hung up without ceremony. Maggie's collection of aging actors and hangers-on in Manhattan would certainly dampen Victor's ardor. Maybe. He swung his legs over the side of the bed and reached for the telephone receiver but replaced it at once. He had an urge to call Sarah, but Maggie with her childish enthusiasms, which were usually destructive, made him want to clear the bad taste of that telephone call out of his mouth.

And what the hell. Victor looked like a man who'd been around the block once or twice. The Maggie Romans of the world had probably stepped into his well-ordered life before and it was obvious he had resisted them.

Ty was through poking his two cents' worth in. Maggie was a big girl, and if she and Victor wanted to trip the light fantastic, it was all right with him. Sarah had better learn that lesson, too, and stay out of Maggie's way.

Sarah of the cerulean-blue eyes. She had leaned into him, clutching the doll, her eyes, even in that faded light, glittering with happiness. Her cheek against his, her arms around his neck. She smelled faintly of a crisp gentle perfume. Her skin was soft, cool. Her lips tasted of something impossibly good. He felt her defenses crumble, felt a quick, almost perceptible shiver shake through her. No little girl, Sarah Crewes. Sensuality waiting just beneath the surface, and he had almost inadvertently tapped it. He had pulled back, sensing it was there to savor, wanting it yet knowing when the time came it would be complete and thoroughly fulfilling.

He closed the yellowed diary with an impatient gesture and put it aside. Addie Schermmerhorn Ranger in the main had led a quiet, steady existence even in the midst of a civil war. Rooting around in the cellars of the past might fascinate Sarah Crewes. The truth was it bored the hell out of him.

The carton of papers, diaries and deeds lay on the bedroom floor at the foot of his bed. He had gone through them quickly the night before in a desultory way. As far as he was concerned, Sarah was welcome to them.

He had better things to do, one of them being a telephone call to the town supervisor, Alec Schermmerhorn. When he reached Alec they made a date for a late lunch that day; Alec would intervene for him with Sarah and that would be an end to it. He'd find what he came for, solve the problem of Riveredge with or without Sarah, with or without Waverly Crewes. Of course, what might happen after that he had no idea. If he married and if he had children, Riveredge could well belong to them. Time enough to make decisions about the future. He had work waiting for him in California, and dallying in Merriman was one way of not facing it.

A half hour later Ty was walking with his quick assertive step down Merriman's main street. The first object was a glass of juice and cup of coffee. He stopped at the corner of Main and Vanderheyden where a place called Smitty's served fresh-squeezed juice and respectable coffee. He took a seat at the counter and was a little surprised when the counterman filled his coffee cup and said, "Compliments of Mr. Gardner." He gestured with his shoulder to the end of the counter, where Ty found Hunt Gardner smiling at him. Ty picked up his cup and made his way over.

"Good to see you again," he said, genuinely meaning it.

Hunt motioned to the seat next to him. "As a matter of fact, I was going to call you."

"Ah, about the stone house."

"That too, of course. But it's because of Maggie Roman. She's been after me about you. Said you should lecture my education students on architecture. Said you're witty, knowledgeable and guaranteed to keep them awake for an hour or two."

Ty laughed. "Sounds like learning has gone to Maggie's head. Once she takes up a cause, nobody's safe."

"Oh, I wouldn't underestimate Maggie," Hunt told him. "I teach education techniques to advanced students about to take up residence in third-world countries. One of the most powerful tools is dramatizing local events in small communities where we're teaching adults to read. Maggie's been a help in setting up an idealized program our students can take into the field."

"Will wonders never cease," Ty remarked. The counter-man brought over a tall glass of orange juice. "Must be something about the Merriman air in general," he said, lifting his glass. "Obviously increases brain cells the same way it does the appetite." The juice was fresh, cold and tasty. He noted that Hunt had only a cup of coffee before him, which he scarcely touched.

Hunt saw his look and smiled. "The virtues of being well married. Jemma, who has redefined the word workaholic, gets Seth off to school, lays on a big breakfast for the two of us, then heads for Whiting Printing after making certain the house will clean itself while she's gone. Incidentally she's in her Merriman shop today."

"I knew she had one in Ramsey Falls," Ty began.

"Oh, she's an entrepreneur. One more place and I'll have to quit my work at Pack and take up bookkeeping."

"You sound like a man who'll follow his wife any-where."

Hunt let out a huge laugh. "You're right, of course. Here I am waiting out time while she goes over the Merriman books with her accountant. I've a class to teach around noon and I offered to help Jemma because one of her pressmen is sick. Lord," he added with a shake of his head, "I came here five months ago, passing through on my way somewhere else. Victor Bosworth set the bait and hooked me into a series of lectures at Pack College. You see the result before you . . . hog-tied and happily married, deep into var-nish remover. . . ." He stopped and turned to Ty, grinning foolishly. "I grew up on a farm in the Midwest and left it as soon as I could to chase rainbows around the world. I found one end of that rainbow right here, where I least expected it."

"Wonder where the other end is," Ty said.

"I wouldn't even venture a guess. How about it?" Hunt asked, turning serious. "A lecture, I mean."

"No architecture department at Pack?"

Hunt shook his head. "The emphasis has been on education, and I'm afraid the arts have gone by the wayside until now. There is a small arts program, a good English department, but our students graduate cultural ignoramuses."

"I'm afraid you're barking up the wrong tree if you think I'm in a position to define architecture," Ty said. He stirred a couple of spoons of sugar into the coffee as soon as the counterman refilled his cup. "You're looking at a man who sold his soul to the Beverly Hills devil a long time ago. I'm a builder of five-million-dollar houses for two with all the hedonistic devices you can dream of contained therein. You want a Jacuzzi whirlpool that seats ten, you've got it. Want a pool in the shape of a dollar bill, Lassiter Associates can submit a bid. How about a glass room that's a quarter mile wide and is dug out of a hillside overlooking the Pacific? No problem."

"No problem? From the frown on your face, I get the impression it's a problem all right."

Ty jerked his head up and gazed at himself in the mirror opposite. Then he laughed. "You're right, of course. I've had it up to here with easy architecture. I do my clients' bidding and, believe me, their bidding is pretty appalling." Ty stopped and frowned once again, wondering why he was telling Gardner what he scarcely wanted to admit to himself. He was a director of a small respected firm that dallied in architecture and had commissions ten years down the line.

"Well, I suppose there's something that can be learned from that, too," Hunt said. "Do the best you can with what you have. What about that skyscraper in Manhattan?"

"I was part of a winning team that submitted a bid. We could have had more, which meant traveling to New Delhi or New South Wales or New York or New whatever. After it was completed the owner of the building suggested I design a house for him on the West Coast, and the rest is Beverly Hills history."

"How come you've fished up in Merriman?"

"Came to do a little research into family history."

"And when you're not researching..."

"Haven't had much of a chance researching. Sarah Crewes guards the keys to the files and she'll make no exception about rooting through them, not even to long lost relations."

"Can't blame her," Hunt said. "The word nepotism is used pretty freely around these parts. A number of people in this town believe Sarah got the job of archivist because of Victor Bosworth and that the two of them are out to protect Victor's considerable interests. Not true, of course. A more sensible and unselfish pair never existed."

Ty raised his hands. "I'm glad to hear it. For a while I thought Sarah was being a little mean spirited to her cousin from Australia."

"Come on," said Hunt. "If you've a half hour to spare, drop by Whiting Printing and say hello to Jemma."

"Great, I'd like that."

"By the way, ever tell Sarah she lost the game of Finesse?"

Ty smiled. "I have to crow every now and then."

"She's a lovely lady," Hunt said, reaching for the check before Ty could and preceding him to the cash register. "I'd hate like hell to see her hurt."

CHAPTER SIX

"FOUR, FIVE, SIX, seven, eight, nine, ten. Wave, pick up the phone, damn it." On the eleventh ring to Riveredge, Sarah slammed the receiver down. "Oh, Reg, hi," she greeted her assistant as he came into the office. "Get your aunt back safely?"

Reg went over to his desk and threw down his book bag, his earphones and a lunch sack from a local hamburger joint. "Yeah, with her nagging all the way. Slow down, pass that car, stop here, go there, whoever said you could drive. *Ssschew*. I'm never going to do her a favor again."

"You drive like a maniac and you know it."

"I do not. Anyway, how would you know?"

"You're a young, healthy, irresponsible college kid, aren't you?"

He grinned. "Man, my Aunt Nellie was up this morning at the crack of dawn. She makes the coffee first thing and when my mom comes down, tells her she has to get a new coffeepot. Then she tells my mom not to cook eggs for me, they'll kill me, and bacon, man, forget it. Not even in our house for twenty-four hours and she's running the place."

"Give her a chance, Reg. Her life has changed drastically. After all, she's been pretty much in charge of the way she's lived all these years."

"That's what my mom says, but I can tell it's not going to be easy."

"It'll all work out. Nellie's going to get her own place, I'll bet, and in short order."

Reg shrugged. "I mean she's pretty neat, funny, too, but it's like this steamroller is about to flatten us. My dad doesn't say anything, just escapes behind the newspaper."

"Let me try that number again." Sarah picked up the phone and dialed her uncle once more, something she had been doing regularly since ten that morning. "He should answer," she told Reg.

"Who should answer?" He opened the bag and pulled out a sandwich. "Want some?"

"My Uncle Wave. I'm a little worried. I've been trying to get him all morning."

"Maybe he went out."

"Clever, Reg. The only trouble is he's got arthritis and he can't really go very far, not in this weather. Four, five, six, seven." She replaced the receiver and checked her watch. It was noon and time for lunch, anyway. "I'm going out to Riveredge. I should be back in a half hour if he's okay. Can you keep your earphones off long enough to mind the fort?"

Reg shook his head and with an exaggerated motion put the radio and earphones into his desk drawer.

Sarah grabbed her bag and jacket and headed for the door. "Keep the home fires burning." Her remark was flip, but she had a feeling of dread she couldn't quite name. The day outside was gray and cold and the damp bite in the air suggested an early snowfall. Usually the feeling gave a lift to her step. The season's first fluttering of snow wrote the end to the beauties of autumn but painted its own fresh picture. With winter her worries about Wave would only increase. He couldn't go on living alone at Riveredge and he had to understand that. She made up her mind to be firm with him and to tell him he had no choice in the matter.

When she pulled up to the great house on the river, she saw a wisp of smoke rising out of the kitchen chimney, which drew a breath of relief from her. At least he'd been able to start a fire that morning. The front door was unlocked, too, which meant he may have gone out for a walk.

"Wave? Uncle?" The house had a preternatural quiet to it, however. She went quickly back into the kitchen and found the fire in the stove nearly burned out. She threw in another log and noticed that the cat lay in Waverly's chair. Its bowl had been filled with food and a cup of half-finished coffee sat on the table.

"Wave?" She walked into his bedroom, which had been the old parlor. The bed was neatly made. She rushed out of the room and began to climb the stairs to the second floor, calling her uncle's name, her heart beating heavily now. She stopped on the landing, ran over to the window and looked out but found no sign of him on the grounds.

"Wave, it's Sarah, where are you?"

The wings on the second floor were closed off with heavy draperies, and the hall was chill and damp. She heard a faint sound from above, a slight movement and what she thought was a groan. "Oh, damn," she said aloud and raced up the stairs to the attic. The door was half open and she took in the familiar scent of dust and wood that recalled her rummaging around in the attic of Riveredge when she was a child.

"Sarah, that you?" Waverly Crewes lay in a bundle on the attic floor, grimacing with pain.

"Oh, Wave, what's wrong?"

"Damn foot, twisted the damn thing. You took your time getting here."

"Oh, Wave, how did it happen? This? The right foot?"

"The right foot, be careful."

"Do you think it's broken?"

"No." His answer was terse and she knew enough not to believe him.

She bent over him and delicately pulled his pant leg back. The ankle had already begun to swell. "How long have you been lying here?"

"How the hell do I know? I came up around ten. What time is it?"

"Noon. Anything else hurt?"

"Just the foot. Help me up, Sarah."

"I'm going to call an ambulance, get you to the hospital."

"Damn it, Sarah, call the doctor and get some compresses."

"Wave, how did it happen?"

"I don't know. I came upstairs to find something—"

"You climbed all those stairs in the shape you're in? Clever, Uncle Waverly."

"I've got a right to do what I want in this house," he said truculently. "I was looking for something. I forget what."

She knew it was no time to discuss the possibility of his having had some kind of episode with his heart. "I'm calling an ambulance, Wave. I'll be right back."

"I said I don't want an ambulance."

She looked shrewdly at him. "What is it about people when they reach their seventies? They seem to think they have a lock on stubbornness. Reg Casedonte was just telling me about his Aunt Nellie. Back in town ten minutes and she's already pulling the strings of the entire Casedonte household. I said I'm calling the ambulance."

"Nellie Casedonte? What did you say? Back in Merriman?" In spite of his grimace of pain, Sarah was surprised by the glitter of interest in his eyes.

"Look, I'll be right back," she told him.

"Funny thing about Nellie," he said. "I was just think-ing about her, but I guess in a way—" He stopped and gave his great-niece a sheepish grin. "The doctor, Sarah. He'll tell me to use a cold compress or a hot one and that'll be that."

But Sarah was already out the door and heading for the telephone in the kitchen.

TY GLANCED UP at the huge cut-glass chandelier in the lobby of the town hall, a brilliant contrast to the gray day easing in through the tall mullioned windows. The hall was old, predating the War of 1812, and in a state of perfect preser-vation. It smelled of wax and lemon oil, the supernal quiet broken only by the sound of his footsteps along the worn tile floor. Ty could grudgingly understand how someone of Sarah's temperament would find the ambience appealing.

He found Alec Schermmerhorn's office easily. The town supervisor came forward to greet him, pumping his hand and offering him a seat and coffee in the same breath. "Glad to see you," he said, and then added apologetically, "We've got a problem up on Route 7 near the old Scott house. Water main broke and there's some flooding. Let me make a few telephone calls and I'm all yours."

Ty took the seat and refused the coffee. He picked up a magazine and began thumbing through it while Alec com-pleted his calls. His mind was on Sarah Crewes. He guessed she'd be in the basement of the building, buried in her mounds of papers. Once he cast a discreet glance at the closed door, wondering if she might now somehow come wandering in. She was too much on his mind, he thought, or rather the picture of her, as though she had been stamped there with some indelible material. No amount of wishing, or washing, could get rid of it. If this were Malibu or L.A. or even Manhattan, he might have taken her to bed by this time. In Merriman, however, things took place in slow motion; the world seemed leaden with reasoned excuses.

She wasn't at all the kind of woman who ordinarily intrigued him. She was too clever, too provoking yet too careful about keeping her emotions hidden. Ty suspected that underneath it all there lurked another woman entirely waiting to be let out. He found himself thinking of her in bits and pieces: her hair shining in the moonlight; her lips red and ripe; her eyes so blue he knew if he were ever lost in their depths, he'd never emerge. Nor could he help imagining her naked on a bed in a room he'd never seen. The image flooded his mind and gripped his body, her full breasts, curved hips and an inviting smile on her lips. He imagined the scent she used, faint in the air. And her flesh, sun-stroked and warm to the touch.

Damn it, he wanted her and the idea didn't enter into his plans at all.

"Okay, got it all squared away." Alec put down the receiver and threw a smile at Ty, who jumped at the intrusion into his thoughts.

"I'll have to get down there and make an appearance," Alec went on. "Celie Decatur wants a picture for the Ramsey Falls *Times Herald*, and the Merriman *Record* was already out there. I put Celie off until we've had lunch." He rose heavily to his feet, ignoring the sound of his telephone ringing. Reaching for his jacket, he began to work his arm through the sleeve. "Like fish and chips?"

Ty grinned. "Ate them through my university years in England, out of rolled newspapers with plenty of malt vinegar."

Alec held the door for him. "We do them up a little differently here," he said. "Besides malt vinegar, we offer up tartar sauce and catsup, take your pick." He nodded to his secretary on the way out. "Back about three. I'm going to inspect that broken water main on Route 7 sometime after lunch."

"Smells like snow," Ty observed when they stepped outside. He drew up his jacket collar.

"What do you Californians know about snow?"

"We keep it in its place, out of the city and on top of mountains, where it belongs."

Alec was clearly in a good mood as he led the way out to the parking lot. "We'll take the car although it's within walking distance. The restaurant sits over the water with a striking view of the Hudson. Problem is you have to pass through the rundown section of town to get there. I'll want to give you a tour before we have lunch." His car started with a wheeze and then tumbled into gear and purred as he moved out of the lot. "The area's an eyesore, but worse than that, it's a plain waste. We could use the warehouses near the docks for any number of purposes—"

"Including refurbishing them and selling them as condos, I take it," Ty said.

"Look, I know what other cities have done. We have a lot of unemployment in the area. We have some slums, and we know the dangers of gentrification. I want—" he stopped and cast a glance at Ty "—damn it, input, and the town budget is strained to the limit."

"Meaning that you can't afford a study into the uses of the land, and you can't afford to pay for plans until you have the study."

"And," Alec added, "we've been arguing in the town council for years about how to handle the problem. Every time someone comes up with a suggestion, half the town council vetoes it and the other half applauds it."

"That's a song I've heard before."

"Take a look." Alec waved his hand to show the run-down area he had swung into. "One block off Main Street and this is what we have."

Two-story buildings of unpainted clapboard seemed to lean into one another the length of the street, which eased in a gentle slope directly to the waterfront. The view of the river and the mountains on the other side was spectacular. Ty frowned. "How in hell does it happen?"

"Slow but steady weakening of our economic ties to the rest of the state. Appearance of the railways. Trucking industry. Manufacturing business moving south or just closing down. Opening of the St. Lawrence Seaway, which diverted river traffic." They reached the river and Alec pulled into a crowded dirt lot next to an unprepossessing building with a garish painting of a fish above the front door.

"Barney's Fish and Chips," Ty read.

"If you give me a few more minutes," Alec said, getting out of the car, "I'd like to show you what I'm talking about." He began to walk with a rapid stride across the street, gesturing toward the sprawling waterfront. Rows of deserted buildings with boarded-up storefronts lined the embankment.

"Used to be a boardwalk here. Families strolling along, safe place for kids, all these stores doing a brisk business."

Beyond the long street lining the embankment, he pointed to a string of warehouses. "Those are the ones that are left. Beyond that, the wrecking ball has demolished at least half a dozen. I could take you over there. The rubble still dots the landscape, and the fair denizens of our city like to use it as a dump for their more arcane treasures, like worn-out sofas and old washing machines. Want to see more?"

"I get the picture," Ty said. What he didn't tell Alec about was the surge of adrenaline he was experiencing, all

too familiar and best kept hidden. He had too many commitments waiting for him back home and he didn't feel a
charitable nature, not now at any rate, not at this point in
his career. He'd come to Merriman on impulse and that impulsive side of his character had landed him in trouble before.

"Let's have that lunch," Alec said, looking at him quiz-
zically through narrowed eyes.

Ty smiled inwardly. His decision to meet Alec for lunch
had been completely self-serving. Who, he wondered now,
was going to flim-flam whom?

The restaurant was long and narrow with wide, newly installed windows overlooking the waterfront. There was a
pleasant, faint scent of beer and fried foods as they walked
through the door. The floor was covered in sawdust; tables
and chairs were placed strategically so that diners had an
unobstructed view of the water. The restaurant was filled,
but a table in the corner had been reserved for the town
supervisor and his guest.

"Nice," Ty commented, sitting down. A barge moved
slowly downriver, riding high on the water. The foothills of
the Berkshires on the opposite shore were a hazy rust color
under leaden skies.

"Off to the right—you can't see it from here—are half a
dozen empty warehouses, maybe a million square feet of
space."

"How much is Merriman town property?"

"Well, that's an interesting thing," Alec said. "Thirty-
four acres in all. Land was in the Bosworth family for generations and was deeded to us seventeen years ago."

"By Victor Bosworth? Man seems to be a fount of generosity."

"His uncle, actually. He left it to the county for development, stipulating that we had twenty years to complete the project. If not, the land goes on the block."

"Money go to the county?"

"That's the damnedest part," Alec told him. "Goes to a private foundation, Bosworth. Money will be used on local projects, but I'm telling you, we're missing the opportunity to really make the thirty-four acres work for the good of the community. Fish and chips and two beers," he added to the waiter, who stood by for their order. "That okay with you, Ty?"

Ty surveyed the condiments on the table. He spotted the bottle of malt vinegar and smiled. "Suits me fine. Preferable if it's served in the London *Financial Times*."

The waiter looked confused. "Just bring him the fish and chips in a basket like always," Alec told him.

"Three years isn't much time to develop the property," Ty went on, once the waiter was gone. "Not when you have a town council that's tripping over its own feet."

"I want to see it under way during my tenure. I'm thinking of retiring at the end of my term. I've been at the job for a dozen years now, time to move on, time to let someone younger take over."

Ty looked out the window. For a while both men were silent, then Alec spoke up once more. "Maybe I can squeeze some money out of the budget for a feasibility study. For the moment what I'd like from you is something very simple."

Ty drew his attention back. "I'm in town for maybe a week or two more. I just came to do a little research into family history. A hobby of mine, you might say." He threw the last out. The beers were placed on the table and he waited while Alec took a hearty slug, which finished half the glass. "If you want my opinion about developing the waterfront, I can tell you in a word or two. It's a good idea."

Alec laughed out loud. "What about your family history? What are you trying to find out? Sarah knows everything. Talk to her."

"Oh, I have." Ty picked up the glass of beer and then nodded appreciatively at Alec. "Good," he said of the crisp, dry flavor.

"Can she help you?"

"The lady guards her cache of papers down in that basement like Cerberus at the gates of hell."

"She has to," Alec told him. "Everybody in town wants a go at them. She has a mandate to straighten out the county's archives and if every Tom, Dick and Harry interrupted her...okay, okay," he added with a wave of his hand. "I'll talk to her. Know what you're looking for?"

"Let's say I'll know it when I see it."

"Who's this ancestor of yours again?"

"Emma Forrester. Married a Crewes and left for Australia just after the Civil War."

"Ah, here's our food," Alec said as the waiter placed napkin-lined baskets in front of them, mounded with deep-fried fish and French-fried potatoes.

Ty reached for the malt vinegar and spread it liberally around while Alec contented himself with a generous dollop of tartar sauce. "Great," Ty said with his first bite, marveling at the knack Americans had for reinventing other countries' national dishes and improving on them.

"Sarah's a Crewes," Alec pointed out. "In fact, Sarah's been researching family history for a long time now. Kind of a hobby."

"That so?" She hadn't mentioned the fact to Ty, but then come to think of it, he'd been playing what he already knew about his ancestor's history close to the chest.

"Well," Alec said, "you sort it out between you. I'll give her a call when I get back to the office and tell her to give the run of the files. Of course," he added, "Sarah can be pretty stubborn when she wants to."

"You mean she'll dig her heels in for no reason at all."

"Stubborn," Alec reiterated. "From way back. I remember when she was twelve, thirteen. She'd come to live with Victor after her mother's death. Wild kid." He smiled with fondness at the recollection. "Her mother was pretty cut up when her husband died, let Sarah bring herself up in a way. Victor tried to solve the problem with a governess, the works. Don't know if it ever took. For all her ladylike ways, Sarah still is a bit of a daredevil. Anyway, for a while she figured she'd be a jockey. And as if to prove the point, Sarah takes out a half-broken horse she'd been forbidden to ride. Stayed on his back, too, till he was worn down. And if the animal hadn't given in, I have no doubt Sarah would be on him still."

Ty laughed. Somehow he wasn't surprised. But the words stuck with him, *daredevil*, *wild streak*. He'd felt it in that last uncousinly kiss. It had lasted mere seconds, but then a flame needs only just so much oxygen to flare up.

"Well, what do you say?" Alec asked suddenly.

Ty looked at him and for a moment failed to understand his question.

"Input," Alec prodded.

Ty smiled and speared a potato. "Projects like the refurbishment of the waterfront can run into half a billion dollars. And you've got the special interests to contend with, the ecologists, the environmentalists, the real estate interests."

"Tell me something I don't know."

"You're looking for it to be mixed use, I gather. Living space, manufacturing, playground, shops, crafts, a careful re-creation of Merriman when it was at the height of its commercial powers."

"Clean up the waterfront and we can expect the rest of the town to follow suit." Alec's eyes lit up. "Employment, the waterfront refurbished, people living in homes they're proud of and feel safe in."

"And your town council is short-sighted enough to vote the issue down each time it comes up."

"What they want is a picture that will tell them what a thousand words can't."

"Architectural sketches," Ty said.

"With that, maybe I can get money for a feasibility study, interest some of the local property owners to kick in, you know the m.o."

"Let me work on it." Ty glanced once again out the window. The project was big, it would cost a bundle, and he hadn't any doubt of its success. What it needed was an entrepreneur with plenty of enthusiasm. And some fanciful architectural drawings that not even the devil could resist.

"Fine. Think about it. I can't ask for any better than that," Alec said. "You come up with something and the first person who'll stand in line to congratulate you will be Sarah Crewes. I'll lie a little and tell her you're knee-deep in ideas."

"Go ahead," Ty told him. "Maybe that's just what I am, about a lot of things."

HER SECRETARY showed Ty Lassiter into Celie's office on the top floor of the Decatur Building on Ramsey Falls' Main Street. Celie, who was sitting behind her antique desk, gave him an uncertain smile and shoved her glasses high on her head.

"I thought we were going to have lunch tomorrow," she said. "What's the occasion for this special honor?" She motioned him to a chair.

"I'd like to say I was just passing through," he began. Instead of sitting he went over to the window that looked out on Main Street. What he saw was a faithful restoration of a turn-of -the-century town, its citizens going about their modern business in an atmosphere that was full of charm and color. "The fact is," he told Celie, "I had lunch today with Alec Schermmerhorn and he suggested I check out Ramsey Falls if I wanted to learn something about historic restoration. I'm impressed," he added, coming over and taking a seat opposite her. "Town looks busy, proud, scrubbed up and without the feeling of being sugar-coated for the sake of tourists."

"You're right on all those counts. Alec, I suppose, is touting the Merriman waterfront restoration. Good luck if he wants your help. The first thing you'll need is an active historic-preservation society. And after that, an interested town council."

Ty suddenly realized that her attitude was adversarial and wondered why. Then the notion hit him. Maggie, damn her, she was somehow blaming him for Maggie. Gazing at the blond, good-looking and very clearly self-sufficient woman sitting opposite him, he thought that flamboyant Maggie would have tough competition. He fished around for a moment, trying to find a way of bringing up Maggie, and knew he had to stay out of it. He settled for the conversation at hand. "You mean there's no historic-preservation society in Merriman?"

"There is, but the meetings are mostly teas, archeology lectures, tours of old houses, that sort of thing. This is a very old area. Much of the original land grant in Merriman County was from the Dutch government to patroons."

Ty nodded. "Let's see if I remember my American history lessons. Patroons were given vast acreage and manorial rights to establish colonies that vowed allegiance to the Dutch government.''

"Exactly," Celie said. "Of course the *Times Herald* is old, but I'm afraid that whole system of patronage can be found in the history books, not here. To get back to any possibility of an active historical society in Merriman County, they need a Sarah Crewes to take an interest, to blast them out of their complacency."

Ty waited a beat. Sarah Crewes, it seemed to him, was as much a part of daily conversation in Merriman County as the weather. "And Sarah's not interested."

"I suppose if she were," Celie said stiffly, "the waterfront project would be under way."

"Bundle of energy, Sarah Crewes."

Celie looked at him closely. "Just why are you here, Ty? I've scheduled the interview for tomorrow, too. The one you promised me."

"Thought I'd do a little checking into the area files. Alec also told me that the *Times Herald* has been publishing without interruption since before the Civil War."

"Are you looking for information concerning the Merriman waterfront?"

He nodded but knew finding pictures or articles of the waterfront wasn't the only thing on his mind.

"As a matter of fact," Celie told him, "unlike the Merriman County archives, the *Times Herald* files are in an excellent state of preservation. *And* filed properly. During the last five years I managed to have everything put on microfiche. The earlier stuff is much too valuable for handling by any and everybody. Anyway, I'm thinking of donating the originals to Pack College, where they'll get proper care."

Ty got to his feet. "Any reason I can't go through the microfiche files?"

She stood also and held out her hand. Her smile, when it came, was suddenly very sweet and apologetic, as though the subject of Maggie and Victor Bosworth was in the air around them and she disliked it just as much as he. ''Library's on the ground floor. Just consult the librarian. She'll set you up.'' Her handshake was firm and Ty, on his way to the library, decided he liked Sarah's friend very much. And if he were lucky and his patience held out, he'd learn something in the files about Emma Forrester's marriage to Greg Crewes back at the end of the Civil War, and maybe even why they both left Merriman.

CHAPTER SEVEN

REG CASEONTE CAME triumphantly back to the office from foraging in the basement of the old country club at the other end of town. "Found it, Sarah. No sweat. It was like it jumped out at me. Here." He pointed to the carton he carried with the name Forrester-Riveredge scrawled in smudged black crayon on the outside. "This what you want?"

Sarah grinned and reached for the carton. "Reg, you genius."

"Hey, no sweat. Almost missed it, though. It was on the bottom of a whole pile. I looked at it, like, for ten minutes, should I, shouldn't I? But I figured you wanted it and you're the boss." He looked over her shoulder as she examined the contents. "There was nothing anywhere else. That was *it*."

"Maybe this is all I need. Now, my boy, I owe you one big fat favor. Just name it, Reg."

He pretended to scream, rearing back and raising his arms as if to ward off a horde of attacking bees. "Get my Aunt Nellie an apartment, get her out of my hair."

Sarah laughed. "Reg, there are apartments available in Merriman. She'll be out of your way soon enough. She just needs to get her bearings."

"Talk to her, then," he said, giving her an inspired grin, as though Sarah somehow had the means to change his great-aunt's behavior. "Tell her to get off my back, I'm a big boy."

"I'll have lunch with her, how's that? I'll talk about nephews who are grown up and can find records in old country club basements just like that, etcetera, etcetera. Is that all? I feel as if I owe you a lot more."

"Right. Buy a ticket to the Pack College production of *Much Ado About Nothing*, because I'm in it, and so is Adriana. That's Friday, two weeks from now."

"Sold. You and Adriana play young lovers, I hope."

Another grin, sly and embarrassed, crossed his face. "One ticket?"

"Better make it two." She had no idea whom she'd invite, and the name Ty Lassiter scarcely crossed her mind. Anyway, he'd be gone, she had no doubt about it.

"Two tickets, fantastic."

"Off with you now," Sarah said.

"Right, we have a rehearsal after dinner. Show up on time or else, quoth Maggie Roman. She's a pretty tough director, but fair."

"Really? You like her, then."

"Yeah, she's pretty neat. Adriana thinks so, too."

"Adriana's taken on a lot, hasn't she?" Sarah asked while Reg gathered his gear. "Between her job at the *Times Herald*, school and now an acting career."

He shrugged. "You know Adriana, she hates to stand still."

Adriana Scott, who lived in Ramsey falls and also attended Pack College, had left her part-time job at Whiting Printing for the *Times Herald*. Celie Decatur liked to encourage young talent and felt that Adriana had exceptional writing ability. As for Reg and Adriana, they had one of those steady, easy relationships that began in high school and would undoubtedly continue through college and culminate in marriage.

"See you, sweetie," she called as Reg waved goodbye.

Once the door closed on him, Sarah stood looking at the carton for a few seconds, then in a quick movement pulled up a chair and bent over it.

She knew a certain amount about Riveredge's beginnings. She also knew about the Forresters. Amazing how easy they had been to trace, after all, those distant owners of Riveredge.

Sarah readily located the early records, those pertinent to the deeding by the Dutch government to the first patroon of the property that eventually became known as Riveredge. The history of Merriman was extremely clear until the end of the eighteenth century. It was only after the Revolutionary War that deeds and rights of ownership became fudged, lost, stolen or packed away in cartons to be forgotten.

What she had before her were deeds that post-dated the Revolutionary War. She began to trace through them, handling the papers in a gingerly manner. There were no longer any Forresters in permanent residence in Merriman or Ramsey Falls, at least no one who went directly back to the original family, the last having died out about two decades before with no issue.

The first thing Sarah did was put the records in chronological order. There was only one problem: they stopped about the time of the Civil War.

The original records were carefully preserved elsewhere in the town hall, showing the deeding of twenty thousand acres to the original patroons. When the Forresters gained possession in 1721, some of the land had been granted to the original tenants. Riveredge became theirs with the manor house and ten thousand acres. The land then passed on to Ebenezah Forrester in 1763. The carton held the deed dated 1801, in which Ebenezah's son of the same name received title. Randolph Forrester was deeded title in 1823 and passed it on to his son, General Ethan Forrester, father of Emma Crewes.

Family lore had Emma Forrester marrying Greg Crewes just after the war. They left for Australia. The general retired to Riveredge and died two years later. Riveredge passed into the Crewes line and remained there ever since.

She sighed. There was nothing in the carton that referred to the succession, no deed, no marriage certificates, no birth records. The world according to Riveredge stopped with the general's inheritance. She looked around the large carton- and file-filled office. Good luck to Ty Lassiter if he thought he could easily find something about his ancestors. It could take a year, it could take ten years.

"Don't you ever give up?"

Sarah looked up to find Gert poking her head in at the door.

Sarah yawned. Her eyes smarted. "What time is it?"

"Seven. Don't you look at your watch? It's freezing in here. Sarah, I'm beginning to wonder about you."

"Gert, I'm so far behind in my work, I'm never going to catch up. I lost almost all of yesterday taking Great-Uncle Wave to the hospital and this morning visiting him once again, the old reprobate. He lies in bed blaming his fall variously on poltergeists, elves and squirrels in the attic."

"He's getting too old to stay alone."

"In that big house, anyway. What he should have is a nice efficiency apartment in the center of town. But when I tell him, I invariably emerge from the skirmish with half my head chewed off."

She had gone with Waverly to the hospital the previous day, holding his hand in the ambulance and looking at the bright side as the paramedics took his blood pressure, measured his heartbeat and pulse and smiled reassuringly at her.

Later the doctor assured her that Waverly had suffered a sprained ankle and there was no evidence of a break. Over her great-uncle's objections, a week's bed rest in the hospital was prescribed. Sarah had assured her uncle she would see that his cat Ginger was fed and, in fact, had stopped in on that errand on her way home. Just before she closed the door to Riveredge behind her, she had stopped and listened, while the cat wove itself around her legs. What had impelled her great-uncle to go up to the attic in the first place? Was it something Ty had said to him? She remembered the cold gray evening now and the odd premonition that had stopped her from going up to find out.

She'd talk to Wave about it.

"What are you doing here so late?" she asked Gert.

"Alec is in a tizzy over that waterfront renovation," Gert said. "He's been trying to get a meeting together with the trustees, and he wanted me to man the front desk until they get here."

"Did they?" Sarah frowned and wondered whether he had met with Ty and how the meeting had gone.

"Just about everyone. Phil Nevins, the old crab, couldn't make it, which should leave everyone quite happy. Incidentally, the gorgeous Mr. Lassiter and Alec had lunch yesterday. Do you suppose he's married?"

"Alec? Certainly," Sarah said.

"Oh, that's a cheap shot," Gert chided her. "He doesn't wear a wedding ring—Tyler Lassiter, I mean."

Sarah stared down at the carton of deeds and then reached out and thumbed her way through them. One more glance at Gert and the receptionist would know Ty had been too much on Sarah's mind. In fact, all during the day she had expected him to call, but every ring of the telephone proved that expectation fruitless. He wouldn't even know about Waverly's accident.

If she closed her eyes she knew she'd still feel the kiss they'd shared, the soft stirring of something she was afraid to name. He had pulled away quickly, leaving her in confusion. Petting in a car outside the Merriman Arms was no way for two grown-ups to act. She understood that, and yet the soft, sudden touch of a deepening kiss had brought a rush of emotion that almost took her breath away.

"Well, look, I'm closing up," Gert was saying. "The front door will be on the latch. Alec said he expects the meeting to last until the maintenance man shows up at least."

"See you in the morning, Gert." Sarah bent her head over her work, deep into what promised to be a long search for the deed proving Riveredge to be Crewes property.

And she really had to do something about getting help for her great-uncle. She had waited too long as it was. When she was at the hospital, she had phoned Victor, and true to his character he had come at once.

"What's he doing here?" Waverly had complained as he was being wheeled into the X-ray room.

"Uncle Wave, Victor's worried about you," Sarah had said. "He only wants what's best for you."

"Don't tell me what he wants. I know what he wants, all right."

Victor smiled and shook his head. "You're lucky I don't take you too seriously, you old hoot owl." He gave Wave an affectionate pat on the shoulder. "Try not to give the staff any trouble...."

"You've given enough money to the hospital," Waverly growled. "Bosworth Pavilion, Bosworth this, Bosworth that. I could kick them in the fanny with my bad foot and they'd smile. And don't forget, I'm sailing out of here tonight to see you don't get your hands on my property." The door to the X-ray room closed behind him.

Victor laughed out loud. "I love that old curmudgeon. Too bad he thinks I want to pull Riveredge out from under him."

Her cousin took her arm and led Sarah to the waiting room. "Is that what his fussing is all about?" she asked.

"I once proposed buying his property. I offered him the blacksmith's cottage you have, free and clear. I wanted to keep an eye on him and also ensure the future of Riveredge."

"Is that all? I always figured you'd done something dark and evil. What do you mean, ensure the future of Riveredge?"

"Well, it would become yours, Sarah, if Waverly has his way," Victor told her. "I'm selfish enough to want to see the house given to the state as a museum. The land, well, that would come to you in any case."

"I didn't want to discuss with Wave what will happen to the land when he dies, and I don't want to discuss it with you, Victor."

"The point is, Sarah, your Great-Uncle Wave figured I was trying to steal his land to resell it at a profit. He hasn't talked to me since." Victor shook his head and regarded her with a smile. "In a way it's been a relief not having to deal with him."

"Leaving it to me. Thanks a lot. Okay, I know," she added. "You pay his food and upkeep bills and he thinks I do. Keeps swearing he's going to pay me back next time. Next time is about due. How long can I go on fooling him?"

"We'll think of something."

Sarah reached over and spontaneously planted a kiss on her cousin's forehead. "You're the nicest man I know."

He gave her a fond smile that held something wistful in it. "Obviously I can handle every contingency and everyone except Waverly Crewes."

And Maggie Roman was calmly handling him, Sarah had thought, but kept it to herself. Maggie was another problem, but discussing her with Victor would have to wait until another day.

Standing at her desk now, Sarah pushed her hand through the carton again. Odd how the records stopped just at the point where the Crewes had taken over Riveredge.

But just how odd, she wondered. Deliberate? Possibly. A frisson of fear crept slowly over her. It was as though a chill of something evil, more than a century old, had suddenly invaded the room. It was possible that the record of succession from General Forrester to the Crewes was somewhere in that vast storehouse of Merriman memory, but Sarah knew otherwise.

What wasn't there might never have existed. The general died. Emma, married to Greg Crewes, was far away in Australia. It was easy enough for Greg's father to take over Riveredge, claim it in Greg's name and, with a little bribe here and there to the authorities, write up deeds of sale and sell off chunks of the estate to unsuspecting buyers.

Which meant that Ty Lassiter had come to Merriman to right an ancient wrong. It meant there was no proof of Riveredge ever belonging to the Crewes line. It meant there were families living illegally on land that belonged to Ty Lassiter. No. Impossible. It couldn't be. She had to continue searching the records, checking through every piece of paper issued in Merriman County just after the Civil War. The prospect was daunting.

But meanwhile Sarah had a box of explosive information sitting on her desk, explosive not because of what it contained but because of what was missing. She should have left well enough alone, should never have sent Reg on a search for something in which a member of the Crewes family had a personal stake. She'd have to keep the carton well hidden until Ty Lassiter was long gone from Merriman.

Footsteps down the corridor roused Sarah. She glanced at her watch. Eight o'clock. There was a light tap at her door but she was unable to move. She stared at the carton, willing it to disappear.

Another tap, then Ty Lassiter pushed the door open and backed in, carrying the Franklin box he had so cleverly stolen from her. "Ah, there you are," he said cheerfully.

At the sight of him, her heart began to beat unreasonably fast. "What—what are you doing here?" Afraid he would catch the words Forrester-Riveredge scribbled so obviously in black crayon on the box, she rose to her feet and picked the carton up, dropped it to the floor and pushed it out of sight beneath her desk.

"I'm a man of my word as you can see," Ty told her, clearly not noticing anything unusual in her actions. "I promised you the cache of documents and here they are."

She was aware of the strain in her voice as she answered. "How'd you know I'd be around to take delivery?"

"Checked with the reception desk around five. Found you were in your office not taking calls. Checked again at six. Same news. Then ran into Gert a little after seven and she said you looked as if you were in for the long haul. Heard about Waverly. How is he?"

She drew a heavy hand across her brow but was glad of the diversion. "Sprained an ankle. Hospital is keeping him for a week. I'm feeding the cat."

"Baby-sitting the house?"

"Oh, Riveredge can take care of itself, it's been around that long." She stopped for a moment, realizing that the more she said, the more she would back herself into a corner. Yet at his interested look, she couldn't resist adding,

"It's locked up solid against all intruders." She pointed to the carton. "Found what you were looking for?"

He came over to the side of her desk, put the box down and dusted his hands. "Would you believe me if I told you no?"

She shook her head. "How can I?"

"You can't. You can just take my word for it. Incidentally, the diaries are a wonderful soporific if you have trouble sleeping." He hadn't moved. He was inches away, staring at her as if he had invaded her lair and could take possession with ease. "But of course you sleep the sleep of the just, don't you?"

"Oh, absolutely. And you?"

He bent close enough for her to feel the faint touch of his breath on her cheek. He held her gaze, a slight smile playing about his lips that struck right at her heart. Conflicting feelings fought for control. She wanted to reach for him, to touch him, to be reassured that this was the present and that the past was only a preoccupation of the bored or the foolish. And then again she wanted to push him back, to heed the warning that had been struggling within her from the first. He was bad news.

"Sleep has eluded me the last couple of nights," he told her. "Must be something about the night air."

"Must be."

He continued to hold her gaze. "I came bearing gifts. My motives are the highest, and I'm a man of my word. Yet I detect a slight coolness in the same night air." He pulled Reg's chair over to her desk and straddled it.

"Why wouldn't there be?" she said. "It *is* November. Thanksgiving is a couple of weeks away. We usually manage a light blanket of snow about now."

"Old-fashioned Thanksgiving?" he asked.

"As a matter of fact, yes, with lots of your cousins, uncles and aunts. Maybe you should consider sticking around."

"Continue looking at me like that and I'll have no choice."

She smiled involuntarily when she wanted to be serious, wondering just what kind of payment he really expected for donating the cache of documents to the county. "Find anything about your ancestor Emma in the diaries?"

He smiled. "Fell asleep on Addie's description of what she wore to church on Sunday. That was about one-eighth of the way through. Her handwriting's faded, barely legible and only for the determined. No, I found no specific mention of Emma, although Addie's life seems to be dotted—or dotty with—Emmas, Amys and, incidentally, Sarahs."

"What did you find?" she asked, keeping her voice low and insistent.

He smiled, lightly shaking his head at her stubbornness. "Sarah, I haven't heard a word of thanks for the gift to Merriman County. The least I'll expect is a plaque."

"A plaque? For this?" She reached into the carton and took up one of the velvet-covered diaries. Then with her free hand she poked through the deeds. "The entire county of Merriman is eternally grateful for your generous gift, Ty. I'll put a notice in the newspaper."

"Ah," he said, leaning back, "that's more like it." Then he added, "As for poor Addie's soporific journal, I'm sorry to tell you that Addie died."

"Too bad. Just think, she'd be a hundred fifty today if she'd lived."

He pointed to the carton. "If you look in the box you'll find a thick leather embossed journal. That's by one Peg Hanson."

"This?" She smoothed her hand over the leather, still fresh and soft even after all those years.

"Peg's handwriting is a little harder to read than Addie's, which puts it at a ten on a scale of difficulty of one to ten. What she said was quite clear, though. Addie Schermmerhorn Ranger died in childbirth."

"Oh." Sarah let out a deep, shocked sigh, as though the event had happened the day before. She clutched the diary to her breast.

"Almost four months, to the day after Addie received word of her husband's death in battle. Hey," he added, noting her reaction, "women died of childbirth more frequently in those days."

"I wonder what happened to the child, who brought it up. Boy or girl, that sort of thing."

"A girl, adopted by Addie's family."

"I'll take these diaries home with me to read," Sarah said, picking up her bag and tucking them inside.

"Apparently you need sleep more than I do. How about having dinner with me? You name the place. You know Merriman better than I."

Sarah didn't answer him. The smartest thing she could do would be to go home, bury her nose in the diaries and forget Tyler Lassiter.

"We could always have fish and chips at Barney's," he said. "Alec was responsible for tapping into my fish and chips syndrome. Thought I'd buried it in English soil."

"Sarah's." She gave the invitation spontaneously and at once would have given anything to take it back.

"Want to run that by me again?" His smile told her he understood her quite well.

"Sarah's," she repeated with a certain reluctance, although as she went on, the idea began to appeal to her. She'd cook up a pasta with vegetables in a light cream sauce, all quickly made. "It's a sort of small joint near the river. Not a bad place. Cook sticks to down-home stuff, meaning whatever's in the refrigerator that can be whipped, stirred or beaten into submission."

The quickened look in his eyes told Sarah that he was interested, and she knew at once that she was stepping into something she should have stayed clear of. If she looked back at all the mistakes she had made as far as men were concerned, she would never again issue a spontaneous invitation, especially to the sophisticated Tyler Lassiters of the world.

"Sarah, you're not having second thoughts, I hope."

"Wherever did you get that idea?" If there was a pitfall anywhere, she was certain to find it, but all at once it was time to face the danger head on. He'd be certain to make a pass, and she either had to head it off or not. "I think we ought to stop at the market for some things," she said, regarding him with a serious look.

"I'll follow you anywhere," he told her. "Gotcha."

IT WAS THROUGH Tyler Lassiter's eyes that Sarah took in the small blacksmith's cottage her cousin had lent her. Ty, walking in behind her, carried the packages from the supermarket.

A stained-glass lamp on the corner desk cast a rosy hue over most of the small, low-ceilinged living room. It struck her for the first time that her little cottage seemed impossibly crowded with all the bric-a-brac she had collected over the years. The living room was undeniably charming with a late addition brick fireplace and rough white-washed walls with crowded bookshelves and old gilt-framed paintings. Facing the fireplace and flanked by two Windsor chairs that had belonged to her parents was a comfortable, flower-covered chintz couch.

The whole house was also stuffed with the detritus of her life and her hobby. She thought of the old wooden sled behind the kitchen door. Now why had she kept it and why there?

"The kitchen," Ty reminded her, still holding the packages.

"Right. Follow me." She led the way and gestured to the butcher-block table. "There's fine."

"This all the stuff you don't sell at the flea market?" He looked around the tiny kitchen with its oak fixtures and fireplace, the overbearing china cabinet filled with gewgaws, the early-American chairs placed around a small round table, the gingham curtains at the window and planters of late-blooming mums.

"I don't sell everything I buy." She went quickly back into the living room as though there she might be able to defend herself better.

He followed her and began prowling the room, picking up some little thing only to put it back and reach for something else. She had the strange feeling that he was trying to read some message locked into the objects she had so carefully placed around the room.

"Ah, our red-haired doll." He reached for the doll he had given her, which sat on the fireplace mantel, but he was diverted almost at once by an enlarged snapshot in an oval elmwood frame. "Your parents?"

"Yes." She came over to him, feeling her cheeks burn for a reason she couldn't quite name. She wanted to take the photograph out of his hands and hide it from him.

"Parents were very good-looking."

"Yes, they were."

The photograph showed her father in his Air Force uniform. He clutched her mother tightly in his arms. They were both looking out at the camera as though caught by the photographer in a moment of extreme intimacy. Her mother, a pale blonde with light blue eyes, exuded the most extraordinary happiness, although she must have known that her husband was going to Vietnam.

"They look like two people who were very much in love."

"They were." She took the photo away from him and held it for a moment, then carefully replaced it on the mantel.

"Were you a glint in their eyes when that was taken?"

She laughed. "I was about six or seven at the time, but often wondered if I were ever a glint in their eyes."

"What the hell is that supposed to mean?"

She backed away, feeling the rush of blood to her cheeks once again. "I just mean...well, frankly, they were such an enclosed couple. I mean, I often found them kissing...a strange, strong, wonderful love. It was as if I was an intruder."

"That's a rather odd emotion for someone so young. Odder still to remember it all these years."

"Look, just forget what I said." Sarah tried to hide the anger his words evoked. "I'm sentimental about them—and yet maybe my memory is a little selective, after all. Of course they loved me, they adored me."

"And," he said in a very quiet, serious voice, "they left you."

"I don't think being called up by the United States government to fight its wars qualifies as leaving one. As for my mother..." She stopped, sorry she had brought him there, sorry she had allowed him a glimpse of her private life. Sarah picked up a small china dog from the mantel and stared at it without quite seeing it. She rubbed the china creature between her fingers and could feel the cool glaze and the bump of its tail. "I'm sorry," she said after a moment. "I've no idea why I blew up. You want to know about my family."

"I want to know about you."

"My parents owned a large, handsome stud farm and went broke when they gambled on a stud purchase that didn't pay off. My father was in the Air Force reserves and they called him up. My mother received a small inheritance and she bought a modest stud farm, but it never got off the ground. I guess she thought if she could just keep it running, my father would take over when he came back. And he never came back. Then my mother died. The stud farm ceased to exist, the land was sold, and Victor took in the little orphan from the storm." She did not tell him how her mother died and in fact often wondered whether anyone in Merriman knew the true story. Victor had done all he could to hush it up, but she had often wondered. She ought to ask Celie or Jemma Gardner but had never had the nerve.

"And then I grew up at Bosworth Stud, end of story," she said, averting her eyes.

"Not quite the end of the story." When she looked up, she found Ty watching her, his gaze unwavering.

"Well, I went to college, became an archivist and puttered around with antiques. End of story."

He gestured toward the doll. "And Ferdy? What happened to her.?"

"You mean did the bank take her along with all the other fixtures of the farm?"

"Something like that."

"Could be. Suddenly I woke up in Victor's house and my young past was consigned to history."

"Which you've been looking for ever since."

"No." Her retort was short and sharp, and when Ty regarded her it was with a shrewd expression in his eyes that told her he was through asking questions since the answers she gave were dishonest ones. She felt stripped naked by that single glance. She moved away from the fireplace and only spoke when she felt calmer. She went over to the window and gazed out at the night. "Incidentally," she said, "you should be interested in the architecture of the cottage. Victor had the windows enlarged to let in the northern light. Stunning, isn't it?"

He seemed willing to play the game her way. "Hasn't hurt the lines of the house, Sarah. The idea is not to change the shape of history."

For a moment his remark stunned her, but of course he couldn't know. "Is that what you really believe?"

"Maybe not."

"In other words, if you had the ammunition, you'd change the course of history."

"I didn't say that, either."

She continued to stare out the window. The moon had not yet risen. "When there's a full moon, it's as if it shines just for me." She said the words irrelevantly, scarcely aware of them.

"I'm sure it does," he agreed, joining her and yet standing a careful foot away. "I've a certain envy of the man in the moon."

She thought for a moment that he was going to reach for her. "How about an aperitif while I prepare dinner?" she asked, moving deftly away from him and heading toward the kitchen. "Sherry? I've some splendid stuff, thanks to Victor, who has an excellent wine cellar and is generous enough to share it."

"Sherry's fine. A drink I'd call aristocratic right down to your cousin's toes."

She laughed, glad that the stiffness between them was gone. "Lay off Victor or else. He's the perfect person."

He followed her into the kitchen and accepted the small incised and delicate glass of sherry she offered. "Mmm," he told her after a sip. "The perfect person knows a good dry sophisticated aperitif when he sees one. Ever think of setting up your own establishment and moving out from under Victor's shadow?"

"I'm not under his shadow," she told him angrily. "Perhaps you'd like me to move out of the way so Maggie Roman can have him, lock, stock and Bosworth Stud."

Ty let out a huge laugh. "Okay, I asked for that one."

"He should marry—Celie Decatur. It's about time, damn it."

He shook his head slowly. "I'm stepping away from that one, too, Sarah. Trouble with you is you came back from the big city and slipped right into the small doin's of a small town when you should be mindin' your own business."

"I'll get dinner started," Sarah said. "You can offer to light a fire in the fireplace."

"There's some stuff in here that fits into the microwave," he told her, fishing in one of the bags.

"What makes you think I own a microwave?"

"It's the only civilized way to live," he said.

"Then welcome to the backwoods and I knew I shouldn't have let you roam free in the supermarket."

"Well, you took so long choosing tomatoes, I had to amuse myself somehow."

"I'm extremely particular, tomatowise."

"So am I, Sarah."

"I ought to report you to the nearest women's group for that remark." She shoved a wedge of Parmesan cheese and a grater at him. "Here, get to work."

Instead of eating in the kitchen they carried their plates of pasta into the living room and sat on the flowered, down-filled couch before the fireplace.

It was only after they had finished and Sarah served coffee that Ty reached for her hand and held it for a moment. "My compliments to the chef. Is there anything you don't do well? No," he added with a laugh, "don't answer that. Some things I'm looking forward to discovering for myself."

"Oh, I'm a deep study," she told him. "I'm like an attic stuffed with all sorts of everybody's throwaways."

"Are you really?" He gazed at her for a moment as though her remark both charmed and disturbed him. "You're right, of course. I've only to look around this cottage to wonder where the real Sarah Crewes is."

"You're looking at her." She drew her hand away. "Obviously you think she's present and accounted for."

"Not accounted for," he said, shaking his head. "You've taken on life with a vengeance, your own and everybody else's. You run Waverly's life for him, Victor's, Celie's."

"That's not fair. Wave needs my help. He's old, he's—he's..."

"Not that old, but sinking fast if you don't give him a little air. You're helping him into *helplessness*, damn it."

"You don't know anything, Ty. You don't know Wave, you only want what he has."

She stopped, aware of her gaffe, but he only shook his head as if in wonder at the foolishness of her remark. He reached out and drew his fingers along her cheek. "Beautiful Sarah, you look like your father, I think. And get off Victor's back, too. He must think you a proper little pain in the neck. As for Celie, she's a lovely, strong woman whom I admire more each time I meet her. Step back. The only trouble is, every time you step back, you crash into something."

She felt his warm dry touch caress her cheek and knew she couldn't speak for the lump in her throat. He was saying all the wrong things if what he wanted was to make love to her. But he couldn't want to, not tearing away at her like that.

"What right do you have to step int my life, my domain, and then tell me I'm breathing of tune with everyone else." She said the words slo and carefully, afraid the moisture at the back of her ey uld spill over. She glanced over at the mantelpiece and ie photograph of her parents. In love, so in love she always felt like a third wheel peering at them, wondering what it was about.

"Sarah."

She looked back at him. He was regarding her with a deadly serious expression. "Beautiful, wonderf touchable Sarah." He took up her hand again and kisse er open palm. "I don't think you have the vaguest ide who you are."

"Then why do you care?"

He kissed her palm ag and then pulled her close, his lips coming quickly d n on hers. For a moment the warmth of his mouth was disorienting, as though she had never been kissed before. He smelled good, a faint masculine scent she couldn't quite identify. When he pressed close, his mouth insistently moving over hers, an enormous shudder ranged through her body as though removing every vestige of resistance. Love, that was what she wanted, sensual, powerful, all-consuming love, and she'd never had an idea until that moment what it was. She was aware of the deepening of his breath, of time moving to another dimension. She had no idea of the moment when she raised her arms and clasped them around his neck. His tongue prodded her lips apart and with a deep, unexpected sigh she opened her mouth to him. The kiss lingered, changed subtly to create a warm, irresistible fire. His hand slid over her body to find the soft flesh under her breast, and yet even as she moved closer to him she heard herself make a small noise of protest.

He pulled back and shook his head slightly. His hair was faintly mussed. Sarah drew her hand across his cheek and thought that in spite of all her misgivings he was a man to love, a man to trust, a man of deep seriousness and commitment, a man to give her heart to.

"It was a mistake to bring you here," she said.

"No, it wasn't. We had to touch, to hold each other, to know." His mouth came down on hers again in a slow tantalizing movement, then once again he drew away and released her from his arms completely.

"To know what?" she asked softly.

He stood and reached for her hand and in a quick gesture kissed her palm once more. "To know that the next time there'll be no stopping. Not for you and not for me." He went quickly over to the door, but before stepping into the tiny entrance hall, he turned to her. "I was an only child, too. My parents love each other, and when I was with them, they focused that love on me. I was the one who left, but the break was equally tough on me. They sent me away because they wanted me to be a proper English gentleman. It was equally tough being in an English public school with your mum and dad gone from your sight almost as completely as though they no longer existed. I had no Victor Bosworth to rescue me, and all I had to do was toughen."

"And did you toughen?" Sarah asked from the couch, where she still sat.

"Toughened."

"And not looking for love because you knew no matter where you were, you held it in your heart."

He gazed at her for a long moment. "Oh, looking for it all right, knowing it happens with fireworks." He seemed about to say something. Instead he turned away. She heard the outer door open. "I'll call you," he said, his voice floating back.

She sat listening as the door closed behind him. After a while a car engine started. She heard the sound of his wheels in the pebbled driveway as the car spun away. "Fireworks." She put her hand to her lips. "Fireworks."

CHAPTER EIGHT

WHEN SHE HAD LIVED in a sublet apartment in Manhattan, Sarah had inherited a streetwise old tomcat named Pablo. He came and went at will through three inches of her open fire-escape window four stories above ground. One ear had been chewed off in a fight he apparently lost, and he often came back home with fur missing and a scratch or two above his nose.

Pablo possessed an uncanny knack of knowing just when Sarah needed something warm to cling to. He had been there whenever anything went wrong in her life, his usual menacing growl replaced by a soft purr as she stroked him.

With Tyler's kisses still fresh on her lips, Sarah realized she was in trouble. She knew so by the simple, amazing fact that she wanted Pablo desperately. She wanted to hear his footfall as he jumped from the window to the wooden floor, and she wanted the warmth of his fur, his simple acceptance of her unique role in his life. But he was still in Manhattan, still in the same apartment and, no doubt, still getting into scraps and then coming home for assurance that all was right with the world. And still wondering where his next mouse was coming from. As for Sarah Crewes, the giant who stroked his ears and opened up tins of food for him, she was miles away, wondering if she were going to be the mouse in someone else's dream.

It was twenty minutes after Ty left, as the fire died down in the fireplace, that Sarah finally stirred from the couch and made her way into the kitchen. She cleared the dishes and put the silly little packages of microwavable food away. Then she undressed and took a long slow shower, knowing that no amount of water could wash away the feel of Ty's hands, the touch of his lips, nor did she want it to.

Oh, she seemed to be his quarry, all right. The question was why. And what was she going to do about it. She had known sophisticated men in her life; had flirted with them, dated them, kissed them and even on occasion gone to bed with them. Yet she had always eschewed long-term relationships as though to continue them meant ultimate rejection. Men who wouldn't or couldn't marry or tarry were the ones she usually chose to fall in love with.

She slipped into an old-fashioned nightgown and climbed into her pristine white-covered four-poster bed, turned out the light and, in another gesture, flipped the radio on. A half-moon winked through the window, as a soft melody, an old love song, stirred the still air in the room.

After all these years,
Where do you find that old love?
Look around every corner
Behind every tree...
Where's that old love...
It's hiding from me.

She lay with her hands behind her head staring at the ceiling and the strange patterns made by the movement of the leaves outside her window.

Where's that old love? But there never had been any. No love hiding from her, no long-remembered happiness of being in the arms of a man she adored, no regrets for something gone sour that had once been so good. She had always felt apart, standing back, no matter how much she chattered or interfered in the lives of those she loved, no matter, in fact, that people depended upon her. She was always the outsider, even in the bosom of her family or under Victor's protective wing.

And now she was more scared than ever, scared of Ty and what she might have to learn about herself. Scared of doing something she might be sorry about. Scared of not doing it and being sorry about that. She had wanted him and he knew it. Yet it was he who pulled back, who said all the kind words, even told her of the inevitability of their making love.

And yet she knew that sometimes things could change, and the moment in time could be pinpointed exactly. Now a crack of light had shone in and brightened a dark corner of her life. Ty had reached for her; she had melted into his arms for that instant when all reason disappeared and sensation took over.

She had wanted to step back but couldn't, even though she knew the next logical step would be for him to lead her into the bedroom. It took but a moment for him to pull away, and that gentle act, his leave-taking, was what confused her most.

She knew now what she could feel for him, and with that knowledge came the uncertainty of her childhood. How strange it should come back to her like that.

Yet . . . yet there was something about the way Ty smiled at her that touched the wounded place in her soul. Only she knew that wanting and needing the love of one person was far too dangerous. Fate, she decided, was playing a dirty trick on her. Of all the men in the world to set before her, it had to be the one man who could not only wreak havoc with her heart but, if he had a mind to, tear the town apart.

In spite of the cool night, the cool sheets she lay between, the heat he aroused still coursed through her body, leaving her unfulfilled.

At last Sarah gave up every pretense of trying to sleep. She turned on the lamp, got out of bed and walked barefoot across the cold pine floor to her bag. She fished out the diary belonging to Addie Ranger and padded back to bed. She propped up her pillows and then gently touched the worn green velvet cover and at last opened to the first page. It was an hour later when she rubbed her eyes. Addie's handwriting was spidery, the ink a pale brown, the paper foxy in spots. She yawned, read a couple more pages in a desultory way, then came upon the name Emma, and all at once she was wide awake:

I can't believe Emma really means it. I'm sworn to secrecy and I'm not allowed to tell a soul, except you, dear diary. But is Emma right in doing this thing? She had gone to the hospital in Herkimer every day and so I know that what she tells me must be the truth. But a Confederate soldier! He was wounded just as the war ended and brought here for treatment. She says he is very handsome. She says his accent is soft and sweet but I believe she's under a witch's spell. No, that isn't true. Emma has always been headstrong and independent. Once she makes up her mind to do a thing, there, it's done.

The entry stopped there. Sarah flipped a few pages, scanning the words for Emma's name, and found it a few weeks farther on.

She's done it. Gone into Herkimer County and married Kurt Hoving. I am still sworn to secrecy. No one

knows, especially not her father, that old dragon. He'd
disown her sure as I'm sitting here. I haven't met the
handsome Mr. Hoving, either. Emma says he's going
south to tell his family. He wants her to go with him but
she says no, she must pretend to live her life until she
finds the time ripe to tell her father.

There was only one other entry in the diary, and as in the
others, no last name was mentioned, neither Emma's un-
married name nor that of her father, the old dragon.

So sad about Emma. I do hope she tells someone besides me. I can't help and I don't know what to advise
her. But that Emma, you never could talk to her anyway.

Sarah closed the book and put it down on her night table. Once again she turned off the light and lay looking at
the patterns on her ceiling. Emma Hoving. The last name
wasn't familiar, and she wondered with a yawn, as sleep
gradually overcame her, how many Confederate soldiers
captured how many young, Northern hearts.

The next day Sarah left home early to spend some time
with her great-uncle before going to work. Efforts to con-
vince him that he couldn't remain alone at Riveredge failed
to move him. However, while she sat with him, Nellie Casedonte called and told him to expect her that afternoon.
Wave put the receiver down with a smile he tried to hide
from his great-niece.

The first thing she did upon arriving in her office was to
dial Nellie Casedonte and make a luncheon appointment
with her for noon. She had made a promise to Reg to talk to
Nellie and she intended to keep that promise. When Reg
came by after class, she wanted to have Nellie's assurance

that she'd stop squaring off with her great-nephew. Sarah had given herself no little job when she agreed to talk to Nellie. The woman was very self-sufficient, used to living alone and used to having her way. Sarah at seventy-two, she thought acerbically . Then someone will send around a messenger telling me to lay off somebody, too.

The box labeled Forrester-Riveredge lay under her desk where she had put it hastily the night before when Ty showed up in her office. Sarah pulled it out and sat contemplating it for a while. She and Ty may have tasted each other's lips, they may have aroused something wonderful in each other, but the fact of Forrester-Riveredge remained. Who had the deed to the house and where were the tax records for the year following old General Forrester's death? She had no doubt a call would come into the office from Alec, asking her to give Ty access to the records. If Ty and he had made a deal about the waterfront, then Sarah would have no choice but to say yes.

A second carton sat on the floor, the one Ty had delivered the evening before. Had he found something? She doubted it. She believed in serendipitous events but not magical ones.

When the telephone rang, Sarah reached for the receiver, still wondering what to do about Forrester-Riveredge.

"Sarah Crewes." She even spoke her name absent-mindedly.

"Sleep well?"

His voice was a caress. She felt the small hairs prickle along her neck. "Oh, like a top."

"I never understood that remark. Exactly how do tops sleep?"

"Beats me. How did *you* sleep?"

"Not at all, Sarah. Stayed awake the night through."

"Ty, I don't believe a word you're saying. You strike me as a man who can sleep standing up."

"Try me."

She laughed, a little afraid her voice held too joyous a lilt. "I think I'll take your word for it."

"How about lunch?"

"Sorry, got a date."

"Dinner tomorrow night?"

"Sorry, scheduled there, too." Maggie Roman had invited her and Victor along with Celie to a rehearsal of *Much Ado About Nothing* at Pack College. She had been adamant about cornering Victor so they could talk about Wave's problems and, if she could subtly manage it, Maggie. The rehearsal seemed like a good excuse, especially since Victor had invited her to dinner first at Bosworth Stud.

"Too bad," Ty was saying.

"I'm sorry, but—"

"You're a busy little beaver," he finished for her.

Whatever was happening was too soon, she thought. She didn't want to be alone with him, not quite yet. There was too much to be straightened out. He was coming on too strong. It shouldn't be.

"Saturday, then," he said. She detected a certain amount of anger in his voice. He was clearly a man who didn't like to be thwarted.

"I was thinking of the flea market Saturday."

His voice was a growl. "Forget the damn flea market. What time do you get home tonight? Never mind, I'll call you later."

"Ty, wait."

He hung up and for a moment she sat staring at the receiver, then replaced it only to have it ring once more. She picked it up expecting to hear Ty's voice, but it was Alec.

"Sarah, when Ty Lassiter calls, let him poke around the archives for a while. He won't be in town long and he's interested in finding something about his ancestor Emma Crewes. Stuff's a mess down there, anyway, what's the harm if he shoves things around a bit?"

"Hold it, Alec. I won't say no if you give me a real reason why I should make an exception for Tyler Lassiter."

"He promised to produce a set of drawings of an idealized waterfront for Merriman. No fee. Good enough reason?"

"Good enough. I don't suppose even Phil Nevins would accuse me of doing a favor for a relative."

She hung up and stared at the Forrester-Riveredge carton. Let Tyler look all he wanted. He'd said nothing to her about the waterfront deal. He was set upon conquering her, perhaps, but thought little enough of her to talk about the development of the waterfront. She picked up the carton and carried it out of the room. It took a little while for her to find a home for it—facing the wall, behind and at the bottom of a double layer of similar cartons piled to the ceiling in a back storage room. It would take some time before it came to light. Let him try, she thought. He was impatient, as witnessed by the way he had given Addie Schermmerhorn Ranger's diary a summary look-through. He was a quick study, Tyler Lassiter, but Sarah doubted he possessed the ingredients an archivist needed: quiet, calm and incredible patience.

The rest of the morning Sarah fielded a dozen telephone calls, managed to match some official inquiries with the appropriate tax records and disposed of an urgent query on town property having to do with a poorly performed survey a quarter-century old.

At noon she realized she was going to be late for her luncheon date with Nellie, but all attempts to find her failed.

As she flew out of the office she greeted Reg arriving from school. "Meeting Nellie. Talk to you later."

"Don't forget."

"Won't. Back about one-thirty."

Nellie was seated at the window of the restaurant, a martini with an olive set before her. She held a cigarette in her hand. "You're late and you look harried," she said at once, motioning to Sarah to sit down and acting as though they met frequently and were about to continue a conversation inadvertently left dangling the last time. She was a tall slim woman, with a sharp nose and deep inquisitive eyes. Her silver hair was worn straight with a girlish line of bangs across her forehead.

"Harried, I suppose I am," Sarah replied, sitting down opposite her and pointing to her drink. "And you look as if you haven't given up one of your vices."

"I haven't." Nellie's eyes twinkled. "And I'm not planning on living forever, either."

The waiter came by and Sarah ordered a cola with a twist of lemon and plenty of ice. "So you're back home and out of a job, Nellie. I had to see you with my own eyes to believe it."

"Retired is how we in the civil service put it. I'm going to see Waverly this afternoon. What does the old curmudgeon need?"

"A friend. I think he's happy you're coming to see him. You've known him ever since you were youngsters. What was he like as a young man?"

"Very handsome," Nellie said with unexpected enthusiasm. "Laconic. You couldn't get much more than boo out of him. All the girls were in love with him. He was a very good athlete, good student. Went up to Boston to college and took a lot of broken hearts with him. Of course he never knew it. I think he was painfully shy."

"Did he take your heart along with him, too?"

Nellie gave a hearty laugh. Her face was almost free of wrinkles, her teeth the Casedonte teeth, white and regimented, as though they intimidated toothbrushes. "Are you trying to find out whether I've carried a torch all these years? Why I haven't married?"

"I know why you never married, Nellie. You were married to the New York State Education Department."

Nellie picked up her martini and sipped it. "A mite on the wet side," she said with an air of wanting to change the subject and daring Sarah to go on with it. "Some little pip making them who doesn't know the first thing about mixed drinks."

"Nellie, if you could be a friend to both Wave and me I'd appreciate it."

"I'm an acquaintance of your great-uncle's," Nellie corrected. "We knew each other as kids, then he went off to college and so did I, at opposite ends of the map. We've only met on occasion back here. At the tri-bi, for instance. All right," she added, as though Sarah's asking something of her were inevitable, "what is it?"

"He shouldn't be alone in that great house any longer. If you could just manage to find out if his accident has changed his mind any about having someone live in with him." Sarah waited a moment. "If Victor or I mention it, he has a fit. You know," she added with an apologetic smile, "family. He thinks we have his worst interests at heart."

"I'll find out," Nellie said. "Families are always a pain in the neck when they mean to be most helpful."

"Believe it or not, we're deeply concerned about him."

"Oh, I believe it," Nellie remarked. "Settle the senior citizens and get them out of your hair, that's the motto of the younger generation."

"Oh, Nellie, that's unfair."

"Unfair but true, Sarah my love."

Sarah's cola was served and she was glad of the interruption. "How about ordering fish and chips," she suggested, expecting an argument. She remembered now what Nellie was like and understood Reg's feelings. His great-aunt was the kindest-hearted of women but she had long ago given up being polite for its own sake.

"I looked the menu over while I was waiting for you. They haven't changed it in a century. Fish and chips will be fine," she agreed, surprising Sarah. Once the waiter was gone with their order, she went on. "So my great-nephew is working for you."

"Yes." Sarah gave her a bright smile. Wave was out of the way, at least temporarily, and now she had Reg to deal with. "He's bright, funny and willing to work long hours. Good company, too. We really get along."

"He'd do better if his ears weren't glued to those headphones listening to that music. He'll go deaf before he graduates."

"Nellie, he's doing just fine, in school, at work. His mother should be proud of him."

"Doesn't even have a handle on how her son operates. I want him to go on to graduate school. He thinks he's had enough schooling. She shrugs and says the boy knows his own mind."

Sarah reached out for her glass and closed her fingers around it. "Nellie, don't nag him." There, she told herself, I've done it, I've paid off Reg and probably infuriated Nellie for life.

Nellie looked at her, then put out her cigarette very methodically in the ashtray and promptly lit another. "Reg tell you to talk to me?"

"Do you think you need talking to?" Sarah asked carefully.

"Damn, I'd hate to have the boy hate me. What did he say?"

"He's not a boy. He's a man."

Nellie stared at the blue smoke and then suddenly smashed that cigarette out, too. "The trouble is retirement. It's not all it's cracked up to be. I discovered as much in the first ten minutes at the Casedonte household. My nephew hiding behind his newspaper, his wife all solicitation. They wanted me to come stay with them, but they don't want their lives disturbed, either. I'm a drill sergeant and I can't help it. I want out of there, but if I leave at once I'll hurt their feelings, Sarah. And the trouble is, I've the most appalling sense of failure. Retirement should be full of wonder and adventure."

"You've always traveled—"

"I've lost my taste for it. Sometimes I think it would be nice to settle down in some distant place just to get the real feel of it, but no. Something's there, just out of sight, waiting to be discovered. I don't know what." She gave an embarrassed smile.

"There's always charitable work. They can use you up at the college."

"I know. They've a fine education program. Do you know what, Sarah? I'd like to have some fun in my life, shake the establishment, take up flying balloons or piloting an airplane, do something outrageous for once."

Their baskets of fish and chips arrived. Nellie drank the last of her martini and picked up a chip with her fingers. "Outrageous knock-their-socks-off stuff," she said, biting into the chip. "Got any ideas?"

Sarah thought of her Great-Uncle Wave and that big old house at the river's edge, but all she did was shake her head no. "You'll think of something, Nellie. Take your time, and when you come across it, shove right in, don't take no for an answer."

"Sounds all well and vague, my girl," Nellie told her. "Where's the malt vinegar?"

"In front of you," Sarah said patiently. "But remember, whatever it is could be staring you in the face. Just make sure you see it."

WAVERLY CREWES knew someone was in the room without even opening his eyes. One of those damn nurses who were always fussing over him, no doubt. He could smell the perfume. But no, maybe not. He couldn't hear the telltale squeak made by their rubber-soled shoes. He opened his eyes a crack and let the sunlight in. If he turned his head to the right, he'd get a clear look at who was sneaking around.

"Ah, good, you're up. You shouldn't be sleeping this time of day, anyway."

Wave opened his eyes wide, blinked at his visitor, then pulled himself up, feeling the slight twinge in his foot as he did so. He managed a smile, not even wanting to admit to himself the pleasure he felt at the sight of Nellie Casedonte. "Well, well, well, so you came after all. Did Sarah ask you to call?"

"Waverly, just say hello and don't start an argument right off the bat." Nellie came over to his bed, took his pillow, plumped it and set it comfortably behind his head.

"Well, go ahead and deny it."

"About Sarah? I met her for lunch today, as a matter of fact, but I make my own decisions and my own telephone calls. I don't need your great-niece telling me what to do and how to run my life." She gave a sudden laugh. "Although she managed to ream me out about something, anyway, and she was right."

Her voice, Waverly thought, still held the same girlish lilt he remembered; probably managed to keep it in shape from having to sweet-talk politicians in Albany. Her flaming red hair had turned silver, but she had the feisty appearance he had never forgotten. She was still a damn good-looking woman. Her skin was smooth and her eyes bright. The small amount of makeup she used only enhanced her air of self-possession. It annoyed him that the first real time they had to talk found him so vulnerable, in bed in striped pajamas with his foot bound up.

"I came to see how you're doing," Nellie said. She thrust a package at him. "Here, I brought you some homemade cookies. Sugar-coated with nuts. Can you eat them?"

"Damn it, Nellie, I hurt my leg, I didn't knock my teeth out. I eat whatever I please. Hospital food could kill you, anyway."

Nellie pulled a chair up and sat down. "How're you really doing, Wave? You don't have to put an act on for me, you know that."

"I twisted my ankle, period. That's enough about me. So you're back home in Merriman for good. Where are you staying?"

"With my nephew. But believe me, not for long."

Wave thought he detected a note of embarrassment in her voice, as though she hated the idea of letting someone else take care of her. Well, damn it, so did he.

His mind slipped back over the decades to a one-room schoolhouse on the outskirts of Ramsey Falls. Somebody was using it now for karati lessons; it had been painted blue on the outside and all the memories inside varnished away. Funny how he still remembered everything about that time so long ago. It was summer, the last day of school before vacation. Nellie wore her bright red hair in pigtails and she had on a ruffled dress with the hem of her petticoat sticking out. She had a book in her hand and she was standing alone by the big oak tree in the grassy yard behind the schoolhouse. He and Tommy Morgan sneaked up on her and pulled at her braids. He remembered grabbing her book and throwing it to the ground; then he and Tommy chased her around the yard yelling Indian war cries until she collapsed in a heap, full of tears. He'd started the whole thing because she was the prettiest girl in class and he didn't have the nerve to talk to her.

"Wave?"

He opened his eyes.

"I thought you fell asleep."

"No." He gave her a sheepish grin. "Just thinking. Do you remember that time—?"

She laughed softly. "Very well, and it doesn't bear repeating. Oh, how I hated you when I got home. Cursed and ranted. My father was all for demanding you be strung up, but I begged him not to say a word."

They smiled at each for a long moment. Then Wave said, "How come you never married? You always were the prettiest girl in town." He knew the question was presumptuous, yet knew it was also the one that most needed answering.

She reached into her bag and extracted a pack of cigarettes, then changed her mind and put them away. "I almost married," she said. "My first year in Albany. I was just out of graduate school."

"I suppose I was in South America at the time. What happened?"

"As a matter of fact, he died—bus accident. That happened a month before we were supposed to be married. He was a traveling salesman. Funny," she added, "the telling of it seems so pedestrian, but I'd been wildly in love with him. After that—" She stopped, staring off into space.

"Damn waste if you ask me," Waverly observed, not unkindly.

"I know you mean it as a compliment," Nellie said. "Sarah thinks I was married to my job all those years and maybe I was. How's the foot, anyway?" she added, as if a change of conversation were needed at that point. "You still haven't told me if it still hurts."

"Slight twinge," Waverly told her. "They figured I could be out of here by Monday."

"How's your heart? Blood pressure?"

"I'm ticking away, Nellie, no complaints but for a bit of arthritis."

"You're still living at Riveredge, then."

"And meaning to go on living there."

"Alone? That house is too big."

Wave screwed his eyes up. "Victor send you?"

"Listen, you old bear," Nellie said, "first it was Sarah, and now it's Victor. Mind telling me why they sent me? I'd be interested in hearing it."

"They'd like to move me out of Riveredge, lock, stock and barrel."

"What the devil do you want to go traipsing about that big old pile for, anyway? You've been all alone there ever since Ruth died. It was too big even then. You had no kids."

"Ruth had a big family," he told her. "Place was always mobbed. They all drifted away," he added, "one by one."

"Wave, don't you think you'd be better off in a small place closer to town?"

"No, I don't think I'd be better off in a small place closer to town. You got a car?" he asked abruptly.

"Of course, but it's over at Monty's getting a tune-up."

"What'd you take it there for? Monty's a crook."

"He's my nephew," Nellie said.

"Doesn't change my mind any."

"What happened to your car, Wave?"

"Nothing much. They took my license away."

"Really," Nellie said. "They took your license away. And what did you do to deserve that?"

"I suffer from night blindness and I had an accident."

"Or two, I'll bet. You can't borrow my car, it that's what you're getting at."

"No," he said, watching her. "What are you doing with your time, Nellie, now you're retired?"

"Winding down, that's all. Smoking too many cigarettes, getting in everyone's hair."

"And do you like winding down?"

Nellie shook her head, smiling thoughtfully. "I hate it, every minute of it. I'd really like to kick up my heels. Got any ideas?"

"Kicking up my heels?" Wave let out a deep breath. "Doctor would have my head. How about my paying you to toot me around town? I can call a taxi but I've got reasons for not wanting to."

"I'll toot you around town, but not for pay," Nellie said. "Mind telling me the reason?"

"Riveredge." He leaned toward her, lowering his voice. "I've had something on my mind for a long time about that place. Took me a little time to get my act together." He stopped, surprised by the look of interest on Nellie's face.

"Is that what did it, your fall?"

He shook his head. "Maybe I was daydreaming it for a long time, but the appearance of that architect . . ."

"What architect, Wave? You're being very vague."

"Lassiter, Tyler Lassiter. Claims he's a long-lost relation. A charmer, all right. He wants something, maybe even Riveredge."

"Wave, what are you planning?"

He needed her help, Wave thought, and now here she was at precisely the right time. Odd how things worked out. "Can you keep a secret?" he asked.

She smiled and reached out to place her warm hand over his. "Try me."

CHAPTER NINE

"Looks as if Tyler Lassiter has made an offer for Franklin Orchards."

"What?" Sarah stared at her cousin, unable to hide the look of incredulity that she knew colored her face. "How in the world did you find that out?"

Victor smiled at Sarah. She was sitting on the same settee he had shared with Maggie Roman a week before, the fatal night when the actress showed up at Bosworth Stud with Ty Lassiter. Victor handed her a glass of cognac, then sat down on the chair opposite. "You seem oddly unsettled by the notion. Celie mentioned it, as a matter of fact. And," he added, "the only reason she brought the subject up was because I'd been considering buying the place."

"Buying Franklin Orchards? Whatever for?"

"Saving valuable, rare old apple trees from the wrecker's ball. And it does link up with Riveredge to the north."

"You mean," she interrupted him, "he has his eye on Riveredge."

"No, I mean if Wave ever decides to sell the acreage, Ty Lassiter could add on a healthy chunk if he planned on developing the land. Didn't know he was interested in the Franklin place and I didn't act fast enough."

"But I don't understand," Sarah said. "Ty never mentioned—"

"Ty. That friendly, are you?"

"Victor, you know everything," Sarah snapped. "You tell me. You always know everything. You're the czar of Merriman County."

Victor continued to smile, shaking his head and clearly allowing his cousin to vent some steam.

"I suppose you know Ty went with me to the Franklin house."

"I didn't, although I'm pleased you're letting me in on it."

Sarah blanched, feeling her face grow warm. "You're being unreasonably smug lately, Victor. What's come over you?"

He continued to smile in a maddening way. "I'd say the full moon, but I don't believe it's due yet."

Maggie Roman, Sarah decided. The actress was responsible for Victor's unbearable smugness, but she'd get to Maggie by and by. In fact, it occurred to Sarah that she had never seen her cousin looking better. He was wearing an English-style tweed suit with a paisley scarf tucked into his open shirt collar. His hair had been newly trimmed, too—styled was more like it, so that it looked fuller, made him seem handsomer. She was about to comment on it but decided to wait. Right now she had Tyler Lassiter on her mind and what she thought of as his traitorous act.

There was something going on that she couldn't afford to ignore. She was certain Ty and Jed Franklin had never met before, that he had never been to the orchard. Yet she wondered at the convenience of it all: property coming on the market right next to Riveredge, the one place in all the world that Ty coveted. Next he'd be applying for a strip of the Hudson River. "I mean, he didn't even know the orchard existed until I took him there. At least I don't think so."

So why did you take Tyler Lassiter to the Franklin orchard, Sarah?" he asked, raising his brows. "Are you into real estate now?"

"He'd dropped by the office just as I was on my way there." She stopped once more and gave an exasperated sigh. "Buying the orchard, I'll be damned. He didn't even show an interest except in the carton I'd gone specifically to buy."

"You're talking riddles, Sarah."

"I went out to see Jed Franklin on business. He had some old deeds to sell and I wanted to look at them. I mean, what reason could Ty have for offering to buy the place?"

"Sarah, Merriman County is ripe for development. Overdue, I'd say."

"Neat little cluster housing," Sarah offered. There was no reason, as yet, to share her true suspicions. She took a sip of the cognac, then held the glass up and examined it through the firelight. "Cluster housing. All those beautiful old trees coming down. Traitor. He used his interest in Riveredge as a cover-up for far more nefarious deeds."

"Take it easy," Victor said, using his calmest most sensible tone, the one that always infuriated Sarah. "You're getting hot under the collar about the sale of an apple orchard. Maybe he has other reasons for buying the place. Maybe he isn't the marauder you think he is."

"I thought you wanted to save those trees," Sarah snapped then, when he looked reproachfully at her, added "I know, you'd like to save the world from itself, Victor."

He laughed. "I think I could've made the orchard pay, but you can't win them all. According to Maggie—"

"Maggie!"

"According to Maggie, Tyler Lassiter has been looking for some real estate ever since he set foot in Merriman

County. He came here to do some research into his past and in his spare time has been checking out properties for sale."

"He never said a word about it," Sarah remarked indignantly.

"Was that a requirement for your friendship?"

"Oh, you know what I mean. What would he have to hide? I mean he's been perfectly open about wanting to find out all about his Ramsey Falls ancestors. In fact, today Alec called and asked me to give him the run of my office. Or else."

Victor grinned. "Alec giving you an 'or else'? Doesn't sound like him."

"Apparently Ty has offered to come up with some architectural plans for the redevelopment of the Merriman waterfront."

Victor took a sip from his brandy glass and then peered over at Sarah. "Town board approve?"

"It doesn't have to. Apparently Tyler is doing it *pro bono publico*. Otherwise known as I'll do this for you if you do this for me."

"Wait a minute," Victor said, interested. "There's a big difference between looking for your ancestors' history and mocking up plans for waterfront redevelopment."

"Victor, do you remember those old stories that make the rounds every now and then? The Merriman newspaper runs a series about somebody's ancestor or other, then everybody has a story to tell. Wasn't there one about Emma Forrster?"

"Certainly." Victor gestured toward the cocktail table and the slim volume of his family's history that he had written several years before. "I make reference to it, but only as hearsay."

"Right, of course. Emma married a Crewes and they took off almost immediately for Australia."

"Banished is the word," Victor told her. "Greg Crewes was a bit of a bad egg and an embarrassment to the family."

"If you used that in the book, how'd you do your research?"

Victor shook his head. "I just mention it in passing as part of the Crewes line apocrypha. My relationship to the Creweses is decidedly peripheral. I gave a brief sketch of the history of Riveredge, if you remember."

"Yes, yes, I remember," Sarah said hastily, although she remembered no such thing. She cast a glance at the leather-bound book and made a mental note to reread it at the first opportunity.

"I asked Celie's permission to go through the *Times Herald* newspaper files, but that was before they were put in order and on microfiche. They were in a rather delicate state and I could see Celie dancing around me, worried I'd tear them. I gave up. Besides, I was tracing Bosworths, not Creweses, and if I went down every byway and pathway, that volume would be a yard thick."

"Riveredge belonged to Emma's father, a General Forrester," Sarah went on carefully. "When he died, the Creweses inherited. Am I right? I mean, why not Emma? Why didn't Emma pack up and come back and claim her birthright?"

Victor gave a slight shrug. "You're the record keeper. Look it up."

Sarah flushed. They were moving into waters that were a little deep and a little dangerous. She *had* looked it up and had been very careful about hiding what she felt was the truth. The Creweses had stolen the property out from under the dying general and calmly fudged the official record. Hadn't she now "stolen" and therefore fudged the record?

"Look what up, Victor?" She was aware of the tightness in her voice. "You know the mess things are in."

"Check the tax records."

"I have to find them first."

"Then find them, my dear Sarah."

"You're incorrigible, my dear Victor."

"We've had dinner, we've had our after-dinner drink, we've even had our official family chat," Victor said amiably, apparently refusing to be drawn into an argument. He put his brandy glass down. "Time for Pack College and the rehearsal of *Much Ado About Nothing*. Ready?"

Sarah didn't move. That was the irony. Much ado about something. She had come to talk about Waverly and about Maggie, and neither had been accomplished. And all she would come away with was fresh fodder concerning Tyler's duplicity.

"Sarah?" Victor was watching her patiently.

She stirred. "I wanted to talk to you about Maggie Roman."

He frowned at her and his jaw set in the line she knew as intractably stubborn. "No, it's nothing I'm going to talk about. I haven't asked you to explain any of your relationships to me, at least not since you graduated from college and took off on your own. I expect the same respect for my privacy."

Sarah clamped her lips together. He was right, of course, but she realized that her cousin was watching her expectantly. He wanted both to talk about Maggie, yet keep her to himself. "Look, I know that Maggie must seem exciting and unusual," she said, "but for heaven's sake, she's been married four times. *Four times.*"

"Sarah, you don't know anything about her." Victor's eyes brightened. "She's the most electrifying woman I've ever met."

"She's an actress. She knows all about setting off sparks in men. It's her business, remember?"

"Sarah," he said softly, "the simple truth is I've only felt this way once before. And even then, that other time, it was part of being young with the sap rising in me."

She was about to speak, then held her silence because his confession seemed extraordinary to her.

"You were very young at the time, you wouldn't remember," he went on. "I was a little unsure of myself, then. Her name was Anna." He spoke as though he had forgotten Sarah was in the room. The words began to spill out as though he had just lifted the lid on a jewel-filled treasure chest. "She was the daughter of my father's caretaker."

"Anna," Sarah echoed, trying to recall some memory.

"Strange, I remember her hair most of all. A magnificent shade of brown like the shiny coat of a prized mare. I used to find all kinds of excuses to follow her around, and when at last I managed the courage to ask her out, I didn't trust her, simply because she agreed to see me." He looked at Sarah as though willing her to accept the reason he had never married. "After awhile she told me she loved me, and all I could think of was that she didn't love me, she loved Bosworth Stud, the house, the grounds, my inheritance. Least of all me."

"But if *you* loved her, why didn't you just let it happen, anyway?"

Victor didn't respond for a long while. "I went off to Europe," he said at last. "I told her I'd make some decision about us while I was away. I was gone longer than expected and stopped writing. Damn it, I was testing her. Like a fool," he added. "When I returned, she was gone. She'd married and moved west. And left me a letter that burned a hole in my heart."

"A letter!"

"Saying she loved me but understood why I'd never marry her, that it was clear money was so important to me I couldn't risk involvement with an ordinary mortal. That I lived in the rarefied atmosphere of privilege, but it never taught me a thing about love."

"Sounds wonderfully like a Russian novel," Sarah remarked. "What happened to Anna? Certainly not what happened to Karenina, I hope."

He laughed suddenly. "I lost track of her for years, then heard that she was living in Kansas City and that she had three children. And asked about me."

"Asked about you. But that's how Russian novels always end, on a simple little note like that. Asked about you. You know what you've done all your life, don't you?"

"I haven't been able to act differently."

"Until now. Until now you've used your fortune as a barrier to love, marriage, children."

"I haven't lived a celibate life and you know it."

Sarah colored. "Oh, I know that, too. You've had the most remarkable long-term relationships with appropriate women, and you've never loved any of them." She thought briefly of Jemma Whiting Gardner. She had believed for a while that he had fallen in love with Jemma, but then Hunt Gardner appeared on the scene and Jemma never had eyes for anyone else.

"Appropriate women," Victor murmured, "women whose lives parallel mine. No, no sparks, never any sparks."

"But, Victor—Maggie Roman!"

"Don't interfere, Sarah. I don't appreciate it."

Sarah waited a long beat, then took the plunge. "I always thought you and Celie—"

"Celie?" He looked nonplussed. "We're friends, nothing else. I knew her husband. I ushered at their wedding. She's a wonderful woman. And there's never been anything between us, not from her point of view, not from mine. Come on," he said, "let's go, it's late." He reached for her hand and pulled her to her feet. "The simple truth is Maggie's a breath of perfumed air. She's vibrant and exhilarating and she makes me feel alive. Is that enough for you?"

"I suppose," Sarah observed, feeling that somehow the entire evening was getting away from her, "we all make choices from the heart that have little to do with what's good for us."

"You might loosen up a bit, too, Sarah. Maybe you need a little drama in your life."

"Drama," she said, following him out of the room. "I rather thought I had too much to begin with."

The rehearsal was under way in the darkened Pack College auditorium by the time Sarah and Victor arrived. There were several people seated down front; otherwise the auditorium was empty. The bare stage was brightly lit. The actors upon closer examination turned out to be Reg Casedonte and Adriana Scott. Maggie was sitting downstage facing them. She didn't notice when Sarah and Victor arrived and took two aisle seats. Celie, in front of them, turned and gave them a welcoming smile. At her side was a member of the college board of trustees.

"How bad is it?" Sarah whispered to her, motioning to the stage.

"Amazing what Maggie can wring out of those kids."

Sarah settled back to watch. The parts Adriana and Reg were reading were of the young lovers, Adriana as Beatrice and Reg as Benedick.

"Darlings," Maggie cried from the stage, "no British accents, please. And please remember, we're out to interest our audience in the story and characters, so let's not put them to sleep by declaiming. I want them to understand the meaning of every word. Conversational, darlings, as though you're two wary and clever young people in modern-day America, with rock music blaring out from the stereo. Adriana, continue from 'Scratching could not make it worse.'"

Adriana smiled prettily and gave a little curtsy as she repeated the words. "Scratching could not make it worse an 'twere such a face as yours were."

"Well, you are a rare parrot-teacher." Reg put his hand stiffly out, then dropped it as though suddenly seeing it as an unfamiliar appendage.

Adriana, who seemed perfectly at home in her role, tossed her beautiful black curls. "A bird of my tongue is better than a beast of yours."

"I would my horse had the speed of your tongue, and so good a continuer. But keep your way, a God's name! I have done."

"Almost perfect, Reg," Maggie broke in, "but remember, these two are quarreling, yet their words quite clearly preface their fascination with each other. A fascination they refuse to admit quite yet. Want to try again?"

Adriana giggled, and Reg, with a broad grin, began his speech once more, this time with a respectable interpretation.

"Perfect," Maggie said.

Then Adriana as Beatrice gave a saucy smile. "You always end with a jade's trick. I know you of old."

Sarah was faintly aware of the slight rustling in the seat behind her. As Maggie called out some instruction from the stage, she felt the touch of warm fingers along her neck.

"And do you know me of old?" Ty said in her ear. "Maybe in some historical form of life? Come on, let's go for a walk."

Sarah knew that Victor had stiffened slightly before turning around to greet Ty. Celie also turned and smiled at him. "Don't go far," she said to Ty. "Adriana has a few more questions to ask you."

"I'll see her outside after the rehearsal."

Sarah stood and squeezed past Victor, and when she looked down at her cousin, she saw a small, self-satisfied smile on his face. The action had stopped on stage while Maggie consulted with someone standing in the orchestra pit about the lighting. She could hear the words "spots" and "mix" and "too bright" as she went rapidly up the aisle with Ty at her side.

Once in the lobby, she turned hotly to him. "I didn't appreciate that, Ty."

"Dragging you out of the rehearsal? Let's go back then, she's a pleasure to watch, Maggie. In spite of all the sophisticated saloon keepers she played in the movies and on television, she's paid her dues in the legitimate theater."

"I'm talking about your proprietary air."

"What you really want is to watch your cousin in action with Maggie to see the effect on your good friend Celie Decatur. I told you once before, mind your own business."

The lobby was a big pedestrian affair built in the twenties when the college was first accredited. Sarah stalked across the marble floor to the soft-drink machine in the right-hand corridor. "You put in a bid to buy Franklin Orchards, why?"

He reached out, placed his hand on her arm and spun her around. "Where the hell did you hear that?"

"What difference does it make? I suppose you're going to uproot all those wonderful old trees." She dared not accuse him of trying to surround Riveredge, of keeping his eye on the house and land that he might one day claim as

Forrester property. It was too preposterous, too far-fetched. The idea made no sense and yet scared the hell out of her.

He dropped his hand away and then dug into his pocket and extracted some change. "What's your pleasure?" he said, referring to the choice of soft drinks.

"Oh, apple juice by all means."

He laughed and tossed a coin into the air, grabbed it and slapped it on the back of his hand. "Heads I kiss you for being a smart aleck, tails I kiss you just to keep your mouth shut."

"Oh no, you don't," Sarah said, ducking out of his way.

"Ah, but I do. This is a game I can't lose." He backed her effectively against the wall, then leaned in toward her, bracing himself with his hand. When he spoke, his lips were just above hers. She could feel the soft exhalation of his breath. "Why in hell do you think I owe you any explanations at all for my behavior? Exactly what interest do you have in the Franklin property?"

"None," she stammered, "none at all. I didn't even know it was for sale until Celie called me about the documents he was offering."

He interrupted her, a look of satisfaction crossing his face. "You mean there's something going on in the general vicinity you don't know, someone whose life you're not attempting to direct? Amazing. Even so, you've become an expert on Franklin's apple trees and the disposition thereof. I'm trying to decide whether it's your upper lip or your lower."

"What in the world are you talking about?" She attempted to move out from under his hard gaze, but he put his hand on her arm.

"Which is more sensual, your upper lip or your lower? Both, I think. It's the combination. Wonder someone hasn't spirited you away before this just to spend a lifetime kissing them, upper and lower, I mean.'' He placed his lips on hers in a tender kiss.

Sarah heard someone's step on the marble floor, heard a slight hesitation, then heard coins inserted into the soft-drink machine. She pushed her hand against Ty's chest and broke away, moving quickly and unseeing past the figure reaching for a can of soda. She ran through the lobby and past a couple of students just coming in, and it was only when she was out in the November cold that she halted and took in a deep breath.

Ty came up behind her. ''Sarah, stop taking yourself and your position in the world so seriously.''

She turned around abruptly, aware of the soft imprint on her flesh that the touch of his lips had made. She wished desperately that he would go away, far away, to the ends of the world, and yet she wanted to be enfolded in his arms once more and soundly kissed. ''You're the most, most *blatantly* mysterious character I've ever met.''

He cocked his head and grinned at her. ''Blatantly mysterious? I've let Celie's part-time star reporter, aged nineteen, interview me and ask me the most outrageous questions. Answered all of them. If you want to read about Tyler Lassiter, I'd suggest you open up next week's copy of the biweekly Ramsey Falls *Times Herald*.''

''I can't wait.''

''No,'' he said, taking her arm and leading her along the drive to an avenue of trees that ended at a fountain in the distance. ''No, I don't suppose you can wait. Cold?''

She shook her head. The night air was vigorous, but the wind that had played around the Hudson Valley all day had died down. The sky was black, the moon low, the stars hard and glittering. She was bundled into her down jacket and wore boots. Her plaid skirt whipped around her knees. And she was warm, as warm as though it were a mild summer's day.

There was a massive oak tree off to the left, used by students all summer long as an oasis of cool. It was bare of leaves now, its heavy, muscular branches raised against the dark sky. Ty took her arm and led her over to the tree. She leaned hard against it, knowing she was becoming increasingly powerless to do anything more about him than submit to his love-making, that evening or whenever he asked.

How amazing that her emotions should change from moment to moment when she was with him. A roller coaster of emotions, highs and lows, then hot, then cool. Suspicion followed by the most intense desire to bare her soul to him. If he had waved a wand over her and cast a spell, he couldn't have done better.

"What are you thinking about?" he asked.

"You."

"Ah, we're making progress."

"And why you're here, in Merriman, buying property as if you mean to stay."

"I came to Merriman on a lark," he told her. He leaned in toward her, but instead of touching her, he put his hand on the lowest limb of the tree. "Just walked off the beach at Malibu, called for a ticket east and grabbed the next plane. Why? I decided it was time to learn something about the Forrester-Crewes line. Make sense?"

His face in the dark was merely soft light and shadow. He reached over and drew her hair from across her forehead and then tucked it gently behind her ear.

"Yes," she said, aware of holding her breath even as she spoke. "You never kept that a secret."

"I'd no idea there would be a lioness at the gates and that I'd have to resort to special means to get past her." He leaned over and kissed her briefly.

"This one of your means?" she asked.

"This is the last thing I counted on." He kissed her once more and yet again. "At first, before I met the lioness, I thought of taking her out with one shot. Ping. A dead lioness." His lips were on hers for a moment. "Then I met the lady and the game changed. Finesse. It called for a great deal of finesse. The trouble was I figured on three, maybe four days, and back to California. I retreated to think things over and gave myself more time to plan the operation."

He kissed her willing lips again. Sarah closed her eyes, let the heat course through her body and, when he pulled away, knew that it mattered very little to her what he had to say.

"Suddenly there I was with time on my hands. I had already tried smiling my way into Riveredge but found myself dealing with a man far cannier than I. How is the old reprobate?"

Sarah shook her head, laughing. "Had your number, did he? In fact, I don't know how or why, but your visit somehow spurred him into action, which is why he ended up in the attic with a sprained ankle."

"I'm not sure what the lineage is, concerning Riveredge," he began.

"Why do you say that?" Sarah asked sharply, unexpectedly afraid that he would confirm what she already suspected was the truth.

"My ancestor Emma was a widow by the time she made her way out of Sydney. She had enough money to invest in a small piece of land good for raising sheep, but neither the ranch nor her bank account would have been enough to keep her in Australia if Riveredge had come to her in her father's will. The question is, what happened?" He waited a moment, watching her closely.

Sarah instinctively turned away, casting her eye over the long shadow of the tree upon the silvery ground. She was afraid he could see her expression, know what she surmised about her family and the possession of Riveredge.

"Why didn't she make her way back home, a widow with four young children? Why not come back to Riveredge?"

"And you expect to find the answer in my office at the town hall?"

"Sarah, I'm not even sure what I'm looking for. I'm not even certain I'd know it if I stepped across it."

"Then why bother?" She stopped, then frowned. "Why didn't you spell it out right away instead of turning on the mystery? You could've written me a letter to keep an eye out for it."

He smiled and drew her close, pressing his lips to her forehead. "Clever of me not to think of it. It was a trip I wanted to make. I frankly wanted to see Riveredge again, wanted to see the ancient family homestead and if the old gentleman still lived there."

"Still? Are you talking about Waverly?"

"I came through Merriman once before," he told her. "I stood outside Riveredge and thought of the way it once was and might be again."

She stiffened under his touch. "Really? Such as?"

"Adding twenty stories and turning it into a condo, what do you think? Anyway," he added, smiling at her consternation, "this time around I became intrigued with Merriman in general and some people in particular. Because certain persons have been guarding the gates to the files at the town hall, I've had a little too much spare time, which I've been using to check out properties for sale. The Franklin house appealed to me from the start. Maybe," he added, "because it fit around you so well."

"You haven't answered me about Riveredge, Ty."

He kissed her again. "I wanted it with all its contents. Give you something to do on a cold winter night. Franklin agreed." He stopped as though caught by the look of astonishment on her face. Reaching over, he drew her collar up. "Come on, your teeth are beginning to chatter in the cold. Besides, I promised Celie I'd let her star reporter have another go at me." He took her hand and drew her back along the walk. "How much sense have I made?" he asked.

"None," she told him in a breathless voice, "none at all."

He stopped on the steps leading up to the auditorium, turned and gripped her arms. "Sarah, I left California to come here for a long weekend, meaning there's a pile of work waiting for me. I talked with my office today and one of our projects is in trouble. I'm going to have to go back."

"When?"

He shook his head. "I've been handling it by phone but I can't wait it out."

"Come in Monday," she said in a resigned voice, knowing the choice was no longer hers to make. "The files are all yours. You know, of course, that we have more files stashed all over town. It's a monumental job. Think you're up to it?"

His smile held something of self-congratulation in it, but she was already prepared for his visit. "I'm counting on a continuation of my good luck. Let's go." He turned and bounded up the stairs ahead of her.

Adriana was waiting for them when they came back into the lobby. Sarah saw Victor off to one side with Maggie, who had her arm draped around his shoulder. Celie, engaged in conversation with a couple of students, smiled at Sarah and beckoned to her. Sarah shook her head and excused herself to go into the ladies' room. There she stared at her reflection in the mirror. She looked well and thoroughly kissed. It struck her that a flush of happiness had been painted onto her cheeks. She turned on the tap and drew some cold water over her face. She applied lipstick and carefully combed her hair and just as carefully tried not to think about Ty. When she came back into the lobby, Adriana, her brow knitted, was dutifully holding up a tape recorder and trying to balance a notepad and pencil at the same time. Ty, hands dug into his pockets, was talking with a good-natured smile on his face. Sarah went over to them.

"Gee," Adriana said, her light blue eyes widening, "I'll go over the old clippings in our files and try to find out something about the Forrester family. Oh, I think Celie said something about your coming up to the office and going over our microfiches."

"I was and I did, and gave up soon enough. I'm nothing if not impatient. If you find anything, let me know."

Maggie was still talking head to head with Victor while Celie was striding purposefully toward Sarah.

"Hi," Sarah said in a bright voice, which she realized sounded a little high and brittle. She had no idea what to do about Celie.

"Hi," Celie replied, tucking her arm through Sarah's and drawing her over to the far end of the lobby. "Sarah, your feelings about Maggie are written all over your face. You're going to embarrass Victor and then you'll feel very bad if and when something develops between them."

"If and when? Celie, are you blind?"

"No, pet, not blind, just very, very sensible. What if I tell you one or two things you may not know about me so you'll understand that I won't fall apart no matter what happens."

"Oh, Celie," Sarah said, "I've known you for such a long time."

"Then you know I was in love with my husband. He was years older than I but I thought him the wisest, funniest, most charming man who ever lived. When he learned he was dying, he made certain that I'd be independent, that I'd use every bit of wit I ever had to carry on. We had no children and he wanted me to marry, wanted me to have children, but for a long time it didn't matter.'' She cast a glance over to where Victor and Maggie stood.

"That was then and this is now,'' Sarah told her. "And I know you love my cousin.''

"Yes,'' Celie said, "I think I do, after all. But what I feel for him has grown slowly, and maybe it's atrophied along the way. He's certainly never taken an interest in me, not the way he did with Jemma and now Maggie. Look,'' she added, "Maggie's the upstart in our midst, but she has talent, she has glamour, and what's most amusing is that she's Merriman born and bred, like one of Victor's Thoroughbreds.''

"Wouldn't it be Loverly,'' Sarah murmured. "Of course we know the bloodlines of that loverly creature.''

"You snob.'' Celie shook her head, but regarded Sarah with a fond smile, nonetheless.

"I didn't mean that. I just wanted you for my cousin.''

"And oddly enough,'' Celie told her, "I want your cousin's happiness first and foremost.'' Her eyes glistened with what Sarah thought were tears.

"Maggie won't make him happy. Four husbands, imagine. She's probably a cold mackerel in bed.''

"Victor and Maggie are going away together,'' Celie said. "To Manhattan for the weekend.''

"Fine. I assure you when Victor comes back it's going to be as a disappointed man.''

Celie leaned over and hugged her. "I love your cousin. He's good-hearted, wonderfully smart, a little insular...''

"Not your basic charmer,'' Sarah threw in, "but then he's never had to charm anybody in his life, not even Anna.''

"Anna?'' Celie looked at her nonplussed.

"I'll have to tell you about her sometime. Meanwhile, I think they're going back into the auditorium."

Across the lobby, Adriana solemnly shook Tyler's hand, then went back into the auditorium. Maggie was gone also and Victor made his way over to the two women. "How about coming back to the house for a drink?" he asked Celie.

Sarah saw the look of loving interest on Celie's face, which she erased almost at once. "No, I've got a long day ahead of me tomorrow, Victor. Some other time."

"We have to talk about the fund-raising dinner."

"We will." She bent over and kissed Sarah on the cheek. Ty had joined them and Celie laid her hand on his arm. "Give Adriana what she wanted?"

"Bared my soul," he said.

"I'll save a copy of the article for your scrapbook."

"Ready, Sarah?" Victor asked.

Sarah looked at Ty and realized he was about to offer to take her home. She knew she couldn't deal with him that night. She wanted to go home, put a fire in the fireplace and climb into her pajamas and wool bathrobe. She wanted a glass of hot tea on the side table, a good book in her lap, and she wanted to stare into the embers and think about him. But she didn't want him with her. She gave him her hand. "Good luck with the Franklin house," she told him as he grasped it warmly. "Just don't cut down any trees I wouldn't."

"The trees stay, the cider press stays, the horse stays, even the chickens, Sarah. And I wish to hell I could." He shook Victor's hand and then turned quickly away and hurried out.

CHAPTER TEN

A FLUTTERING OF SNOW on Saturday morning dampened Sarah's enthusiasm for her paid-in-advance booth at an indoor flea market. She'd have to carry tons of merchandise from her car to the Grange Hall, a trip that would be repeated a dozen times before she was fully set up. For the first time in memory, she had no taste for the work entailed, nor even for manning the booth through the long day.

Instead, over a cup of coffee in her tiny kitchen, she sat and gazed out her window at the plump and lazy snowflakes that seemed in no hurry to reach the ground. Snow. Well, there was no turning back; winter's icy ballet was a little early this year and Thanksgiving a scarce two weeks away.

Usually the progression of seasons and its marker holidays excited Sarah, but all of a sudden everything seemed a little askew. The snow could be rising upward for all she knew. Victor could lay on Thanksgiving dinner and serve frankfurters and hamburgers. Mickey Mouse might be his honored guest. She wondered whether Maggie would be present. And her son. Victor with a built-in family and a college-age son. All things were possible when it snowed. And Celie, of course. The new, calm, absolutely resolute Celie.

Not Ty, however. Sarah had no idea when he would leave for California, but sometime during the long night she decided to pretend it was the next day and, if not, the day after that. Or the day after that. Deep into her sleepless night she had believed her lips still burned with his kisses. Sweet kisses, tentative kisses, kisses that told her he enjoyed the touch of her lips and would keep coming back for more. But when? She remembered the cold outdoors and the way she had felt as his lips descended on hers. Her cheeks had burned. The tip of her nose was frosty, her ears tingled, and his lips brushed hers again and again as though he were tasting morsels of food, savoring each bite. She thought she ached for him and then told herself she was a fool; he was a man used to charming women and she was a willing victim.

But if she was no longer worried about Ty's reasons for being in Merriman, it was because she held almost all the cards. She had deliberately hidden the Forrester-Riveredge file of records, knowing they'd come to light eventually, but only after Ty was back on the west coast.

She supposed he'd come to her office on Monday. She'd wave and say, "Help yourself."

He'd never find the carton, of that she was certain. He embarked enthusiastically on a project, but details bored him. Odd enough behavior for an architect. He'd have personnel skilled in details, she imagined. All he ever had to do was sketch in the grand vision. Perhaps a grand vision had brought him to Riveredge in the first place.

And all he had to do was answer the questions about his distant grandmother and he could lay Emma's ghost to rest. Or come into possession of Riveredge.

Riveredge. At the heart of it all lay a huge old gray elephant of a house with twenty-five rooms inhabited by one retired gentleman and his cat, Ginger. Sarah had made the documents "disappear" to protect the house, its land and all the land surrounding it that was now owned by unsuspecting householders.

Had she hidden the file to protect Riveredge or her own heritage? Was she fooling herself into thinking what she had done was for the good of the town? Perhaps she should pull the records out again, drop the whole kit and caboodle on Alec's desk and let him decide how to handle the problem.

But no, she had deliberately gone after the history of Riveredge and it was up to her to follow through.

The Forrester-Riveredge records stopped dead after the Civil War because her family, more than a hundred years before, had deliberately stolen the house from Emma Forrester Crewes. They'd had no right to the land and apparently convinced their distant relative Emma Crewes that she had not inherited her father's estate.

And now she, Sarah Crewes, was doing precisely the same thing, hiding the truth because it was expedient to do so. She wondered if she could be mistaken. If somehow the truth lay in Riveredge itself. What had her Great-Uncle Wave really been looking for when he went up to the attic?

She hugged her arms, feeling an unexpected chill. When she first came upon Wave lying on the floor of the attic, she knew she'd have to come back later, alone, to explore. She swallowed hard, wondering about the feeling of dread that almost overwhelmed her. This was what quicksand felt like. Hope was the only thing to sustain her, hope that something might come to light to keep Tyler Lassiter from claiming Riveredge.

She stood and gazed out the window. The snow wasn't sticking to the ground and she wanted suddenly to escape her little cottage, to do something, anything, as long as it wasn't a flea market.

She made a quick decision to drop by the hospital to see Wave and then make her way over to Riveredge. After all, she had to feed the cat.

At the hospital she found Wave looking quite cheerful. He was sitting in a chair, gazing out the window, when she bustled into the room.

"Hello, darling," she said, bending to kiss his cheek. "You look chipper today."

"I feel chipper. They're going to unshackle me on Monday and send me home."

"What time? I'll pick you up."

"Don't bother," he told her, his eyes twinkling with an unexpected light. "Nellie's doing the honors."

Sarah tried not to show her surprise but failed completely. "Nellie? But that's terrific."

"What's so terrific about it? The woman's retired and she's turned into a regular Good Samaritan. I'm doing her a favor by giving her a reason for getting up in the morning. Have a cookie in that box over there."

"No thanks. Wave, is there anything I can do for you now?"

"Not a thing I can think of. How's Ginger taking it?"

"I'm on my way to feed him now. He's fine. I've kept the oil burner on low so the pipes won't freeze. Remember, there's been no one to feed the wood-burning stove."

"How low is low on the heat?"

"Low, Wave, just enough to keep the pipes from bursting, believe me. Ginger's doing fine. His coat looks nice and thick."

"I miss that rascal."

"You'll see him on Monday. Uncle, I'm going to go up to the attic this afternoon, your attic, if you don't mind."

He gave her a sharp glance. "Scene of the crime?"

"Right. Scene of the crime."

"Don't trip over anything."

"Uncle Wave, why had you gone up there, anyway? It's a rough climb with your arthritis, I know that."

He frowned and shook his head. "Squirrel, I suppose, or a mouse. I just thought for a moment—hell, I was distracted and here you see the result."

Sarah thought it odd that her great-uncle wasn't fussing more about her wanting to wander through Riveredge alone. "I took a quick glance around the attic when I was there, waiting for the ambulance. It's strange how familiar some of the things seemed, but I don't ever remember being there before. An old dresser with a broken mirror..." Her voice faded away and only when Wave stirred did she draw her eyes back to him. "Did my mother store some things up there by any chance?"

He shrugged impatiently. "How do I know? My wife kept filling up the place until there wasn't any room to move around. History! You want to know the history of Riveredge, you'll see it written in the cobwebs. Attic hasn't been cleaned out since—" He stopped, shook his head and lapsed into silence.

"Why did you lie about it?" Sarah asked, trying to keep the irritation out of her voice.

"When did I lie to you?"

"You know my penchant for researching family history. I asked you a long time ago if you had any papers I could go through. I specifically asked about the attic. You told me it was empty, cleaned out."

He fastened his bright blue eyes on her. "It wasn't a lie, it was a convenient way of telling you to keep your hands out of the honey pot. You wanted things to sell at the flea market. I told you there wasn't anything worthwhile."

"Semantics, Uncle Waverly. You let me believe the only things still in the attic were dust motes."

Wave reached for her hand and held it tight. "I didn't want to cheat you, Sarah, but I didn't want you to remove things one by one to sell to some damn stranger."

"I wouldn't have," she protested.

"It'll all belong to you in the long run. You can do what you want then, but right now it's all part of Riveredge, part of me."

"Oh, Uncle," she said, bending to kiss his cheek once more.

"I'd gone up there to find an old tin box of papers. Truth is I haven't really done much about Riveredge since I came back from India to take possession. That was sometime in forty-eight, I believe."

"But why now? Why did you go charging up there now?"

"Lassiter's coming around did it. It gave me the idea I ought to have the deed in my hand."

Sarah waited, feeling the absolute quiet in the air. "And did you find it?" she asked.

"No." He took up her hand once again. His eyes caught and held hers. "Sarah, Riveredge is very important to me, do you hear what I'm saying?"

She nodded, waiting expectantly.

"I'm giving you carte blanche to go through the attic, find that tin box and whatever else you're looking for. But I want you to promise me one thing: to keep silent about it, to tell no one what you've found."

"What am I supposed to find?"

"Maybe nothing, maybe nothing." He gave her a canny look. "Why are you so curious about what's up there? I don't want to see anything for sale at the flea market."

She laughed and assured him that it was simple curiosity about her past, nothing more.

It was late afternoon when she arrived at Riveredge. The snow had stopped and the ground was dry. There was still that anticipatory scent of snow in the air, however, and the sky was clouded over.

She sat in the car for a moment and stared up at the beautiful old house as if for the first time. It was desperately in need of paint both inside and out. Bushes required trimming, and the hundred-year-old sugar maple tree on the north side had cracked a branch, which sagged forlornly to the ground. The wreath she had placed on the front door the Christmas before was still there, the ribbon faded. Funny she hadn't noticed it before.

She got out of the car towing two bags of groceries and let herself into the front hall. The place had never seemed more deserted, or quiet, and she experienced an eerie feeling of having somehow stepped into the deep past. Then Ginger appeared, meowing belligerently and rubbing against her leg.

"There you are, you lonely old thing." Sarah put the packages down and bent to scratch the cat's ear as he stretched along her leg. "Do you miss Waverly?" She picked the animal up and nuzzled his soft warm fur. "Want something to eat?" He purred and pushed his head against her chin.

"I guess you want something to eat."

In the kitchen she stacked the groceries and then opened a can of cat food. "Here you go, old fellow." She was talking to fill the uncanny quiet, to brace herself for what she felt would be an unrewarding enterprise. If she found nothing at Riveredge pertaining to its true ownership, then her suspicions might be correct. Somehow her ancestors had wrested the house and property from Emma and claimed it as their own. It was too terrible to contemplate, especially if Ty had reached the same conclusion.

The cat walked carefully around his plate, sniffing at the food and giving it a tentative lick with the tip of his tongue. He then gazed up at Sarah, and as if giving up the idea that Waverly's absence would at last be explained, he began to eat. Sarah watched him for a while, then refilled his water bowl and made her way into the living room.

The shutters were closed against the gray day and the room was dark. She felt the cold chill of the house sink into her bones but didn't raise the temperature. Wave was a fusspot about how much heat he was obliged to pay for. Nor did she turn on the lights. Wave had been involved in an ongoing feud with the electric company and he was an ogre about turning lights on.

"Oh, what the hell," she said, and touched the light switch near the stairwell as she started for the second floor. High above, a crystal chandelier came to life. Tiny, exquisitely cut glass mirrored the light and cast a twinkling reflection against the faded yellow brocade wallpaper. She wondered when Wave had last touched the switch, perhaps not since Ruth had been alive.

She remembered the chandelier aflame with lights when she was a child and attended a party at Riveredge. She had a sudden, very clear vision of her mother in some soft swirling dress being whirled around the floor by the tall handsome man who was Sarah's father. Their faces were close, eyes brilliant, their smiles showing they existed for each other alone.

Sarah frowned. Where had she been standing at the time? In the corner? A shy thing with long curls and a party dress and shiny Mary Janes, looking on wide-eyed, not part of them, merely an observer of her parents' incredible love?

She left the chandelier glowing as she made her way up the stairs, past portraits of Crewes family members long gone; they returned her curious gaze with frigid stares.

"What have you done?" she asked, feeling foolish as the words pierced the silence.

The center landing contained an alcove with a worn pale blue silken seat and high arched windows that gave out on a view of the back lawn. The wings leading to the bedrooms on either side were draped with heavy cloths. Beyond them she knew the bedroom doors were shuttered, as well. Once a month, in spite of Wave's grumbling, Sarah sent someone over to dust away the cobwebs and air the rooms out.

It was late afternoon, and the sky was darkening. Sarah turned on a wall lamp. A fresh magical glow made romantic shadows of worn wallpaper and carpets in need of replacement. As she climbed the stairs to the attic, she found Ginger at her feet, romping ahead of her as if eager to get there before she did.

"Looking for a mouse?" She pushed the attic door open. He raced in as though spooked and disappeared almost at once. The musky scent she loved drifted out, the smell of cedar wood shavings, even of mothballs and leather, and old, dried lavender hanging from the eaves. A fly buzzed lazily against the window. She had no idea how it managed to find its way into the attic or remain alive there. A gray mist, the result of the fading day, fought its way through the dust motes like a busy ghost.

Sarah found the small glass light pull near the door and tugged at it. The light went on overhead and illuminated the near side of the attic that stretched the width of the house.

The attic was a high, beautiful place with arched windows that looked out on the river. It was filled with old furniture, antique trunks, frames covered with cloths, peeling cartons piled high with books—the detritus of a hundred years, perhaps two hundred years of living.

Dust lay over everything; it was clear that no one had been up there for a long time, with the exception of Wave on his ill-fated visit. The furniture for the most part wouldn't survive a trip to a flea market, but Sarah hadn't any doubt there were occasional gems to be discovered.

She went immediately over to the old dresser with its broken oval mirror. She caught a glimpse of herself, strangely faded and disembodied like a portrait of her own ancestor. The top of the dresser was made of gray marble. She touched the surface and remembered the cool feel of the marble when she was a little girl and it had seemed so impossibly high. The dresser had stood in her mother's room, she was certain of it. She opened the top drawer. It was scented with powder, and in fact an old compact lay open as if jarred in the moving. Its contents had spilled over everything, brushes that had been hastily thrown in, a pin cushion, bottles of perfume. She closed the drawer quickly, aware of the shock of seeing all those small personal things belonging to her mother.

Then, unable to resist, Sarah opened the second drawer and discovered an old handmade quilt. Had it covered her mother's bed? She couldn't remember, although her mother had loved antiques as much as Sarah.

She raised the quilt and drew in a sudden deep breath. Her heart gave an unwilling lurch. Ferdy. It had to be her doll of so long ago, with its dark red hair tied back in a ribbon and its white dress spotted with juice stains. Of course, Ferdy, that funny little doll she had searched for all those years. She bent over and picked it up.

Odd, Ferdy was smaller than she remembered, yet there was no denying the lovely doll face with its wondrous glass eyes and serious, pouting mouth. Sarah could remember the exact moment she had spilled juice on the dress and how it never did wash out. She felt a lump in her throat and fought the sensation to give in to tears.

The old fury rose to the surface then, and Sarah found herself clenching the doll, as if the doll itself were enough to handle her anger. "I don't forgive you, mother, I don't. Never, never."

She put the doll back in the drawer and covered it once more with the blanket. Perhaps one day she would ask Waverly for the true story of how it came to be there. How odd, she thought, she need never look for Ferdy again.

It didn't seem to mean so much after all. The little redhaired doll Ty had given her had taken its place. Now Sarah couldn't even have said why searching for Ferdy had occupied so much of her time.

Perhaps the doll signified a time that could never be recaptured, a time that was hazy and full of shadows, a time she was too fearful to examine. If she ever had a child, she promised herself she'd come back and haul Ferdy into the here and now.

The boards creaked under her feet as she went over to a large humpbacked trunk with brass locks. Ginger came out of hiding and entwined himself between Sarah's legs as she struggled with the catch.

"Out of the way, Ginger, you're a pest."

When she raised the lid a faint scent of mothballs and lavender drifted out. The lining of the trunk was in perfect condition, a faint dimity print with a narrow band in a darker print as edging. Beneath a layer of delicate yellowing copies of the *Times Herald*, she found an old photograph album in incised leather. She opened it to discover some valuable photographs of stiff unsmiling folks, perhaps her long-gone relations, perhaps Ty's.

Beneath the album was a pile of neatly folded clothing, and the scent of lavender was stronger. Each piece was encased in faded blue tissue paper that was so light and brittle, some of it came away with her touch. There were garments of lawn cotton and muslin as soft as silk, petticoat edging that had been carefully removed and preserved and the remnants of a black silk dress that someone obviously could not bear to part with.

The most beautiful piece of all Sarah discovered last. It was a long flowing dress of silken blue velvet with an ecru lace collar and wrist-length puffed sleeves edged in the same lace. The stitches were perfect little dots, obviously hand-worked. She guessed it dated from the end of the nine-teenth century. She held the dress up and with a shake all the creases fell out. It was in perfect condition except for one little tear in the lace collar at the back. Sarah got to her feet. She went over to the old dresser and its dusty broken mir-ror and held out the skirt in front of her, her head bent in contemplation.

The tin box, she had come for a tin box of old papers where Wave thought the deed lay. She'd come looking for...what? Her past? Riveredge's past? She glanced around the attic but the tin box was nowhere in sight.

Then, unexpectedly, the closeness of the attic, the scent of lavender, the soft light, the buzzing of the lone fly at the window seemed almost overwhelming. It came to Sarah that she had spent her whole life looking for something, look-ing, searching, wondering. Well, Ferdy lay resting in the middle drawer of an old dresser with a broken mirror. Picking up the blue dress and the photo album, she shut the trunk, then closed the attic light, leaving her past behind. The cold in the stairwell felt very good.

Ginger bolted down the stairs ahead of her but Sarah stopped on the second-floor landing. She remembered staying overnight at Riveredge when she was very young; the night of the party, in fact. Hers had been a corner room in the left wing with a view down the rolling lawn of the Hud-son River. Her father had scooped her in his arms and car-ried her to bed, hugging her tight and telling her that he loved her. Then he was gone, down to the party below and her mother's waiting arms.

Later Sarah had sneaked out to watch them between the carved spokes of the stairway, glittering and smiling as they danced the night away.

She turned and lifted back the curtain that closed off the left wing and went quickly along the corridor to the room she thought of as hers. Night had fallen, and when she opened the door, she reached inside for the switch and found it easily enough. A small bedside lamp glowed; the room took on an amber hue and she thought with a tremulous sigh that nothing had changed. There was the four-poster bed with its ruffled canopy and matching quilt, the walnut dresser and beveled mirror. On a small table in the corner she discovered the ancient Victrola that had fascinated her so. An album of records lay next to it, music that at the time had seemed to her to be very sweet and yet quite grown up. "Music to Love By." She smiled, remembering that she had played one record over and over again but had no recollection of the title. She reached for the album and then realized with surprise that she still held the blue dress and the album of photographs, as well.

What had possessed her to take the dress? It was of museum quality and belonged...where? In the Merriman town hall museum that was only a gleam in everyone's eye? She forgot the records for the moment and in a quick, almost unconscious movement tugged off her boots, removed her skirt and blouse and slipped into the dress. It fit snugly, the buttons just closing. She drew in a deep breath and stepped in front of the mirror, pulling her hair up high on her head.

Twentieth-century Sarah in nineteenth-century garb. Just who was she? "Memories," perhaps that was the title of the song. It was certainly the title of her life. She had come to Riveredge to wallow in memory, to discover some part of her past in a dusty old attic. And all she had found was a dress, a photograph album and Ferdy.

She turned away from the mirror. Sarah who was always digging and probing but never finding out about herself. Her life was filled with bits and pieces of other people's lives while she studiously avoided having any real commitment of her own.

Memories. She went over to the Victrola, picked up the first record and put it on the turntable without even checking the title. "Music to Love By," the strains of a song dating from the late thirties drifted around the room, faintly tinny and appealing.

Sarah went over to the window and pushed aside the curtain. The night was black and clouded over. There was no vestige of snow upon the ground. She took in a sudden breath as she saw a tall figure move out of the shadow and stand at the edge of the lawn. Then she realized that she wasn't at all surprised. Ty Lassiter. He'd been hovering around the edges of her mind all day. She hadn't dared speak his name, even silently, until now. And seeing him there filled her with the most eager joy, yet she didn't smile, didn't even try to attract his attention.

In another moment, however, he turned and gazed up at her and then with a quick stride moved toward the house and out of her line of vision. She remained at the window waiting. She heard the entrance hall door open, then close. Heard him run along the pine floor and take the stairs two at a time. Heard his footsteps down the corridor. She gazed down at the river. A barge glided past on its way north. On the opposite shore a train moved along the river edge. She heard him hesitate at the door, then he was behind her, his hands on her arms drawing her close. His lips were on her neck and when she turned in his arms she was aware of the music filling the room, of his exciting male scent, of everything around her that she must hold in her memory forever.

"Sarah." It was just a heartbeat before his lips found hers. She felt her knees weaken as he rained quick kisses across her face to find the hollow between her throat and shoulder.

"I knew the next time I saw you that there would be no turning back," he murmured between kisses, his lips moving back and forth over hers.

Sarah gave up any hope of reasoned thought. She had been waiting her whole life to be held this way, to feel a desire rise up in her that told her she had come unexpectedly on the meaning of life. The big, drafty old house had taken from their warmth and seemed to Sarah to be as radiant as it was on that magic night when she was a child.

She arched forward, crushing her breasts against the strength of his body with an abandon that was new to her. She found herself kissing him in a way she had never dared before.

He pulled away and gazed at her and once again whispered her name. "I thought I knew something about you," he said.

"No, you know nothing about me. And I believed until this moment that I knew everything about myself."

"And now?"

She drew her lips along his and didn't answer. She knew with an absolute certainty that what she had to say was not an answer but a brand-new statement all its own.

"And now?" he asked her once again.

She stretched luxuriously and put her arms around his neck. "I want you." She said the words quite simply and knew it wouldn't be the first time he'd heard such a remark and it might not be the last. Still, it didn't matter to Sarah. It was her statement for him and Ty had to know that for her this feeling was new, different.

The record stopped. There was a faint, funny little creak as the arm lifted and came to a rest. The room was suddenly silent, although Sarah knew he must surely hear the drumming of her heart. She caught his intake of breath but his lips descended on hers in a long careful kiss, as though he meant for her to reconsider.

She repeated the words, tracing his lips with her finger. "I want you, here, now."

After a long moment, he said, "I think I wanted you from the moment I saw you at the Merriman flea market, smudged nose, Confederate soldier and all. I've never stopped wanting you." He held her and kissed her eyes, her nose, her forehead and then her lips again. "Sarah, beautiful Sarah, challenging me all along the way. You don't even know what you do to me."

She didn't want to think of tomorrow, of his not being there for her. She only knew there was no history, no past, not even any future, just the present. And the present was making love to him, and having him make love to her.

He took her hand and moved toward the bed. In one swift gesture Ty threw back the spread. He turned and with a gentle touch undid the buttons on her dress as though the very slowness of his movements was a tantalizing act. When he removed the dress he held it for a moment in his hands as though sensing its value. "The blue of your eyes," he said. "Did it belong to some long-ago Sarah who gazed at her lover with the same smoldering blue?"

She stood before him in her short white chemise and for one breathless moment she wanted to run away, to tell him it was all a mistake. It wasn't a mistake, however, and when he drew her into his arms and found her lips again, she felt herself grow limp. Her mouth flowered open, his tongue filling her and plundering sweetly.

"Darling, beautiful Sarah," he whispered. He lifted the chemise, drew it over her head and let it fall to the floor. Then in another moment he had removed her lacy bra and panties and lifted her up, his lips on hers. There was no longer any chance to draw back. She knew as she felt the cool cotton sheet along her back and his body covering hers that it was right, that this moment belonged to them both and she wanted to savor every nuance of it.

He pulled back to look at her, his gaze heated and demanding. "You're so beautiful." His voice was husky and his breath came quickly.

He lifted himself off and removed his clothes, never taking his eyes from her. Sarah held his gaze and then took in his body. She felt her own breath quicken at the sight of his tanned chest covered with fine dark hair, the muscles in his chest and shoulders. The image of his body, the golden planes and dusky hollows, would burn into her memory. And that, she realized, was what frightened her so much, that he could ignite something in her she wouldn't be able to control.

He was fully aroused. She shivered with a devastating desire and raised her arms, reaching for him. He was on her again, his hands roaming her body. Sarah heard herself moan with a longing that seemed torn from her soul. A shudder ranged through her as his lips found her breast. When he touched her nipples, it was with a tenderness that told her he understood just how much she needed and how soon.

He found her lips and his kiss plunged deep into her. His hands moved to draw her close but he used the space between them to tease and test her, touching her lightly, exquisitely, delicately, as desire throbbed through her body. His mouth and tongue played her with a pulsing rhythm that simulated the movement of his body over hers. He was slowly taking possession, slowly leaving his imprint on her soul.

Sarah knew he was holding back; she could feel the urgency of his movements and his restraint. But then, so suddenly it took her breath away, she wanted him in her, wanted to know all of him, his weight, his breath, his flesh moving against hers.

"Now... don't wait," she whispered.

He raised his head and for a long moment held himself poised over her.

"Ty, I haven't—" she began.

"I know. I'll take care of it."

After, there was no more hesitation. With his eyes locked to hers he entered her body, slowly, filling her until she arched under him, crying his name.

It was a moment like no other. Sarah clung to him as he moved with her, and then with a moan of ecstasy, he crushed her close, crying her name.

SARAH OPENED HER EYES. He was smiling down at her, his arms still enfolding her.

"I'm afraid to let you go," he said. "I don't want to find out it was all a dream."

"I don't remember anything ever being this real."

For a long moment they lay entwined, breathing softly.

"Ty, how come you found me here?" she asked.

Sarah reached up as his tongue flicked the corners of her mouth and she captured his head between her hands.

"I stopped at the blacksmith's cottage and you weren't there. On my way back to Merriman I used my old Australian logic. There was a cat at Riveredge that needed feeding. It was no sweat to chance by. Your car is in the driveway, the house ablaze with lights. And there you were, standing at the window, waiting for me."

"I wasn't waiting for you."

"Thinking about me. Thoughts so powerful, I material-ized."

Her mouth found his in a long kiss. "I don't think this is purely spiritual," she said at last.

"No," he laughed. "I don't suppose it is. Are we spend-ing the night here, just like great-great-great-grandmother Emma used to with—"

"Greg Crewes," Sarah told him firmly. She lifted herself on her elbow and looked down at him. With her index fin-ger she traced Emma's and Greg's initials on his chest. "It was a hot love affair, so the scuttlebutt has it."

Ty laughed and grabbed her hand. "You're a little liar, Sarah, but it doesn't matter. Nothing in this bed, in this house has ever equaled the heat going on right now."

"We're going to have to leave this bed, and this room, and this house."

"Maybe we can get visitation rights," Ty suggested.

"If my great-uncle ever—"

Ty laughed. "He'd congratulate us for putting it to good use."

"I wouldn't bet the rent money on it." She moved to get up but he grabbed her and pulled himself over her.

"Was it magic for you, just as it must have been on that other long-ago night?" He breathed the words against her lips. She ran her hands down his back, the smooth skin a contrast to his hard muscles. He was heavy on her and yet the pressure of his body was comforting. "Was it?" he asked once again.

She looked at him long, her eyes smoky with fresh de-sire. She didn't answer him but drew her arms around his neck and placed her lips against his in a long, hard kiss.

It was almost an hour later that Sarah stirred. Ty lifted his head from her breast. When she opened her eyes she felt disoriented and thought she was in the middle of a dream. When he spoke, murmuring her name softly, every moment of their lovemaking returned. She stretched luxuriously. "Did you say something about dinner?"

"Too bad we aren't in Manhattan." He lifted himself and turned on his side so that he could look at her. "I'd take you to Lutece or Aurora for a fancy meal and then I'd hire a yacht for a boat ride around Manhattan."

"And then," she interrupted, "we'd rent a plane and fly down to New Orleans for breakfast to this little place that serves those wonderful doughnuts...what do you call them?"

"Then on to Paris on the Concord to finish out the weekend at George Cinq with a stopover in London on the way back—"

"To see the Queen—"

"And afterward," he said, placing a kiss carefully on her nose, "we'd have to find someplace to stay because I'd want to make love to you again."

"You'd be too tired."

"I'll never be too tired." He took her hand and ran it down his body.

"Show-off." She squirmed out from under his touch and reached for the coverlet at the foot of the bed. She wrapped it around herself and rose.

"Hey, don't cover up all that creamy skin. There should be a law against it."

She ignored his remark. "I hate to offer you a mere homemade dinner after the feast you planned for us, but Chez Sarah Crewes is the only establishment open at this hour."

"I accept," he said, propping up the pillows and leaning back. "Oh, on one condition."

"And what's that?" Sarah waited, not quite knowing what to expect. She thought his smile was the most self-satisfied one she'd ever seen.

"Get rid of the cover and let me watch you dress."

Sarah hesitated. Normally she was quite shy, but it seemed silly now to hide herself after the lovemaking they had just shared. She dropped the blanket and stood before him. He held her eyes for an instant and then allowed his gaze to travel the length of her body. Sarah shivered and crossed her arms over her breasts. "I'm—"

"Perfect," he finished for her.

She sat at the edge of the bed and began to dress slowly under Ty's quiet scrutiny.

"Not the blue dress?" he said as she reached for her skirt.

"That was just a moment's fancy," she told him. "I found it in the attic."

He drew his arm behind his head. "Ah, an attic. I've an affinity for attics, smelling of mothballs and dust and history. I wouldn't mind a tour of Riveredge's."

"Oh, it's just your basic, pedestrian attic," she told him lightly. "Surely Maggie has given you the tour of Kimberly Hall's nether regions."

He laughed. "As a matter of fact, she has. And a proper one, too. How about a quick tour of Riveredge?"

She turned and gave him a canny look. "Didn't my great-uncle give you a tour?"

"He stopped on the second landing and after a while complained of arthritis."

She pulled her boots on, and only after standing up and adjusting her blouse did she speak. "Ty, you never did tell me why you came to see Wave. I mean, not really. I'd think now, after..."

"After making incredible love, we owe each other total honesty."

She gave him a serious smile. "Have you been honest with me?"

"In the matter of making love?"

"No," she said, shaking her head. "I believe and trust in your honesty there. What I'm afraid of is subterfuge in other ways, for purposes I don't understand." He reached out his hand and she enclosed it between her own. "It connects with Riveredge, I know that. What is it, Ty?"

"Would you believe me if I told you it doesn't matter anymore."

"It?"

He pulled her down onto the bed and drew his arms around her. "Stop taking yourself so seriously. You hand me those wide-eyed, hurt looks as though I were the enemy come to throw you out of your home. I'm not. I'm the man who daily thanks fate for dropping me in Merriman. I must remember to leave a few coins in the alms box in gratitude."

At his attempt to kiss her, Sarah pulled away, wondering how she could compartmentalize her life with this man. They had just made love; she had carefully hidden information from him that he could use against Wave, and she supposed, ultimately against her if she came into ownership of Riveredge, and she was asking him for honesty.

"What is it?" he asked her quietly. "That sudden rise of color to your cheeks. You're the lady who's been hampering my checking into Emma's history, not the other way around."

"But what do you want to learn? What do you already know?"

He slipped out of bed and came over to her. His eyes had an unexpected hooded quality. He held his hands at his sides and didn't touch her. "I know that you're the most exciting woman I've ever met. I know that I could spend the rest of my life making love to you and it wouldn't be enough. What I suspect, however, is that you don't know your own mind, that something frightens you and you've no idea what the word love or commitment means. Why I came to town has no bearing on what just happened to you and me in that bed." Then, as if he could bear it no longer, he reached for her and drew her to his chest. After a moment he said, "Did you make love to me to secure Riveredge for the Crewes line, because if you did, Sarah, you've more than accomplished your purpose."

Sarah heard the words with a kind of horror. She tore out of his arms and drew her fingers to her lips. Then, without a word, she grabbed her things and ran from the room.

CHAPTER ELEVEN

TY STARTED AFTER HER, then remembered he was naked and took great satisfaction in slamming his fist against the bedpost.

She was gone, dragging the blue dress with her and an antique photograph album. He heard the entrance hall door shut, heard the car start in the driveway and realized Sarah had left him alone in that huge old house.

A blue dress and a simple little reference to an attic and she was off and running. Right out of nowhere she remembered they were at Riveredge and he was on a mysterious journey whose movements she had to thwart.

Hell, had he made love to her badly? No, that couldn't be it. He had felt her response, had seen the fire in her eyes, felt the passion when it rose through her. It wasn't make-believe.

But when things should have been warmest between them, she had turned on him. And he had paid her in kind, accusing her of climbing into bed with him merely to secure Riveredge for the Crewes line.

Damn, he'd been a fool, too, but Ty knew one thing: he was going after her. She wasn't going to run out of his life, treating him like a one-night stand. He grabbed his clothes, dressed, straightened the room and, after making certain the cat was in the house, closed the door behind him and went for his car. He gave one last look at Riveredge before moving out of the driveway. He had just locked away the perfect opportunity to find what he was looking for.

He was ten minutes behind Sarah, and during the drive to the blacksmith's cottage at Bosworth Stud, thoughts that were wholly new flashed through his mind and caused a tightening in his chest. She was both tough and vulnerable, Sarah Crewes, and he had certainly hit her below the belt.

She was a ball of fire in bed, and yet when she remembered his visit to her uncle, she turned icy cold eyes on him. She was full of contradictions, all of them intoxicating and confusing.

Her car was there when he pulled into the driveway. The lights were on in the cottage and he didn't even pretend to politeness. He hit his fist against the door and called her name. "Open up, Sarah, don't play games."

The door opened at once, almost as though she had been waiting for him. She stood there looking slightly breathless. "You're here? Odd, I thought you'd still be rummaging your way through Riveredge. It's what you wanted all along and I gave you the golden opportunity."

He stormed past her into the house. "I never even thought about it. Incidentally, the bed sheets are four-squared and not a trace of what happened between us is left behind. And the cat is securely inside and the front door locked."

He turned swiftly around and found her leaning against the open door, her face flushed.

"You're an absolute martyr," she said. "I don't know how you can live with yourself."

"Easy, as long as I don't have to deal with mad women."

She closed the door and made her way past him into the living room. "I'm hopping mad and I am a woman." Her voice was now calm, and as she faced him, Ty noted that she kept her hands at her sides, fingers biting deeply into her palms. "I asked you a simple question which you neatly sidestepped—*again*—and to make your point you added insult if not injury. I don't need your instant analysis of what makes me tick."

"Instant! I gave it rather a lot of thought."

He went over to the fireplace, poked at the ashes and then busied himself for a few minutes laying a fire. He didn't turn around but heard Sarah walk quickly from the room. When the first sparks caught, he stood. Sarah was coming toward him, still frowning and holding out a brandy snifter.

He took it, held it up and said, "Peace?"

"An uneasy one, perhaps."

"I know how to make it easier."

They regarded each other solemnly. "A few answers would do fine," Sarah told him. He could see that she had begun to relax. "And I don't think I have to ask the questions again."

"No," he said. "I don't suppose you do." He thought, with a feeling he had difficulty in defining, that what had happened between them had ignited too quickly, and that the sparks could die down just as easily if care weren't taken. He'd have to go away quickly, leave Merriman and deal with this newfound feeling far away.

"Ty?" She was waiting, still standing before him, her hands now clasped together.

"They've just celebrated Australia's bicentennial," he told her, watching the flames take hold in the fireplace. "In a sudden fit of patriotism, family biographies have been trotted out and everyone's gone ancestor happy. My mother has written to me on several occasions about our beloved family matriarch, Emma Forrester Crewes. We're curious about why she left Merriman and why she never returned when her father died."

"You might have told me that at the beginning," Sarah remarked with a rueful expression.

"Would it have made a difference in my getting access to the files in the town hall?"

She hesitated. "Why Emma left the country would have nothing to do with our records."

No, he thought, it wouldn't. The core to Emma's mystery lay in the possession of Riveredge. But what mattered now was Sarah. He put the brandy snifter down and reached for her. "Sarah, I'd give my life to blot out forever those words I said to you back there at Riveredge." He drew her close and tipped her chin up. "Tell me you didn't hear it, tell me that every bit of anger is past."

She extricated herself from his arms, all the while shaking her head. "I was horrified, Ty, not angry. I left, and left you to Riveredge." She went briskly into the kitchen and opened her refrigerator. "You've disappointed me," she said, rummaging around for some food as he came up behind her. "I didn't expect to see you again. I thought you'd be in the attic knee-deep in Forrester history. I came home prepared to fume. I hate it when I don't get my way." She came up with the remains of a guinea hen that Victor had sent over from their shared dinner the night before. "Riced potatoes suit you?"

"I can think of a lot of other things I'd rather taste right now."

"Glutton."

"For your kind of punishment, absolutely."

"Here, take this," she said, handing him the potatoes. "Start peeling.

"Peeling? Gladly."

"Dinner, glutton." Her arms were piled with food and she kicked the refrigerator door shut with her heel. "I forgive you for telling me the truth about myself, but I'll never forgive you for suggesting I want to sleep with you for any other reason than that—" She stopped and he was surprised to find her eyes glinting with the sudden possibility of tears.

"Sarah," he began.

"I said dinner, and I meant it."

"We have to talk."

She turned the oven on and spent considerable time fiddling with the temperature. "About what, California? You purport to know all about me and what makes me tick, while giving me nothing of yourself."

"Nothing? Amazing to learn that what just happened between us goes under the category of nothing. Where's the damn peeler?"

"In the left-hand cabinet, upper drawer, right-hand side. Nothing, Ty. All I know about you is that you're a handsome, sexy man who appeared at my booth one day at the flea market and tried to wrest a Confederate soldier away. You claim we're related ever so distantly and behave with ever so much mystery. And *you* tell me that I don't know about love and commitment. Left-hand side, Ty." She went over to him, pulled the peeler out at once and handed it to him. "You're impatient, I know that much—I mean except when it comes to, to making love. Oh, damn." She fled to the other side of the kitchen, then faced him. "Don't make me regret what happened between us."

"I was born in Australia, I was educated in England—"

"I know all that," she said impatiently. "I also know you like to steal apples and cartons and real estate out from under my nose. I want to know about you in California, about Tyler Lassiter. Associated. Beverly Hills."

"That Ty Lassiter. Ah, that fellow I know very well."

"And do you like him?" she asked.

"We live together in a kind of watchful truce. Sure you want to hear about him, about the way he lives?" She nodded. Ty had an unexpected desire to lie to her about what his life was like, to cover the truth and tell her that his work was of uplifting moral value. But she deserved more. If he wanted her love, if he deserved it, then she must have the truth.

"Beverly Hills is full of white stucco and marbled halls and odd-shaped swimming pools, some of which I helped design and build. It's equally filled with money and ego. Want to hear more?"

"The people you know, where you live, what you do with your time." She moved quickly around the kitchen and busied herself with the preparation of dinner.

"I live on the Pacific Palisades in a rented house with a spectacular view."

"Design it yourself?"

He laughed. "No, as a matter of fact, and it might just slide into the sea in the next storm. As for friends, Sarah, most of them are part of the film industry and I can't remember the last serious conversation I had with any of them that didn't deal with . . . *deals*." He stopped short, knowing that he wasn't good at opening up, yet surprised at how much he wanted her to know.

"The ideal life, in other words," she said.

"So I thought, but now I'm not sure. I make money at what I apparently do best, building houses that are too large for people who are too rich."

"Give it up, then."

"Give up success? What an odd notion for an American."

"Are you going to come through with a viable plan for the Merriman waterfront, *pro bono*?"

He looked at the badly peeled potato in his hand, but then an architect knew about stripping away walls, not the skin of potatoes. "I made a promise," he said.

"Sorry about it?"

He shook his head. "Never happier with an idea."

"Come here."

He gave her a surprised smile.

"I mean with the potatoes. I'll finish them or we'll never eat. You're obviously a man who has always had a live-in woman if not a live-in servant."

He surrendered the knife and went into the living room, where he retrieved his brandy glass and checked the fire. When he came back, he leaned against the doorjamb. "You certainly don't fiddle around with subtleties."

"I don't know what you're talking about."

"Of course you do. You want to know about the women in my life."

She looked at him, her eyes clear and challenging. "Yes."

"I'm afraid my sex life, until today, has been a lot duller than you think. There have never been dozens of women in my little black book. Even in my fantasies, I'm conservative." He grinned. "Never more than two or three at a time."

"It's not two or three at a time I'm thinking about," she said with a little laugh. "It's the one at a time."

She touched a raw nerve with her casual remark. Ty had steered clear of involvement long enough for it to become second nature. Hell, what was wrong with him, anyway? Why had he avoided a legal tie with anyone? The women in his life had stayed awhile, then drifted away when they understood he wasn't ready for the long haul. As far as women were concerned, he was waiting to be hit by a bolt of lightning, a simple fact he had overlooked until now.

He watched Sarah bent over her work, hair tucked behind her ears. The picture of her domesticity, the warm kitchen, the scent of wood smoke hit him with unexpected force.

"There hasn't been any one at a time," he told her. "Until now."

"Quart pot on the right side of the stove," she said. "Could you fill it with water? Add a little salt. When," she added with a scarcely perceptible release of breath, "are you going back to California?"

"Sooner than I want to. Damn it, Sarah." He went over to her and pulled her into his arms. "Forget the quart pot, forget dinner, forget everything but Ty Lassiter standing here. I have no women in my life that mean anything to me. My day is filled with the kind of easy glamour that stops you from thinking, from caring. It's not a permanent way of life, but it is the way I live now. When I'm ready to I'll change it." He tilted her chin back and brushed her lips with his.

He felt her soft surrender. Filled with the wonder of her, Ty didn't trust himself one bit. She reached up and drew her fingertips across his cheek and said, "I'm trying to commit you to memory, every bit of you, every taste, every scent, every touch. Is that a scar, right here, at the corner of your eye?"

"Sword wound at the battle of Waterloo."

"Aah, thought so."

"My best friend pinged a dry crust of bread at me in history class. Drew blood and made me a hero for a day."

"Amazing the way these wounds travel with you through life."

"Yours, too, Sarah?"

She was a long time answering, her eyes perusing his face, as though she were trying to assess his seriousness. "You'd have to search me over to find the remnants of even one."

"I could try. Sarah..." The words he spoke next surprised him, but he felt no regret once they were said. "Come back with me. Have you ever been to California?"

"I've been to California. Pretty beaches, lovely mountains, sun all year round. Did you just ask me to go back with you?"

"Your archives have waited this long. They can wait another couple of months." Something hardened in her eyes and he realized he had made a mistake.

"How kind of you," she said sweetly. "Come and romp with me for a while, and when I tire of you I'll send you home on the next plane. Is that how the game is played?"

"It isn't a game." He wondered how he could rescue the moment. "It's a genuine invitation to a woman who interests me."

"So drop everything and hop aboard."

"That's not quite what I mean and you know it."

"I know nothing of the kind." She made no attempt to get out of the circle of his arms, but he felt her resistance. "Amazing how the temperature in this room keeps changing by the minute," she said. "Hot, cold, hot, cold. Right now it's hot, but in a moment it'll be freezing."

"Damn it, we're good together, you know it and I know it. People do this all the time. They stay with each other and then they... see what happens."

She drew away from him. "I don't. I don't live with men to see how it feels. I have my own life, my own job, my own space. And I'm not interested in being carried away to your aerie on the Pacific Palisades. What am I expected to do while you're running Tyler Lassiter Associates? Sit around and eat chocolate and wait for you to appear?"

"Why did you sleep with me?" he asked, and saw her go pale.

"Not for an invitation to California."

"What do you want, Sarah?"

"Today, this evening, I wanted you. I still want you, standing here in the kitchen with the uncooked potatoes waiting to be boiled and a guinea hen being overdone in the oven. I want to look at you and memorize you and spend the winter thinking about you. I'll tell you what I don't want, I don't want invitations to live with someone for a couple of months while we check each other out." She turned and went quickly into the living room, where she bent over the fire, warming her hands as though she were cold.

"I want an absolute," she told him when he came over to her. "I've chosen to live my life with a certain degree of solitude and independence. I don't want to have to count on someone else for my happiness." She paused, then picked up the poker and set off sparks as she moved the logs around.

"No, he said quietly. "Why should you?" He reached for the photograph of her parents that stood on the fireplace mantel. "That's what happened to them, isn't it? They were in love and a war came along and tore them apart."

Sarah put the poker down and took the picture out of his hand. With the briefest glance at it, she replaced it on the mantel. "They adored each other. Loved each other so completely I don't believe there was any room for me."

"That's ridiculous."

She turned on him suddenly. "What do you know about it? You can't know about it. I was deserted, left alone."

Ty shook his head. He wanted to reach for her but didn't. "Your father died in the war. It isn't desertion, Sarah. He didn't choose to die."

"Perhaps he didn't," she said quietly, her face expressionless. "My mother did, however. She killed herself less than a year after the telegram came that really ended her life."

Ty stayed very still. Once again he wanted to reach for her but knew instinctively that she would push him away.

"I came home from school," she went on in a low voice. "She was lying on the living-room couch." Sarah's words were slow and halting as though she were reciting a story that was new to her. She stared into space, dry-eyed. "I thought she was daydreaming. She did that sometimes. You'd talk to her and think she'd be listening but she wasn't. I shook her but she didn't move. I think I knew she was dead the moment I touched her, yet at the same time didn't really understand what it meant. My father had gone away and never came back. And there was my mother, lying there, her eyes open, and she wasn't paying any attention to me. I kept shaking her. I don't think I screamed, but I can't be sure."

"Sarah." He took a step toward her and stopped.

"She left a note saying she couldn't go on without my father. There wasn't a word about me in it, not a word." Sarah looked at him as though she saw him for the first time. "Now you understand, don't you? If I couldn't hold my mother to this life, if there wasn't enough in me to keep her alive, how can I ever hold on to anyone else?"

He reached for her and enfolded her in his arms. He held her tight, feeling the beating of her heart and the heat of her breath. "I don't have any answers," he told her after a long while. "What happened to that child was a terrible thing, but you're a woman now, with a woman's longings and a woman's feelings. History doesn't have to repeat itself in every relationship."

"No," she said against his chest, "but it is a mine field, isn't it?"

"For all of us, Sarah, one way or another." He kissed her then and she allowed his touch, leaning softly into him. It amazed him how quickly he wanted her again, but it was more than the mere touch of flesh, it was something deeper, something he'd have to plumb later, much later when he sorted out his own feelings for her.

"I've never spoken about what happened before," she said at last. "To anyone. About finding my mother, what she did. I've wondered if everyone knows, if anyone knows. The trouble is the pain has never gone away, even though I've pretended all these years that it has."

Ty took her face between his hands and kissed her. "And now you've talked about it and maybe there never will be any answers. She loved with a kind of madness, and not you, my Sarah, nor anyone else could have kept her from destroying herself."

"I've never completely trusted any happiness I've had. I'm always waiting for some crack to develop that I'd fall through, fall and fall forever."

At that moment Ty had no idea what his feelings were; he couldn't have found words for anything that had happened since he first met Sarah Crewes. All he knew was that saying goodbye to her wasn't going to be easy, and perhaps harder for him than for her. She might relinquish him quickly, knowing he was just another crack in the odd surface of her life.

"Ty?"

"Mmm?"

"What are you thinking? Are you thinking I'm a basket case?"

"I was thinking about California."

"And your invitation?"

"That, too."

"And all the women who'd jump at the chance."

"I'm not interested in any other woman."

She lay back against his chest. After a moment's silence, she said, "Do you want to stay the night?"

He cleared a small lump in his throat before answering. "Yes."

She straightened and smiled at him, then took both his hands in hers. "I'm glad, I'm so glad."

He followed her to the bedroom door. The room was small and furnished in delicate antique pieces, and like the others it was filled with an eclectic mix of china and toys. The bed was large, almost too large for the room, a sleigh bed with a velvet patchwork quilt on it, handmade throw pillows and a stuffed calico cat in the center.

"I wonder who lives here?" he asked with a smile on his face.

"A lady with a penchant for collecting things."

She went over to her bedroom closet and removed a wool paisley robe from a hanger.

"My cousin's," she said. "I swiped it when I first moved back from New York and stayed at Bosworth Stud. My clothes and furniture were sent by the moving van to someplace very odd like Nova Scotia and it was weeks before I could get myself together properly."

She tossed the robe at him, and when he caught it, he was glad she had told him the story, even if it weren't true. He might not have been able to put it on if its owner were nameless.

He waited while she plucked a nightgown from a dresser drawer. "Right back," she said, heading for the shower. As he undressed he heard the shower turned on. An uncontrollable urge came over him to follow her into the shower and take her wet body in his arms. He threw the robe on the bed and quickly removed his clothes.

She hadn't locked the door and Ty didn't bother to knock. The steam had already fogged up the room so that he could scarcely catch his reflection in the mirror. Yet when he glimpsed the outline of her body against the glass of the stall shower, he felt himself grow hard.

She expelled a short breath when he opened the stall door but didn't try to cover herself. Instead, she stepped back to allow him room. The water poured over them as he pulled her into his arms. Their shared kiss was long and deep, his lips moving hungrily over hers, his tongue hard and restless.

She clutched his shoulders, her kisses eager and abandoned. She shifted her body and he eased his leg between hers. It would be uncomfortable to take her there, he thought as he felt her move invitingly against him. Reaching behind her, he closed the spigots.

"Not here," he said. "This is just a sample, a tasting."

"Better surprises to come?" She smiled with a joyous, adventurous light in her eyes.

He lightly kissed her lips and then stepped out of the stall, grabbing a large bath towel, which he placed on the tile floor. When he turned to her, her eyes still held a brightness that seared his soul.

He pulled her down and she was under him and he felt as if his world had tipped. He wanted to touch every part of her at once but knew he had to keep control. His mouth found her still-damp breast and he plucked the firm nipple. He felt a shiver rack her body as his hand found the center of her being. When she arched forward she sighed, whispering his name, and began a random exploration of his body that stilled his breath.

He would take his time, he told himself, his lips locked to hers. He'd draw it out as long as she allowed, as long as he was able. When he pulled back to gaze into her eyes, he found her expression hot and heavy with desire. Ty realized he wanted to tell her things, say words he'd never used before, but he didn't know how, nor did he even know how she'd react.

"Lying on this floor is dumb," he told her. "Want to go to bed?"

"I don't really want to move," she said dreamily, "but I'll change places with you." She turned suddenly, pulling him with her, and then he was under her, feeling her breasts pressing against his chest, her legs wrapped around his thighs.

"Sneaky," he managed just before her lips met his.

She took charge and he let her. Her skin felt like silk and his hands roamed her body with an ease that brought a brand new pleasure. He had suspected all along that she'd be wonderful to make love to, that her cool self-control was merely on the surface, that a slow peeling would reveal a passionate, almost wanton woman.

She sunk onto him rotating her hips, taking him in deeper and deeper. He heard his own moan just before he cried out her name. His breath was harsh and uneven but he held onto her lowered mouth as if it were a well and he were a thirsty man. An exquisite thrill rocked his body and he could hold back no longer. He gripped her hips, anchoring himself to her, and holding her tight he thrust into her again and again until he felt her body quake and knew the swirling that swept through her. Only then did he release his own final spasm of love.

Later, tucked into his arms under the quilt, Ty listened to her quiet breath but knew she wasn't asleep.

"You're going to think about it, aren't you?" he asked.

"I am thinking about it, every luscious minute."

"I'm talking about California. Coming back with me?"

He felt her grow taut and it was several seconds before she replied. "I'm sorry, it's not the way I do things."

"Then nothing's changed between us."

"Ty, everything's changed, everything, but not this. You're reaching for a solution that seems simple enough to you, but it's infinitely complicated for me. It's your old formula, isn't it? Hey kid, let's hang around together, see if it works. We get tired of each other, what the hell, what did we lose, a little time?''

"I don't do things that way," he told her, but knew she had hit the mark. Only this time it was different. He sensed permanence, he knew enough to give it the name of love: he wanted to be with her, yet instinctively wanted time apart; needed her but wanted to take commitment slowly. "You're a complicated lady," he added, "and what I'm beginning to feel for you is pretty complicated, too."

"Ty, you've brought me a measure of myself I was afraid to admit was missing. It's enough for the time being." She laughed gently. "I'm afraid everyone in the greater Merriman County is going to know what happened to me. I've no idea how to scrub my happiness away."

"Don't ever." He kissed her closed eyes and lay still while she fell asleep in his arms. Her dreaming seemed deep. He brushed her hair back from her forehead and carefully eased himself out of bed. Perhaps she was right. Perhaps it was enough for the time being. He needed to be alone, to take her image back with him, to think about her under warm clear skies far away.

He gazed at her sleeping figure, her hair spilling across the pillow, the feathering of her long, dark lashes. Something deep inside him was frightened, but of what he couldn't quite say.

He left a note tacked to the kitchen door, turned out the lights and left quietly.

CHAPTER TWELVE

"MORNING, GERT."

"Morning, Sarah. Bit sniffy out there in the cold. You look great, though. I don't know what you do with your weekends, but they sure agree with you."

Sarah picked up her Monday morning telephone messages and glanced quickly through them, afraid Gert would catch the rise of color to her cheeks. "All that lovely autumn air," she said absentmindedly. She established quickly enough that Ty hadn't called.

"Do any flea markets this weekend?"

"No, as a matter of fact. My enthusiasm is beginning to wane with the temperature."

Oh, your Uncle Waverly called. I put it all down. Something complicated about his leaving the hospital this morning but don't bother looking for him as he'll be out all day, so call him this evening at home when you get a chance."

"My Uncle Waverly?" Sarah gave the receptionist a startled smile. "My laconic Uncle Waverly said all that in one breath?"

Gert shrugged. "Frankly, he sounded kind of hyper to me. Make any sense to you?"

"Not exactly. I know Nellie is picking him up at the hospital, but I figured she'd take him right home. He didn't happen to say where he's going?"

"No, sorry."

"Well, if he calls again, locate me wherever I am, okay? I brought that old photograph album with me. I wanted to stop by and discuss it with him tonight on the way home."

"What old photograph album? No, don't tell me," Gert said as her telephone went off and she reached for it. "I hate history."

When Sarah unlocked the door to her office, she knew the day wouldn't be a good one for concentrating, but then Sunday hadn't been, either. When she woke Sunday morning, Ty was gone, a message stuck to her kitchen door: "Think about it."

Will you stay the night, she had asked, and he had answered yes, an answer with strings, obviously.

Think about it. But she had refused to, and busied herself all morning in the garden clearing out old leaves and pulling up spent flowers by their dead roots—and not thinking about it. At eleven she heard the phone and raced indoors. The call was from Celie, who invited her to lunch at Decatur Hall along with a spontaneously invited half-dozen other guests including Jemma and Hunt Gardner. Conspicuously absent was Victor, and no one mentioned that he was in Manhattan for the weekend. No one especially mentioned that he had gone there with Maggie Roman.

Everyone had commented on how well Sarah looked.

The spontaneous Sunday lunch lasted until four and she had gone back to the Gardners' house and spent the evening with Jemma and Hunt. There, the general topic of conversation had to do with the restoration of old houses. Sarah remembered the old photograph album she had grabbed when leaving Riveredge. She had no idea why and planned to return it Monday evening when she visited Waverly. The album was a curiosity and she hoped he might be able to identify some of their Crewes ancestors.

When Sarah had finally reached her own little cottage at ten on Sunday evening, she was exhausted, not at all ready for work the next day, and her body ached to be stroked once more by Ty.

She had deliberately stayed away from home, afraid he'd call her, afraid her defenses would be broken down. *Think about it.* No, she would not follow him, would not live with him, would not be so in love that she'd lose all sense of identity, like her mother. What she had done all those years was establish her independence, her ability to survive alone. When love came it would carry a healthy dose of commitment to marriage, to careers, to children, to solidity, to everything but following a man to his lair because that's what he expected.

But on Monday the memory of Ty's kisses was still too much on her mind. She couldn't fool herself that life would go on as usual. Ty had made a dent in her heart as wide as the Grand Canyon, and there was no repairing it. But she would not follow him to wherever he willed it. His stake in the relationship was the same as hers; he had as much to lose or gain as she.

At ten, Sarah stopped to brew herself a fresh cup of coffee in her office. As she sipped at it, she contemplated the old album she had taken from Waverly's attic. It was a pretty piece of work, containing a dozen pages made of cardboard and pasted over with hand-decorated paper. Each page was attached to the spine by an ingenious use of heavy canvas, but time had taken its toll, and the canvas and glue were coming undone.

At five after ten her telephone rang. She jumped at the sound. The morning had been unusually quiet. Still, she did not expect to hear Ty's voice at the other end.

"I tried to get you all day yesterday," he said at once.

"I was busy." She had to force the words out. They had made impassioned love. She had fallen asleep in his arms and he had gone, telling her to think about uprooting herself for California on a whim.

"You know where I'm holed up," he said, the hurt apparent in his voice. "You could've called me, Sarah."

"Yes, I suppose I could have. You left in the middle of the night. Why?"

He hesitated before answering. "Practice, maybe."

She opened the album at random almost as though she needed something to hold on to. She stared without thinking at the first photograph that presented itself, a man and woman stiffly regarding the camera. "Practice for the grand goodbye?"

"Practice for getting up in the morning and not finding you there. Have you thought about coming back with me?"

She turned the next page and then the next. "I've thought about thinking about it, Ty. Then I decided not to—think about it, that is."

"You won't mind if I try a little pressure."

"I do, but you can try anyway. Can't guarantee results, however." Another turn of the heavy pages, carefully to avoid damage.

"I'll guarantee the results," Ty said.

Sarah was about to close the album when she came upon something that made her gasp.

"Lunch?" Ty was asking.

"Yes, no, I'm afraid it's impossible." She found herself staring at the blue dress, the one she had tried on at River-edge. The same dress, she was certain of it, worn by a frail, pretty woman. Someone had carefully painted in the color and added a touch of rouge to the woman's cheeks.

"Sarah, make sense."

"That blue dress," she told him excitedly, "you know, the one—"

"I know exactly the one."

She caught the smile in his voice. "I'm looking through an old album and here it is." She held the album up to the light, forgetting its frailty. The interior glue of the spine gave way completely. "Oh no, no," she cried as the heavy pages spilled all over her desk. "Look what I've done."

"Sarah, what the hell are you talking about? No, don't bother telling me. I'm coming over."

"Ty, wait, don't." But he had hung up.

She stared, disconcerted, at the pages and the photographs, some of which had fallen loose of their moorings. Waverly would have a fit and he'd be perfectly within his rights. Then, slowly, keeping as calm as she could, Sarah began to compile what she thought was a reasonable match of photograph to page, page to its position in the album.

When she was half-finished, she came upon her next surprise. Tucked into a window from which a photograph had slipped was a folded piece of paper, yellowed with age.

Sarah stared at it for a long moment. Then she clasped it between her thumb and index finger and carefully picked it up. The edges were ragged, the paper stiff. It could easily come apart with rough handling. She carefully unfolded it, aware of the minutes ticking by, afraid Ty would come bursting through the door.

"A marriage license!" Faded angels were painted at the top, and a ribbon of pale blue framed the document. The names of the betrothed were clearly legible. Emma Sarah Forrester was married to Kurt Hoving on March 12, 1866.

She sucked in a breath, trying to take it all in. "Eighteen sixty-six." She spoke the words out loud. No, there had to be some mistake. Emma had married Greg Crewes in 1866.

She picked up the telephone receiver and punched in the receptionist's number. "Gert, could you take my calls for the next half hour? Oh, and if anyone comes by asking for me, I'm in conference."

"He's on his way back." A conspiratorial smile was clearly heard in her voice.

"He?"

"Mmm, that gorgeous Australian."

"Thanks, Gert." She replaced the receiver and grabbed the album and marriage certificate. The implication of the marriage license was sickeningly clear. The proper owner of Riveredge might just be coming through the door. She managed to put the marriage certificate away when Ty knocked briefly at her door, then stuck his head in. "What's this about a blue dress?"

"Oh, right, I found a picture of it in this album and the whole thing became unstuck. Forget it. You shouldn't have come running."

"You sounded as if you'd been attacked by a horde of killer bees."

She shook her head slowly, knowing that her shameless happiness at the sight of him was causing her to become as unstuck as the album. "I guess I just wanted you to come running."

He came around her desk, pulled her up, gathered her in his arms and kissed her. "Let's get out of here, right now. I needed you yesterday. What possessed you to take off like that?"

"My other life," she told him. "The one I lead when your not around."

"That's no life."

"You were the one who climbed out of bed and snuck away in the middle of the night, remember?"

"I needed to think, Sarah, same as I wanted you to."

"And what conclusion did you reach?"

"That I want you to come back with me."

"Odd," she said slowly, knowing she would score a point he would never take her up on, "I decided that you should stay here in Merriman, with me. Move into the blacksmith's cottage with me, get in my way and make a general nuisance of yourself."

All the while she spoke, Ty looked at her with a crooked grin, shaking his head slowly. Then he put a finger to her lips. "You win. Case closed. We're equals careerwise and everything else. Nothing like a bicoastal love affair to keep the fires stoked. Meanwhile what do we do about the fact that I want you, right now?"

"We separate. We show our moral strength. I'll see you later, after work. Wait, not possible," she said. "I have to check on Waverly. It's his first day home from the hospital."

Ty placed his lips on hers in a kiss to stay further words. "I'll see you at your cottage at eight."

"Dinner," she began helplessly.

"I'll take care of it. You take care of your uncle and whatever else. Eight," he cautioned and left her, closing the door behind him with a firm little click.

Sarah sat abruptly in her chair, her knees weak. What was she going to do? She felt as if she were surrounded by a phalanx of Confederate soldiers with Ty on a white horse commanding them. They were moving in tighter and tighter. She was without a weapon at hand to defend Riveredge and Waverly and all those innocent owners of land sold wrongly to them by her ancestors.

She opened her desk drawer and took out the marriage certificate once again. What, she wondered, did Ty know? What had he come to Merriman armed with, and when did he intend to use it? She passed her hand across her brow, then touched a finger to her lips in imitation of Ty's gesture.

With the marriage certificate open once again on her desk, she contemplated the tangle of information it contained. Kurt Hoving, according to the diary she had read, was a Confederate soldier who lay wounded in a northern hospital. Emma Forrester, visiting the wounded in the hospital, met him, fell in love with him and ran away to Herkimer County, where she married him *the selfsame year in which she married Greg Crewes*.

The conclusion Sarah drew was that Kurt died of his war wounds, Emma married Greg and left for Australia. Sarah breathed a sigh of relief. Of course. Kurt died, and Emma, the little flirt, married quickly. So much for love, undying and otherwise.

Unless... but there were too many unlesses, and the trouble was that Ty Lassiter was undoubtedly in possession of some of them. She looked around her office. Odd that he should have spent so much energy trying to gain access to the files and, when he had broken down her defenses, turned away from them.

If he had something up his sleeve, he was doing a remarkable job of hiding it.

Meanwhile Sarah had some choices, too. Assuming the marriage certificate to be true, then Emma had parted from Kurt in one of three ways. The marriage was annulled, they were divorced, or Kurt had died.

If all or part of it happened in Herkimer County, then it was to Herkimer that Sarah had to go. She reached for her telephone receiver. An old school friend, Remy Snyder, was the managing editor of the Herkimer County *Gazette*. She'd go right to the source, the newspaper's microfiche files, which went back to the last century. She checked her watch. Reg was due in at noon. She'd make Herkimer County in forty minutes, spend a couple of hours rummaging through newspaper files, then make her way over to the county hall to check their records. She'd be home by late afternoon.

THE *Gazette* was large, popular newspaper with a circulation that covered areas of both Herkimer and Merriman Counties. Celie's newspaper, out of Ramsey Falls, had a respectable circulation but its main coverage was in the southern tier of Merriman. She often talked about enlarging, about taking on the *Gazette*.

When Sarah walked into the *Gazette*'s bustling city room, the contrast between the papers was strong. Phones were busy, there was a great deal of movement to and fro. Celie, on the other hand, didn't even have a full-time reporter on staff but depended upon news gathering from strangers— retired people and college kids such as Adriana.

Sarah was immediately taken to a small office where the microfiche files she had requested were already waiting for her. There was also a good supply of pads and pencils along with a thermos of coffee and a couple of oversized pieces of Danish pastry.

"What are you looking for?" Remy Snyder stuck her head in the door.

"I'm not sure, but I'll know it when I see it." She smiled at her old friend. "You're looking pretty good, Remy. Success agrees with you."

Remy smiled. "Thanks. Something agrees with you, too, but from the light in your eyes I'd say it has little to do with business. Have time to come home with me and visit with the husband and infant?"

Sarah groaned. "Impossible, but let's make a date."

"Deal," said Remy. She nodded at the stack of microfiches. "Our files are in very good shape, Sarah. We've received a dozen bequests of old newspapers over the years and now they're all on microfiche. The originals are in a vault down in the basement. The owners of the *Gazette* had a sense of history, but then the area has always been in love with its past, don't you agree? Well,'' she added as someone came up to her and handed her a piece of paper, "stop by on your way out and we'll set up that date."

"Thanks, Remy."

"And if you need anything—" The last was lost as the door closed.

Sarah bent to her task with her usual obsessive concentration. Under the magnifier the little blue plastic film brought to life the troubles of the Civil War and its aftermath. She found confirmation of the Forrester-Hoving marriage almost at once in the marriage notices for March 12, 1866.

Buried below an account of a horse auction and an advertisement for a medicine show was a small headline:

Forrester-Hoving Nuptials

Emma Forrester of the town of Merriman and Private Kurt Hoving, late of the Southern Confederate Army, were married today at a civil ceremony at Herkimer town hall. Private Hoving was recently a patient at Herkimer County Hospital, where he had been sent for treatment of wounds received in the late war.

And, Sarah thought, left unsaid is the fact that the bride raced back to Merriman and the groom took himself south. *And* the fact that her father, General Forrester, never read the Herkimer County newspaper.

The easy part was over; now Sarah had to find evidence of an annulment, divorce or death notice. After an hour of unsuccessful viewing she rubbed her eyes, poured a second cup of coffee, went to the window, stretched and stared at the busy street below.

What struck her as remarkable was the fact that Emma had managed to marry twice, that the Herkimer *Gazette* printed the fact, and that the news had never traveled back to Merriman. Certainly if it had, the story would have become part of family lore.

She returned to her work and twenty minutes later discovered a small article on the back page of the *Gazette* dated June 23, 1866.

Kurt Hoving Succumbs

Private Kurt Hoving, member of the late Southern Confederate Army, died yesterday at Herkimer County Hospital of wounds received in the war.

The nurse on duty found the soldier just after midnight in a feverish coma. She heard him calling for his wife, Emma, and bemoaning his fate at having to die before his baby was born.

Dr. John Peerless, director of the hospital, later explained that Mr. Hoving had been away from Herkimer County for three months. He had returned to the hospital for further treatment, but the state of his wounds had developed too far along. The body will be shipped back to his home in Georgia for burial.

June 23, 1866, a bare three months after their marriage and Kurt Hoving was dead. And where was the enchantress Emma at the time? Possibly on the road to Australia as the bride of Greg Crewes. Which meant more research. There had to be an annulment somewhere or a divorce. She'd check the records at the Herkimer town hall and then those in Merriman County. The last caused her to laugh out loud.

There was no sure way to check the Merriman record, was there?

"I LIKE THAT," Celie Decatur remarked when Sarah showed up in her office later that same day. "Imagine, the archivist of Merriman County coming to me to check out my records because she can't find a damn thing in her own office."

"Try not to make front-page news out of it, Celie."

"You don't want to deprive me of a living, do you?"

"In this instance, yes."

"Eighteen sixty-six," Celie mused. "What's so important about the year that has Adriana and now you rummaging through it? And come to think of it, Ty Lassiter too, except he was doing some research for the Merriman waterfront project, I think." She gave Sarah a shrewd look. "What's all this about, anyway, the pack of you?"

Sarah kept her face frozen in a dumb smile. Ty apparently was one step ahead of her.

"Never mind," Celie said. "Adriana's doing a story on Lassiter and I told her the most interesting thing about him is his roots in the country. She's been researching his family's history—yours, too, I take it. You and he are related through Waverly Crewes, am I correct?"

"So the scuttlebutt has it."

"You know where we keep the microfiche. Enjoy yourself. Place closes at five-thirty to outsiders, but of course you're welcome to stay as long as you like."

"Thanks, love, see you later."

Herkimer County records had yielded nothing about an annulment or divorce, and after an hour of plodding through three months of *Times Herald* records, Sarah came up blank.

Neither divorces nor annulments could have been easy to obtain in those days, especially without the consent of both spouses. Of course, Kurt Hoving in a coma and calling out for his beloved wife, Emma, was in no shape to remember whether he was married or divorced.

If General Forrester learned of his daughter's marriage to a Confederate soldier, he might have arranged an annulment very quietly. *If, if, if.* No, Sarah decided, if the general had managed to annul the marriage to Hoving, he'd have been careful about having the marriage notice removed from the Herkimer County records.

Sarah did come across two other notices in the Ramsey Falls *Times Herald* concerning the Forresters. Both were dated in late May, 1866.

The first reported a burglary at Riveredge in which some valuable pieces of silver and gold had been taken. The culprits had not been apprehended.

The second concerned the marriage of Emma Forrester to Greg Crewes, immediately after which they departed on a journey that would end in Australia.

And Kurt Hoving dead the following month in the Herkimer County hospital, calling out for his wife.

Was it possible that Emma Forrester Hoving married Greg Crewes without a divorce? Sarah caught herself in a smile, which she at once wiped off her face. The word she had avoided thinking was *bigamist*, and it was decidedly not a laughing matter. The line of succession to Ty Lassiter would then be quite clear. The Creweses, never owned Riveredge, because Emma was a bigamist and only her first marriage was legitimate.

If Ty wanted to claim the land, he could put Merriman out of business and wreck a hundred lives. He might not win the case in court, for there it would surely end up, but fighting it would take time and cost a lot of innocent people a great deal of money. Surely the court wouldn't find for Ty: the current owners were completely innocent in the matter of real estate transactions more than a century old. Still, money and time; both were always in short supply in such matters.

She could not know Ty's intentions, of course, but Sarah knew where her duty lay. She would have to let both Victor and Waverly know what she had discovered and how she had hidden the Forrester-Riveredge records. *And* she worried about Waverly and how he'd take the possibility of losing his beautiful home.

Victor wasn't in when she called, and his butler had no idea when he might return. Waverly had left a message with Gert asking Sarah to call him, but she decided to run over to Riveredge to break the news in person. She picked up her bag and made her way out of the newspaper offices without saying goodbye to Celie.

As she came up the driveway of Riveredge, Sarah recognized the rental car parked in front. Waverly, not out of the hospital a day, and he was beset upon by Ty Lassiter. She was also surprised to find all the curtains pulled open on the lower floor and the house lights on. She remembered the party of long ago, seeing the house aglow as she drove up with her parents. But that was the past. Riveredge was now the lonely abode of a crotchety widower, although perhaps not for long.

Something's happened, she thought, rushing out of the car and up the stairs. She had no need to use her key. The door was open and she stepped into the well-lit entrance hall, which was several degrees warmer than she expected.

She could hear music emanating from the kitchen and the sound of voices. She went quickly back, but what she came upon was so astonishingly normal that she was caught up short at the door. Nellie Casedonte was at the kitchen sink washing some cups. Ty, sitting at the table with his back to her, was talking quietly to her great-uncle, his words swallowed up by the music. As for Wave, he relaxed in his chair, his foot raised on a stool, Ginger shamelessly comfortable in his lap. Wave regarded Ty with interest, nodding his head as though agreeing with him. There was an iron pot bubbling on the stove with the scent of some rich sauce emanating from it. The kitchen was warm; there was a fire in the fireplace.

No one noticed Sarah, and for a moment she remained at the door watching Ty. She was beginning to know exactly what the back of his neck looked like, the soft line of hair that met his collar, the sound of his voice just before it broke into laughter. If she weren't careful, her heart could shatter right there in front of them all.

"Well, how cozy," she said at last.

All three turned to her. She heard her name spoken three times in varying degrees of surprise. Ty got to his feet and came toward her as though he were the host of Riveredge and not Wave. His smile was warm and intimate, but Sarah backed away.

"We saw each other earlier today," she declared. "Don't you think you should have discussed it with me then?"

He gave her a puzzled look. "Discussed what?"

"Being here, talking to Waverly."

"Sit down, take a load off your feet," Waverly told her. "Did you bring me any of those frozen biscuits I like?"

"The last time, you said you didn't like them. And hello, Nellie," she called, going over to Waverly and planting a kiss on his head. "Excuse my fit of temper."

"Was that a fit of temper?" Nellie asked. "I'd like to see you when you're calm. Sit down and I'll pour you some coffee." Nellie's manner was very proprietary in a way that both surprised and confounded Sarah.

Sarah, who had brought the photograph album with her, quickly sat down next to Waverly, the album on her lap. "How are you feeling, Uncle? You look rested," she commented, trying to gain some mastery of the moment.

"Speaking of fits, fit as a fiddle," he told her. "Mind telling me why you're frowning? And what's that album for? Don't I recognize it?"

She glanced at Ty, who had picked up his cup of coffee and was leaning against the doorjamb. "What have you been talking to my uncle about?" she asked him.

"Nothing much," he said. "Incidentally, I came here looking for you."

"You knew where I'd be at eight o'clock."

"Sarah, did I miss something? I thought—" Ty stopped and shook his head.

"What are you two talking about? Speak up. I don't understand a word you're saying," Wave complained irritably, then added, "Ty's been telling me this place is too big and old for me."

"Really?" Sarah addressed her disdain to Ty. "I had a feeling the house might come up in the conversation."

"I'm not quite sure I put it that way," Ty said. "I merely told Wave that heating a house this size for one person was an exercise in futility."

"Wave has always been quite comfortable here," Sarah told him. "Not that it's any affair of yours."

"Funny," Nellie remarked. "I remember my mother saying a man, or a woman, can only sit on one chair at a time."

Wave frowned at her. "You with me or agin' me, Nellie?"

"I'm only quoting my dear departed mother. She had many such clever sayings, Wave. You believe the same thing."

Wave grinned and Sarah thought she saw an expression pass between them that was both wise and secretive. "If Wave wants to sit on ten chairs at one time, he's earned the right to do what he wants with Riveredge," she said angrily to Ty. "If he wants to heat all of it or none of it, if he wants to use one room or...or...or *all* of them, it's no business of yours."

The situation was getting away from her, Sarah thought, and all she managed to feel like was a foolish intruder.

"Did you get stung by a bee or something?" Ty asked her.

"No, by something a lot more fierce."

Ty put his cup down on the counter and came over to her. His eyes were veiled and angry as he reached for her hand. "Come on." His grip told Sarah she had no choice in the matter. "Let's go." He smiled over at Nellie and then at Wave. He pulled her to her feet, and Sarah, her face red with anger and embarrassment, let him lead her out of the kitchen and into the drawing room.

She heard Wave say, "What the hell's going on?"

"I'll make you a nice cup of tea," was Nellie's response.

The lights were on in the drawing room, a heavy log burned in the fireplace, and the curtains had been opened to the night outside. Ty released her arm and Sarah was caught by the genuinely nonplussed look in his eyes. "Okay, let's have it," he said. "What was all that about?"

"Couldn't wait a minute to crow, could you?"

"Crow? What the hell are you talking about? Are we on the same wavelength or have you gone flying off somewhere into outer space?"

"You came to see Waverly," she said. "He's none of your business, damn it."

Ty threw his head back and laughed. "I said I was looking for you. Answer me, crow about what?"

"Riveredge. It all comes down to Riveredge, doesn't it?" She stood before him, aware of her hands clenched so tightly her fingernails bit into her skin. "You think it belongs to you, don't you? You have some kind of grand design for Riveredge, and that's why you bought the Franklin place, as well, isn't it?"

"Wait a minute," he said in a flash of understanding. "You're still worried because you believe I came to Merriman with a purpose in mind, to take Riveredge and throw Wave Crewes out on the street. Baby—" he pulled her roughly into his arms "—it seems to me I accused you of taking me to bed to hold on to Riveredge. I made the remark half in jest, but I wonder now."

She saw a flicker of pain cross his face and disappear quickly. Sarah knew then that she should have been in control and instead had let everything get absolutely out of hand.

"Sarah, I think I already explained that I came to Merriman to satisfy my family's curiosity about Emma Forrester. You can believe me or not. Why I came no longer matters. I'm willing to lay Emma to rest because I met you, I even met Wave, and things look fine just the way they are. I'm not trying to snooker Wave in any way."

"I wish I could believe that."

"Good Lord, what does it take?" he said impatiently. "Look, I think my actions speak for themselves. If you want to see it another way, there's nothing I can do about it. I came looking for you earlier this evening because I'm going to have to take off for the coast early tomorrow morning. I wanted one long last evening with you."

She felt her heart sink at his words. "I see."

"There's a mix-up in a project we're working on. If I don't go back, we're in danger of losing the job. In spite of

your stubbornness, in spite of the fact that you don't trust
my motives, I want you to come back with me."

"Just like that? Pack a bag, say goodbye to my job, my
family, everything, and hop the next plane?"

"Yes, if what we had together means anything to you."

She shook her head slowly. "It's too soon. Things have
come up. There are complications."

"You're making the complications," he said roughly.

"I can't go with you, Ty, but what we had means everything to me."

Their eyes held for an instant. Then he grabbed her and
his mouth came down hard on hers. At first Sarah held her
lips closed, but then, knowing it was all over between them
and she would be left with nothing but memories, she
opened her mouth and his tongue invaded. All at once he
loosened his grip, released her and strode over to the window. It was snowing outside, small quickened flakes driving to the ground. All day long snow had been threatening
and now here it was to intensify the dark. When he began to
speak it was in a low, reasonable voice that held a slight edge
of finality.

"Emma Forrester Crewes was twenty-three years old
when she arrived on the shores of Australia. The year was
1867. She had already given birth to a baby boy and was
pregnant with her second child. Her husband, Greg Crewes,
died of drink within two years of their arrival. Emma was
left with three small children and was pregnant with a fourth
when he died. I won't go into the details of her life, but she
ended up running a sheep ranch on ten acres of land in the
middle of nowhere. In the true pioneer tradition she saw to
the raising of her children, the building of a house and start
of a small dynasty.

"When she died a little more than a quarter century later,
she was a dignified, revered woman who had lived a moral,

upright life and who gave that same moral strength to her children and grandchildren after that."

Sarah, hearing his words, swallowed the heavy lump in her throat. The Emma he talked about couldn't have been the bigamist she imagined. Once again she had the sense of events sliding out from under her.

"If Emma ever made a mistake, it was here, in the States, at Riveredge. The only reason I returned to Merriman was to try to settle the story once and for all. When Emma lay dying, she called her oldest son to her bedside." Ty turned and leaned against the window ledge, his eyes level with Sarah's. "Her words have become part of family history, handed down like the family bible and the small diamond cluster ring and silver-trimmed net stole."

He moved restlessly, coming across the room to Sarah, who stood with her hands clutching the photograph album that still held Emma's marriage certificate. He reached his hands out for her, then dropped them by his sides and went on speaking in a low voice.

"'He wasn't your father, you know,' Emma told her first-born son, my great-great-grandfather.

"It took him a long time to recover his voice. 'But who, then?' he asked. 'Who was my father?'

"Yet it was as if she hadn't heard his question. 'River-edge,' she went on, 'it doesn't belong to the Creweses. It never did.'

"Her son," Ty said, "wasn't interested in a house called Riveredge thousands of miles away in a strange country called America. He wanted to know only one thing, and that was who his father was, but Emma smiled sweetly, closed her eyes and in a while was gone, as if her confession explained everything, when it had done just the opposite. And there you have it," he concluded, "the reason I came to Merriman, to find out who fathered Emma's son and why she never came home to claim her inheritance when her father died. I'm handing the whole business on to you. Do with it what you will."

"You came all this way based on the hallucinatory words of a dying woman," Sarah said, then was sorry at once. She had shattered the moment with a few mere words.

His eyes blazed. "Damn it, you have a curious way of accepting a gift. Yes, I came here to trace the Forrester line, and yes, I was interested in Riveredge. But I told you it doesn't matter, anymore. What in hell does it take to win your trust?"

"Maybe it's not possible," Sarah said slowly, but she was thinking of herself and thinking of what she would do, *had* done to protect her great-uncle. And still she couldn't confess to knowing the truth about the line of succession to Riveredge, at least not to Ty Lassiter.

"Sarah, we made love because we felt something for each other, don't try to deny it. I want you with me. I don't want to lose you."

The words she spoke were the hardest she ever had to say. "There was never anything *to* lose."

It took him several seconds to recover from the clear impact of her words. "There's no reaching you, is there? You're intransigent. And I won't even take your words personally. You may have thought you'd changed, discarded that shroud of fear your mother's death cast over you, but you haven't. You'd do this to any man who came too close."

Sarah let his words batter her, knowing he spoke the truth and unable to come to her own defense.

"Well, lady, I don't have the time to wait around. Goodbye, it was nice knowing you. If you ever come to California, look me up. We'll have a drink to what might have been."

He gave her a long last look, then went past her out the door, and in another moment the front door closed softly behind him. Sarah went over to the window. She held her breath as she watched him head briskly toward his car, knowing that something wonderful had just stepped out of her life and that she was powerless to stop him.

CHAPTER THIRTEEN

CELIE DECATUR SAT drumming her pencil against the table, trying not to look at Maggie Roman. The fact that Maggie, her deep voice warm and persuasive, was especially radiant in the small gray-walled meeting room of Pack College, only served to put Celie's teeth on edge.

The trouble was, she mused, Maggie made damned good sense, and Celie's penchant for scrupulousness and honesty always got the upper hand even when it came to dealing with people she didn't like.

"Look, darlings," Maggie was saying to the assembled members of the budget committee, who were regarding her with rapt attention, "we can put our actors to work sewing airy little costumes with the seams all inside out, or we can take ourselves seriously and include money for costumes in the production budget."

The scent of freshly brewed coffee rose from a pot on a corner table. The long, center table at which they sat filled most of the room. Although the budget committee for the new Bosworth-Decatur Theater Center at Pack College had only half a dozen members, they had arranged themselves around the table with the express air of wanting to neither touch nor converse privately. They were fascinated with Maggie. At the same time they held the purse strings, and Celie thought they seemed to take pleasure in having the movie actress dangle a bit. Not Victor, of course, who sat stony-faced as if he had already made up his mind and wouldn't budge an inch.

Phil Nevins, whose daughter lost the part of Beatrice to Adriana Scott in *Much Ado About Nothing*, scowled at Maggie's last words. "In the past we had the costumes altered or added to from one play to another to save costs," he said. "I don't see any reason to go in over our head in each and every production. *Much Ado About Nothing* alone has used up half the year's budget."

"Because, Phil," Maggie told him with a carefully sweet smile, "we can't go from Shakespeare to Tennessee Williams by magically waving a dressmaker's yardstick."

"Maybe," he remarked caustically, "we're biting off more than we can chew to begin with."

David Vanderheyden, owner of one of the largest insurance agencies in the township, cleared his throat. "Maggie, it's not a Hollywood production. Why not ask people to donate clothes?"

Maggie regarded him from the opposite end of the table after glancing at Celie as though hoping she'd find someone in the room with a modicum of sense. Her glance did not take in Victor, who had already expressed his negative opinion on the subject and expected Maggie to go along with him.

"The play is Shakespeare. We're not doing it in modern dress, David. All I want, all I planned on doing was to rent costumes from a Manhattan company for the run of the play. That's two weeks and is guaranteed not to break the bank at Monte Carlo. And we don't have *time*, for heaven's sake."

Victor coughed and pulled his chair a little closer. "Maggie, where the devil do you think the money's coming from? The cost of constructing the scenery is already well out of hand."

"Darling," she said with a possessive air that wasn't lost on Celie, "it's not over budget. There was never enough money for the production to begin with."

Celie reached for her coffee cup, took a sip although it was already cold, then made up her mind. "Maggie's right," she said to Victor, gaining some leverage in his look of surprise. Serve him right if he lost this battle, she thought. "We've agreed to help Pack in its theater arts program and to fund this production. I don't even know how the misunderstanding developed and so late in the game. When the school asked Maggie to take charge of its new program, it was with the express purpose of having a professional develop a really fine college theater ensemble. Maggie," she concluded, giving the actress a beneficent smile she didn't quite feel, "send the bill to me and I'll see that it's paid."

Maggie blew her a kiss down the length of the table. "Celie, you're an angel. See?" She turned to Victor with a look on her face that was both triumphant yet extraordinarily intimate, a look that said lovers may quarrel but in the end they solve all their problems in bed. "Celie to the rescue, Victor. I really thought I could count on you, darling."

"No." Victor's face was flushed with barely concealed anger. "Celie isn't picking up the tab." His voice held the finality that ended all arguments, and which he used very seldom because of his power in the community.

Celie gazed curiously at him. She was picking up something else in his voice as well, although she wasn't quite certain what it was. She hadn't spoken to Victor since his return with Maggie from their Manhattan weekend. Earlier, before Maggie's arrival in their lives, they had spoken almost daily, often just to touch base. On several occasions during the week Celie had wanted to call him but didn't. She had found herself devising all sorts of reasons to pick up the telephone receiver, only to decide against them. Victor's own silence confirmed what she felt was the final break between them.

"Oh, darling Vic, be an angel and agree with Celie," Maggie went on. "Of course we should do something about home-grown costumes just as soon as we're out from under. Bring in the art department in terms of theater costume design, that sort of delicious thing."

"Yes, yes," Victor said with suppressed impatience, "the best thing to do would be to establish a committee to go into the matter."

Celie jumped in. "Maggie, what's the name of the costume company? Baron something?"

"Baron Costume Company. We won't be extravagant, I promise you. Everything right off the rack."

"Dave?" Victor was looking at Dave Vanderheyden, who was in charge of committee records. "Will it really break the budget?"

Vanderheyden shrugged. "We expect to fill the theater. Ticket sales have been going well, you know that."

"Some of the profits are earmarked for the theater building fund," Victor reminded him.

"If Celie wants to pick up the tab, I don't see what the problem is," Maggie said. "Darling, for heaven's sake, let's get on to other things." She got up impatiently and went over to the coffee urn and poured herself a cup of coffee.

Victor remained silent until she sat down. He wore his usual careful expression that kept everyone else at the table from conversing. Then he said, "I make a motion that we take the costume funds out of the budget and that there be sufficient to rent them for two weeks." His glance took in the half-dozen members of the committee until he found someone to second the motion, which carried unanimously. Celie had the odd feeling that she, not Maggie, had won the round, although it was a Pyrrhic victory.

Victor shuffled some papers on the table. "Next item. We've scheduled the fund-raiser for February. That's pushing it close perhaps, but it's also mid-winter when most people need a little excitement in their lives."

"We're going to have to give the affair a theme," Phil Nevins said. "They do that sort of thing."

"Oh, darling, hearts, hearts, St. Valentine's Day," Maggie suggested excitedly to Victor. "And I've been meaning to talk to you about this wonderful caterer, Mr. Francis. He's in Manhattan—oh, and of course *tons* of celebrities. They'll come if I ask them. I can't imagine anyone who'd refuse."

Victor gave her a patient smile. "Maggie, relax, calm down. I'm afraid that's not quite what we had in mind." He turned to Celie. She detected the same warm look she always expected from him when he addressed her. "Celie, the last time we talked—"

"Friday," she reminded him, unable to resist the slight dig but then deciding he wouldn't even know it as such.

"We've talked since then," he said, staring at her in consternation.

"I don't think so." She turned to her diary. "But that's beside the point. At the last meeting we decided to schedule the event for February 22, George Washington's birthday. What we had in mind was something that would include students, families of students and everyone in the area with an interest in the theater. We thought about holding it in the school gym and inviting everyone in Ramsey Falls and the college." When she raised her eyes Celie found Maggie regarding her with fixed attention, resting her chin on her hands. "We need the support of the community to build the theater on a really solid foundation."

"School auditorium!" Maggie shook her head. "Darlings, you don't want to be gauche."

"And precisely," Victor broke in, "what don't you consider gauche?"

Maggie had the goodness to laugh. "If it were summer, tents on the lawn at Bosworth Stud, of course."

"But it isn't summer, Maggie."

She watched him out of her violet eyes, a smile playing around her lips. With a sudden intake of breath, Celie realized that Maggie was gazing at Victor with as intimate an air as anyone could offer on the basis of promises already exchanged.

"Let me break the stalemate," Celie threw in, scarcely aware of her words before she spoke them. "I suggest we rethink the fund-raiser, Victor, determine whether we want community support and no substantial monetary return or a solid start on the building fund as the result of a gala fund-raiser. My reaction is to agree with Maggie. Have the gala well-attended by people with generous purses. Build the theater and it will pay off with community interest when the time comes. Now," she said to his astonished face, "I'd like to make a motion that we table the discussion until the next meeting and hammer out the details then."

Celie's motion carried and with that she picked up her bag, offering apologies about having to rush back to work even at that late hour. She slipped out of the meeting room. As she hurried through the lobby, she realized she was shaking and didn't like the feeling one bit.

"Celie."

She turned. Victor came storming up to her. She noted that his tie was undone and he had opened the top button of his shirt like a schoolboy ready to start a fight.

"What the devil's gotten into everybody around here?" he asked.

"I don't know what you're talking about."

"Everything, everybody," he said. "Sarah's been moping around all week muttering about Riveredge and cartons of this and diaries of that."

"Apropos Riveredge and Emma Crewes," Celie remarked. "There's something I want to see her about."

"Better wait a couple of days. Right now she's like some revolutionary full of perceived hurts. I told her I don't have the patience to listen to her. She makes no sense at all. And Ty Lassiter suddenly flies off home with a binder on the Franklin property in his pocket and vague remarks about his lawyer handling the details. Jed Franklin comes to me and says he hopes I'm still interested in buying the place, just in case. Just in case. A binder's a binder, I told him, and Lassiter's good for the money. Is he? What do we know about him?"

"Maybe more than we think. Have Sarah call me, would you?" Celie turned to go. Victor himself wasn't making any sense.

"Loose ends everywhere," he told her, putting his hand on her arm and drawing her around. "And you." He stopped, his eyes narrowing with a look of having seen her for the first time. "You sit at the meeting and side with Maggie on every damn issue, leaving me to look like a complete fool."

Celie couldn't resist a smile. She felt a calm so complete not all the tri-bi fireworks in Ramsey Falls could have dislodged it. "I didn't have to make you look like a fool, Victor. I think you're perfectly able to do that for yourself. And besides," she added at the anger in his eyes, "she was right, you know. It's no use asking a professional to direct the theater department without giving her all the support she needs. And why does it always come down to the bottom line? Us against them in the money department. I'm weary of it all." She sighed. "Let's talk about it another time. I have to get back to work."

"I'll walk you to your car," Victor said.

"Not necessary."

"I said I'd walk you to your car."

"Then suit yourself."

They were silent going out the lobby door, silent going down the stairs and silent all the way to the parking lot. Celie walked rapidly, as though Victor might drop away if she rushed. However, when she tried to unlock her car door, the keys felt like jelly in her hand.

"Give me the keys." Victor took them peremptorily out of her hand, unlocked the door and waited for her to get in. He closed the door, went around to the passenger's side and climbed in beside her. Only then did he lean over and slip the keys into the ignition, saying, "I know I owe you an explanation for my recent behavior."

The interior of the car was cold and Celie pulled her coat collar up around her ears. "Really? I don't recall asking you for any."

Victor smiled. "You've a lot more self-control than Sarah."

"Sarah has every right to question how you run your life."

"But you don't? We've been friends long enough."

"Because we haven't impinged on each other's privacy," Celie reminded him.

"What have you done with your hair?" Victor asked suddenly. "It looks different."

Celie remembered, coloring slightly. She had visited a beauty parlor in Merriman that afternoon and asked for a new styling, shorter and curlier, so that her blond hair made her look a little more youthful, more chic. "Had it cut, that's all," she told him.

"Looks good."

"Thank you." There was a moment of awkward silence, then she said, "How was your weekend in Manhattan?"

"Interesting enough."

She waited. Hanging in the air between them was the simple fact that he had gone away with Maggie and he wanted to tell her about it but had no idea how to begin. In the past they had revealed their thoughts as easily as two people can who don't have a physical involvement. She was good old Celie, the shoulder to lean on, the understanding, accepting friend, and she waited.

"Sometimes things don't turn out the way you expect them to," he said at last.

"Ah, I see," Celie remarked, but she didn't see at all.

"She talks, you know, Maggie, like some wind-up toy that never winds down. Talks all the time in that warm, glowing voice with its perfect diction, talk, talk, talk, until you want to reach for the Off button, only there doesn't seem to be any. Talks about herself, her plans, her career, her beauty, her charm, talks even when—" He stopped and ran his fingers absentmindedly through his hair.

"And after a romantic weekend away, it wouldn't seem gentlemanly to drop the lady." Celie didn't know whether she was angry with him or relieved.

"She's taking too much for granted."

"I'm sorry, then."

"Yet," he added with a deep intake of breath, "I admire the woman. She sets a room on fire, but I know now that she doesn't belong in my life, at least not the way she wants. Damn." He looked away. "Car's cold, you must be freezing. I'll let you go."

"If you want to talk, call me at home later, after eleven." Celie laughed. "Talk—you know, what wind-up toys do."

Victor smiled suddenly, a bright, pleased, open smile. He reached for the door handle and then turned to her.

Celie thought if he bent to kiss her at that moment she would forgive him anything, his weekend with Maggie, his total ignorance of her feelings for him, his inability to say outright that she was important to him and Maggie wasn't.

"Right, I'll call you at home," he said, and stepped from the car. He turned up his jacket collar and headed back toward the building. Celie shivered and switched on the ignition, glad of the work she had waiting for her at the newspaper.

"YOU DIDN'T FORGET anybody, did you?" Waverly had set nine chairs around the dining-room table and was now counting them. "Nine, that right?" He turned to Nellie, who was gazing at him in a fond, indulgent way.

"Wave, why do you keep asking me that? You know perfectly well seven were invited and seven accepted. With us that adds up to nine, it always has."

"Okay, don't get your dander up."

"My dander," Nellie said. "My dander's doing just fine, thank you. And this room is still cold as a snake's tongue."

Waverly growled a few incomprehensible words at her then, shaking his head, went over to the thermostat and turned it up. "Sarah tried talking me into a new heating system a couple of years ago. Place would heat up like a ship's furnace and cost a mint."

"Being comfortable isn't exactly a crime," Nellie remarked in a conciliatory tone. "And besides, you can heat the house room by room. No waste that way."

"Haven't been in most of the rooms since Ruth died," he told her. The best china and silver had been laid out on a pure white linen tablecloth. He picked up a teaspoon and examined it closely before putting it down. "Think the silver is polished enough?"

"Stop fidgeting, Wave. Look at it this way, some old friends are dropping by for coffee and cookies, that's all."

Wave turned to her suddenly, a frown crossing his face. "Damn it, Nellie, I'm having second thoughts. You know I've always been a loner. And what about the condition of this place? Room needs a painting. And these chairs. Looks as if a mouse has been decorating its nest with the upholstery. Funny the things you notice all of a sudden."

"There's going to be a big change in your life, but you haven't any choice in the matter. Things will never be the same."

"I can hold off long as possible."

"It's later than you think. And I don't mean the time of day, either, although the way you keep this room lit is a scandal." The dining room, in fact, was illuminated by one small table lamp that hid most of the imperfections in the wallpaper but made the atmosphere extremely gloomy. Nellie looked up at the ornate leaded glass shade over the dining table. "And it's time that was lit. Where's the switch?"

"I'll handle it." Wave turned off the lamp. They were plunged momentarily into darkness. Then the light went on beneath the shade overhead and the room immediately was warmed by the soft romantic glow of multicolored glass flowers.

"Wave," Nellie said in a pleased voice, "you want the house to come back to life, to be the way it was. You have the opportunity, now go with it."

"Maybe."

"All right, if that's what you want, it's not too late to turn back. We can serve your guests with coffee and cookies on your best china and send them away."

"And what's the matter with my niece?" Wave asked. "Why isn't she here?"

"Since you didn't tell her why you wanted her here, she couldn't know it was important to you," Nellie reminded him. "She said she was too busy and would see you tomorrow."

"You could always count on her, but lately she's been going around with her head in the clouds. Tuesday morning Sarah comes over and tells me we have to find the deed to Riveredge. No reason why, just it's about time it was put in the family safe. We turned the place upside down and there's no deed. I told her that weeks ago. I also told her to check the town record and she said she would if she could, and where had I been if I didn't know the mess the records are in. You'd think she ate something that didn't agree with her."

Nellie laughed. "Wave, nobody ever said you're quick on the uptake. I'll say this for you, you're too busy playing the curmudgeon to remember what being in love is like."

Wave looked sharply at her. "Being in love? You talking about Sarah?"

Nellie shook her head impatiently. "Yes, Sarah."

"All right, get on with it. Who's she in love with?"

"Tyler Lassiter. Have you no sense at all?"

"Tyler Lassiter? She's only met him twice, both times here. She hardly knows the man."

"Twice? That's all? You can swear to it in a court of law, I suppose."

"Nellie, they met here, I tell you."

"Really?" She smiled at the remembrance. "You took no notice of the expression on her face when she showed up Monday night and discovered Tyler Lassiter sitting at the kitchen table with you. She turned a dozen shades of red.

She lost all power of intelligent speech, and she scarcely heard a word either you or I said."

Wave scowled. "What did she want to fall in love with him for?"

Nellie laughed out loud but was prevented from going on when the doorbell rang. "Oh, oh," she said, glancing around the room with a satisfied expression on her face, "they're here. I'll get it."

For a moment Wave looked stricken. Nellie put a hand on his arm. "Are you all right?"

He straightened himself up. "Never felt better in my life."

A half hour later, the seven invited guests were seated at the dining room table under the soft glow of the leaded glass shade. The talk during the interim had been an exchange of news among people who had been friends a long time but met seldom. They had one other thing in common: all were in the process of changing their lives, of selling their worldly goods and accepting new, more cramped lifestyles in unfamiliar surroundings, whether they liked it or not.

"What a wonderful idea, a party," said Marjorie Bensen, a rotund and dimpled woman who had gone to school with Nellie. She helped herself to another sugar cookie and a bit more cream in her coffee.

"It's no party," Wave told her. "It's a business meeting."

Jed Franklin spoke up. "What's that supposed to mean, Wave? I'm about to sell off the house and orchards if Lassiter comes through, and I'm retiring to the desert as soon as the contract is signed. I told you that already."

"You told me a lot more than that," Wave said.

"I don't know what in hell you're talking about," Jed went on, "but then you always did like to talk in riddles."

Nellie cut in. "Why don't we hear what Wave has to say first, then go on from there?"

Jed Franklin sat back and lifted a pipe from his jacket pocket and stuck it, unfilled and unlit, in his mouth. "Go ahead," he murmured. "Be my guest."

"First off," Wave began, "I want to list what we all have in common, why we're here today at my invitation. Go ahead, Nell, read that paper we worked out."

"It's very simple," Nellie said, laying a legal pad on the table before her and adjusting her glasses. "We're all uprooting ourselves for one reason or another, changing our lives dramatically and probably not very happy about it."

"You can say that," Tilly Olsen threw in from the far end of the table. She was a narrow board of a woman with short, straight gray hair, who spoke with the assertive air of one who had worked with children all her life, as indeed she had. "Going to live with my niece. Last thing in the world I planned on."

"None of us planned on developing wrinkles, bad tickers or arthritis," Nellie went on. "Some of us are even beginning to feel kind of stiff-like in our bones, which means we can't go mountain climbing anymore."

"I can't bend to pick up an apple that fell from my own trees without worrying if I can straighten up," Jed Franklin remarked.

"Hear! Hear!" someone else added.

"Some of us have been forcibly retired from jobs—"

"You're lookin' at him," Pat Paterson spoke up. He had recently retired from his job at a manufacturing plant.

"And," Nellie continued, "are living on tight budgets that mean we can't afford to live the way we're used to. Some are rattling around in houses that are impossible to heat." She stopped and cast a doubtful smile at Wave. "And some of us shouldn't be living alone but don't want to depend upon strangers for our care and comfort."

"Frankly, that's why I'm giving up my apartment," Marjorie Bensen said. "Four children and not one of them close enough to count on. I certainly don't want to leave the area and my only choice is to take a room in a hotel residence for seniors in Herkimer County."

"Good Lord, Marjorie, you don't want that," Tilly Olsen exclaimed. "There's nobody in that residence under ninety years."

"You're exaggerating," Marjorie said. "I've visited the home—"

"Ladies," Wave interrupted, "we're just wasting time. Go ahead, Nell."

"The list we compiled," Nellie went on, "covers the alternate choices we've all made as a result of the catastrophic changes in our lives." She looked around the table. "Well, if we start with me, I suddenly found myself out of the government where I spent most of my working life. My official retirement came ten years ago, but the governor asked me to stay on. A computer is what finally outclassed me. I thought I'd come to Merriman and . . ." She stopped and raised her shoulders in a shrug. "I don't know exactly what I thought, but it took me exactly three minutes to decide that retirement isn't what it's cracked up to be."

"I had no illusions when I retired from teaching," Tilly said.

"But then, but then," Nellie reminded her, "you found taxes raised, the cost of living skyrocketing, your car falling apart, etcetera, etcetera. The fact is that all of you, like me, need alternate housing and we've gone about it in ways that are not entirely suitable."

Zeke Smith, a farmer, spoke up. He was a burly man with a great belly and a healthy, robust complexion. Seated next to him was his brother Sam, equally robust and equally well fed. Neither had married and they had recently sold their farm. "It's true we made money when we sold the farm. Land prices skyrocketed and we couldn't afford not to sell out. My sister invited us to live with her in New Jersey. She and her husband run a farm."

"Husband happy about your moving in?"

Sam spoke up. "Doubt it, but they'll get a couple of good strong hands who'll pay their way. It's not," he added, casting a glance at his brother, "the way I'd do things."

"Then what in hell are you doing it for?" Wave demanded.

"How do I know?" Zeke said. "The ball starts rolling, you keep going along with it."

"What's this business proposition?" Pat Paterson asked Waverly. "I'm not sure I really want to know. The last time you got ticked off about something it wound up in a court fight over in Merriman and Judge Vanderhaven had to be talked out of throwing the book at you. You were lucky you had Bradford Kent as your lawyer or you'd still be sitting behind bars."

"Damn fool hunters used to cross my property," Wave said. "All I did was chase them off."

"Yeah, with a high-powered rifle, and when they were on the highway well off your property, you still kept shooting at them until you blasted their car right off the road."

Wave allowed himself a smile. "Got carried away a bit, but it taught them a lesson. Taught everyone in a hundred-mile radius, too, that Riveredge is off-limits to hunters."

"Can you save the stories about your triumphant return to Sparta until later," Nellie said, "and get on with the important business?"

Wave stood up and then leaned over the table, pressing his knuckles into the fine old linen table cloth. He looked at his guests over the rim of his glasses. "Riveredge, twenty-five rooms, river view. Dining room, two drawing rooms, library and an old-fashioned kitchen big enough to accommodate a couple of quarreling cooks. Eight fireplaces, seven bathrooms and a swimming pool out back that hasn't been used in the past half-dozen years. A deep well. That's brand new, or nearly new. Well, it seems like yesterday. I'd say it was put in four years ago. The heating? We'll have to go into that. Maybe I'll have to take Sarah's advice and do something. Needs a painting, maybe the plumbing has to be modernized. Hell, it *has* to be modernized."

"I'll take it, the whole place and how many acres?" Zeke Smith said, laughing.

"Three hundred, but that's not what's for sale."

Mrs. Paterson, who was a small, articulate woman with a particularly deep-pitched voice, suddenly spoke up. "I'll be damned," she said, "what a great idea."

"What is?" Zeke looked nonplussed.

Wave glanced around the table at each of his guests. "I say that we pool our resources and live together at Riveredge."

There was a dead silence and then Zeke Smith said, "You mean run our own old age home?"

"I think the word is senior citizens," Mrs. Paterson chided gently.

"A senior citizens hotel," Tillie Olsen added.

Wave shook his head. "Call it anything you like, but remember this, we'll be in charge of our lives. No administrators, no social workers, no attendants." The excitement was evident in his voice. "Any of us gets sick, the hospital's right in town. We need special help, we're here to assist one another. What I mean is we make our home Riveredge—"

"Riveredge." Marjorie Bensen expelled a sigh. "Imagine, how many times I dreamed of living in a house like Riveredge."

"Riveredge," Wave asserted, giving her a smile, "instead of running off in all directions to places none of us wants to go at just that time in our lives when being with people you know is most important."

Marjorie shook her head. "Wave, I only have my social security and a small pension."

"We're in a slightly better fix," Zeke Smith remarked "but we planned on living on income and not touching our capital."

"Wait a minute," Nellie said. "There's money available in the state budget to help retired people make a go of it. I know people in the state capitol. I think if we wrote up a grant proposal to the state it would be met with interest. They might even want to use us as a shining example of seniors who take an idea and run with it. Anyway, there's such a thing as sweat equity. Cooks cook and carpenters saw wood. We can still use our muscles besides our jaws to make the place work."

"Wave, what about Sarah?" Pat Paterson asked. "She's next in line for Riveredge. If something happens to you—"

"The way I see it, we set up as a corporation complete with a board of directors. Sarah can sit on the board. She was supposed to be here today but begged off." Wave's eyes slid to Nellie, giving her a warning not to say a word.

But Sarah would go along, Nellie reflected, and so would these people with their shining eyes and careful attention. It would take time. Perhaps one or two might back off, but Riveredge was made to come alive and in time it would.

CHAPTER FOURTEEN

JEMMA GARDNER DRAGGED Sarah over to the buffet table. "Your cousin certainly knows how to lay on a Thanksgiving dinner," she told her. "This has to be the most glorious turkey I've ever seen." In a whisper, as soon as they were out of earshot of Victor's other guests, she added, "Now, my darling Sarah, forget that turkey since you've been acting like one all evening. Mind telling me what's the matter?"

"And I thought I was an old pro at covering up my feelings," Sarah said with a smile she didn't quite feel. "The awful truth is I've messed things up and I've no idea how to go about making repairs."

"You're talking about Ty Lassiter."

"I'm talking about a lot of things including my professional self-respect."

"Want to share some of it? I've a willing ear."

"Yes, Jemma, and yes again." Sarah tucked her arm through Jemma's and drew her from the dining room into the small, comfortable den next door. From there she could hear the pleasant hum of happy conversation from which she felt oddly isolated and out of tune.

Victor's guests numbered about twenty, family and friends who had been gathering for years at Bosworth Stud to celebrate Thanksgiving. Added to the usual group were a subdued Maggie and her son Steven, now talking earnestly to Hunt Gardner, who stood with his hands on Seth's shoulders.

Seth was the only child at the dinner, although Jemma's thickening waist told of a new pregnancy. There should be more children around, Sarah thought, and shrieks of laughter as they tore about getting in everyone's way. More children, my children, a whole kindergarten of children.

At any other time she'd have been happy to be there, awaiting a call to a sumptuous dinner from the proverbial groaning board. The feeling of family and friends was always important to her.

Jemma settled down comfortably in a chair. "Tell me what's troubling you," she said, gesturing to the chair opposite.

Sarah sat down. "Oh, you're so blessedly happy, why should I burden you with the boring events of my life, especially on a day like today?"

"I seem to remember you being a tower of strength when I needed you, Sarah. You forced me to deal with the growth of my business, sent Bradford Kent my way when I was about to defend myself against a very tough lawyer, namely my ex-husband. You were a shoulder to cry upon when Hunt took himself off to the other end of the world. How about relaxing and letting it all spill out?"

"I thought...think...oh, I don't even know what I mean. It's about Riveredge," Sarah said. "About Riveredge and Ty Lassiter. I was afraid he had come to take it away from Waverly."

Jemma wrinkled her brow. "But Waverly owns the place free and clear, doesn't he?"

"He does, he doesn't, it's all so crazy. The upshot is, I came across some information that could turn Merriman upside down. The farthest possible scenario would leave Ty in possession of Riveredge and thousands of acres of land that were perhaps once wrongfully sold to the ancestors of the current owners."

"Sounds complicated. And just what did you do with the information?"

"What any archivist would have done. I filed it so carefully it will take another ten years to find it."

"But you know where the information is."

"Oh, in the town hall. I didn't file it in the waste paper basket, if that's what you mean."

"Was the act one of pure unselfish interest?"

Sarah sighed. "Yes...no. Oh, of course I'm out to protect Waverly and Riveredge, but not with any real thought of personal gain, Jemma. I just did what was expedient, and the trouble is I don't like myself because of it."

"Then there's no problem," Jemma said. "Not liking yourself, notwithstanding."

"No problem." Sarah repeated the words wistfully, knowing she hadn't told Jemma what was really troubling her. Hadn't told Jemma how her heart ached and her mind had a habit of wandering at the wrong times and how difficult it had been to get through the past two weeks with Ty gone out of her life forever. That, in fact, this Thanksgiving celebration was full of emptiness and sorrow.

A light snow had been falling all day, and the bushes outside the window wore caps of white. She could see the activity in the dining room as though it were being shown on film. Victor's old pug had wandered into the room. Seth broke away from Hunt and sat down on the floor to play with him. Alec and his wife were there, and Celie, who had joined the conversation with Hunt and Steve Roman. Maggie was entertaining Waverly. Wave had surprised Victor by accepting his invitation and surprised them all by bringing Nellie with him.

There was a smell of pine cones and autumn leaves from the baskets of dried flowers set about the den. On the cocktail table between them was a deep bowl of red apples and a wooden board holding a large cheddar cheese. The stone fireplace was alive with a roaring fire. And Sarah should be happy, and she wasn't.

"Well, Ty is going to come back," Jemma was saying. "After all, he put a binder on the old Franklin place."

"According to Jed Franklin, things are moving rather slowly."

"Do you think Ty's just a hit-and-run guy?"

Sarah pondered her next words. "You know, I don't really think so, but that wasn't even the point. I don't seem to be able to let anyone get close."

"If you know that, Sarah, isn't half the battle won?"

"It takes more than knowing, it takes believing. I just can't make myself believe I could be special enough to hold anyone's love for very long."

Jemma gave an impatient shake of her head. "Oh, I wish I could pound some sense into you. Look, if it means anything, Hunt was really taken with Ty. You know how men are. They either like each other on the spot or not at all. And he felt Ty was interested in you from the very first."

"We had a fight just before he left," Sarah told her. "I think he really meant goodbye."

"Your fault or his?"

"Mine."

"Come on, Sarah, you have wings, spread them."

"But there he is in California, where the living is easy, along with other things. Why should he care?"

"Because I'm willing to bet my favorite printing press that he does."

"I love you, Jemma," Sarah said spontaneously, going over to her friend and placing a kiss on her cheek. Then she patted Jemma's stomach. "And I'm going to love this new baby, too."

"Poor Seth." A sudden frown creased Jemma's brow. "Two blows at once. We're having this baby and his father and stepmother are adopting one around the same time."

"Ouch, poor Seth is right."

"I keep telling him how wonderful it's going to be having two new siblings and he just looks at me with a forlorn and slightly skeptical air. Then I give him the usual pep talk taken straight out of the book: 'Mommy and Daddy will love you just as much as we do now, etcetera, etcetera.' I don't think he believes me."

"I'll have a talk with him," Sarah said. "I'm going to tell him the truth, that he'll always be my special person, no matter who comes along."

As they moved into the living room, Alec Schermmerhorn came along looking pleased with himself. "Sarah, did I mention that Ty Lassiter sent along a nifty sketch about how the waterfront would look after renovation? He said there'd be more forth coming, but it was enough to whet the town board's appetite. I'll tell you something, Merriman doesn't lack for local architects, but there's nothing like a Beverly Hills cowboy to shake up the locals."

"Was there a big price tag attached?" Sarah asked.

"Not for his work, there wasn't. Said cost estimates would be forthcoming. Good thing he's picking up the Franklin property. Gives him a stake in the area. Great guy. I'll have to find some way to repay him."

"Everyone, please." Victor stood at the head of the dining table, which was covered with damask, glowing candles, crystal and silver. "I'd like you all to help yourselves at the buffet and then to join me in a toast."

Sarah forced herself into a holiday mood by filling her plate just as she had every year from the very first time she had come to live at Bosworth Stud. She took a seat next to Waverly.

"I'm surprised Nellie came with you. Her family couldn't have been too happy about losing her to Victor's dinner."

"Oh, we stopped there first. Didn't eat, though. Just sipped a little champagne, then came on here." He eyed her plate.

"Can I get something for you, Uncle Wave?"

"Thanks, Sarah," he told her, "but Nellie's put me on a diet guaranteed to cure me of my arthritis, which means I'll have to do without the stuffing."

"I'll slip you some of mine."

"Great idea. Quick, before she gets back." He reached over and with his fork helped himself to some stuffing.

"But don't overdo it, Wave. I can see Nellie's a great influence. You haven't looked this healthy in years."

Wave alternately beamed and then tried to appear solemn. "What influence? Woman's a regular martinet. I'm just going along to keep the peace."

Sarah suppressed a smile, her first real smile of the day. That her great-uncle should have been saved from himself by Nellie Casedonte came as no surprise—unlike his plans for Riveredge. She'd been procrastinating for a long time over what was to be done about the true ownership of the huge old mansion. And it had been taken care of for her by Waverly Crewes, the old scoundrel. Articles would have to be drawn up over the incorporation of Riveredge House and all the attendant digging out of files. She knew one thing only: she'd do everything in her power to protect her uncle, as she had done already.

"Cat got your tongue?"

It was Waverly, looking at her in a wily manner.

"I'm delighted you made up with Victor," she said. "He's always had your best interests at heart."

"Now that I've gone public with my plans for Riveredge, no one can sneak around the back door and try to take it away from me."

"You're intransigent, Wave." That word. Ty had used it with her. Maybe it went with the Crewes genes.

"Everyone..." Victor stood at the head of the table. "I wanted to offer a toast, but I'd like to wait a few minutes. Maggie has an announcement she wants to make." He looked toward the movie actress and smiled.

Nothing new there, Sarah thought.

Maggie stood up and beamed at them. "All you wonderful people," she began. "I really looked forward to spending the winter in Merriman and getting to know you better. I especially want to stay with the college and I'm going to be back just as soon as ever."

There was a slight humming as guests nodded to each other and remarked on what was coming.

"One of the most enriching experiences I've ever had has been in directing *Much Ado About Nothing*, but oh," she said, hugging her hands to her breasts, "I've been offered a part in a movie being made in Spain. It's such a good role, such a good, fantastic role, a really exciting character. I couldn't turn it down even though the shooting is scheduled to last six months. You know—" she smiled at the assembled guests on either side of the table as though they understood the troubles involved in movie making "—I don't have to tell you." she held her arms up in a dramatic gesture. "I've never enjoyed myself so much, not met a more talented group than the students at Pack." She hesitated, then gave Victor her most dazzling smile. "I'll be back, I promise."

"Oh, Maggie," Alec's wife said, "we adore having you here. What'll we do without you?"

Sarah shot a look at Victor and it seemed to her that she saw a flash of relief speed across his face. "I tried to talk her out of it," he told them, "but I couldn't."

Maggie's announcement was a clear surprise to Celie, as well. Sarah saw her friend's mouth open and then close again before she turned away and coughed into her napkin. Well, well, well, Sarah thought, miracles do happen, after all. She had just resigned herself to Victor's becoming Maggie's fifth husband.

"Wave, change seats with me," Nellie demanded, and promptly sat down next to Sarah. "What cheek, leaving in the middle of the term like that."

"Oh," Sarah said blithely, "I think you should take the opportunity as it arises."

"Reg'll be disappointed. Come to think of it, I'm glad she's going. He's been making noises about becoming an actor."

"A toast then," Victor announced, raising his champagne glass. "To Thanksgiving again next year, with all our friends and family gathered around, and with Maggie and Steve Roman among us."

"Hear! Hear!" Alec boomed.

Maggie glittered and offered a toast to Victor and to Celie and to their joint project, the Bosworth-Decatur Theater. Then there followed other toasts, and it was close to eleven when the party began to break up. Jemma and Hunt had left earlier with Seth, and Waverly and Nellie had gone soon after. But the others had lingered, as though reluctant to see the holiday end.

Sarah kissed everyone good-night, even feeling a little disappointed over saying goodbye to Maggie after all, but Maggie was a survivor, one of that rare breed of women who ride through life believing they've conquered everything and everyone, whether or not they have. They might make mistakes, as Sarah had, but they manage to shake themselves free of self-incrimination and smilingly head on to the next adventure.

"Merriman is my home," Maggie said. "And Steve is going to school here. I'll be back." She reached over and hugged Sarah. "He's one of the best men I've ever known," she whispered in Sarah's ear.

"Victor?" Sarah pulled back, startled.

"Oh, him, too. I was talking about Ty Lassiter. Sarah, I know it's none of my business, but I think you'd be perfect for each other."

Sarah shook her head. "In some movie script, maybe, but not in real life." She placed another kiss on Maggie's cheek and, after saying goodbye to Victor, went to get her coat.

Celie came up to her in the entrance hall. "Hold on, what's your hurry?"

"Too much of a good thing, I guess," Sarah lied. "I was turning sentimental and decided I need to breathe some fresh cold air."

"Oh, for a moment I thought it was something Maggie said."

"Speaking of which," Sarah replied, "if you don't take advantage of her going, I swear, Celie, I'll personally arrange to have your head examined."

Celie laughed. "Maybe I'm way ahead of you but I'll take your advice. Fools rush in where angels fear to tread. I'll try to handle it in a more, shall we say, exotic mode than I'm used to."

"Hooray for you," Sarah said. "If you'd like to borrow the most romantic antique blue velvet dress, only worn for fifteen minutes in this century, I have it waiting for you."

Celie stared at her. "Run that by me again?"

"Never mind. Look, I promised Seth I'd take him out to Saturday brunch, but I'm free otherwise. How about coming over for breakfast on Sunday morning?"

"I'd love to. Incidentally, I've been meaning to talk to you and I keep forgetting to. That story Adriana's been working on about Ty Lassiter concerns your mutual ancestor, Emma Forrester Crewes. Never mind, I'll have the story with me on Sunday and we can talk about it then. Oh, and I'll bring the bagels and cream cheese, as well."

"THE ARTICLE is written with a wonderfully light touch, a bit of tongue in cheek, but it does rake up the coals." Celie buttered a toasted bagel and then spread cream cheese on it. "Adriana has talent. I always like it when my best instincts come true. The trouble is she takes on more than she can handle. Beatrice in *Much Ado About Nothing*, her job here, her schoolwork. That's why she took so long in putting the piece together."

Sarah, who hadn't touched anything except for a sip of coffee, eyed the brown envelope that lay on the kitchen counter.

"The story about your great-great-great-ancestor Emma will open your eyes some," Celie told her.

Decidedly not her blood relation, Sarah thought, but hesitated for a moment before plunging in. "I always figured Ty Lassiter came around because he felt he had a claim to Riveredge. Did Adriana come up with anything to support his claim?"

"No, it's all about Emma Forrester Crewes." Celie's smile held something mischievous in it. "You'll see for yourself."

"May I look at the article now?" Sarah asked quietly.

"It'll keep," Celie said. "You've lost weight, Sarah, and a couple of weeks ago I'd have said you had no weight to lose. Tuck into the cream cheese, my dear. The article isn't going anywhere. Incidentally, I had a Saturday night date with your cousin.''

Sarah drew her eyes away from the manila envelope. "Really? How wonderful.'' Was love seeping out of the corners for everyone but her? she wondered. She was still sleepy from a night spent tossing and turning. She had fallen asleep, then awakened once in the dark calling out Ty's name. She had dreamed of his touch, of his hands caressing her, of his body heavy on hers. She had almost been able to smell the light scent he wore, and when she awakened, Sarah knew she was in for a hard time.

"Victor wanted me to go with him to a concert at the college,'' Celie was saying, "then changed his mind and said all he wanted was to have a quiet dinner.''

"Victor? He must be changing his stripes.''

"I think I'll have to send Maggie a dozen roses. She seems to have put some pebbles in his dancing shoes and he can't stop tapping.''

"Have a good time?'' Sarah asked the question half-heartedly. After campaigning for Celie all this time, she couldn't assemble the energy to be happy for her.

"What's gotten into you?''

"I think,'' Sarah said thoughtfully, "a surfeit of much ado about nothing. The envelope, please.''

Celie handed it to her. "I love your cousin, you know. I have no idea what the future will bring, but I'm determined to have no more rivals.''

Now that Sarah held the envelope in her hand, she paused and let the truth concerning Celie and Victor sink in. "Oh, Celie, Victor's always been slow and thoughtful about everything, except maybe Maggie, but you'll have him, you wait and see. Victor is the best man in the world and worth loving and waiting for.''

"Go ahead and read the story of Emma," Celie urged her. "Ty Lassiter's worth waiting for, too. In fact, he's worth racing after, you know that."

"Just a minute," Sarah said. "Is something written on my forehead that I don't even know is there?"

"In your eyes, Sarah." Celie took the manila folder out of her hand, opened it and pulled out the typewritten manuscript. "Go ahead and read the article. She was a charmer, Emma was. Maybe Maggie can play her in the movie version."

CHAPTER FIFTEEN

THE PLANE LANDED with scarcely a bump at the airport in Los Angeles. The flight had been a late one, connecting in Chicago in the middle of the night. Sarah hadn't slept at all. The action had been an impulsive one, hardly characteristic, but then again she hadn't been walking a straight line since the moment she met Ty Lassiter.

She hadn't called or written to Ty to tell him she was coming. There was every possibility that when she arrived at his Pacific Palisades house she'd discover a bevy of beauties granting his every wish. But somehow it had to be this way, her showing up suddenly on his doorstep dragging as an excuse for her trip a manila envelope containing some old newspaper clippings and an article written with a light touch by one Adriana Scott.

She gave the taxi driver Ty's address. It was early Saturday morning and with luck he'd be home. And alone.

The taxi took the freeway out toward the Pacific Palisades and then exited onto winding roads that passed white stucco homes and lush gardens. The houses became grander, more dramatic the closer they got to the Palisades: huge mansions basking in the western sun with palm trees and vegetation growing ravenously around gates and stone walls.

The sun, even at that early hour, was strong and warm, the light golden. Sarah removed her jacket and shoved it into her overnight bag. She had left behind the cold dampness of a November day to discover within a few short hours another, more translucent world.

Bikers on the road waved to them as they passed, and Sarah, who had always loved the changing seasons of the Northeast, decided that maybe summer all year round wasn't a bad idea after all.

"Here we are," the driver announced, and with those words Sarah's throat went dry. What right did she have to barge into Ty's life? What if he laughed at her and told her to go home? Nonsense. She could always say she had the excuse of Riveredge and Adriana's article. Oh sure, he'd believe that.

She paid the driver and then stepped out of the taxi. As she watched it back out of the driveway and disappear from view, she experienced a moment of panic. Now she had no choice but to bite the bullet.

The house was modern, white stucco and glass. It sat on the mountainside overlooking the sea. She had the odd sensation of taking in everything in the clearest way, as though committing it all to heart. When she stepped up to the front door and pushed the bell, she could hear the chimes ringing throughout the interior as though announcing a momentous event.

She waited a moment, clutching her bag to her breast as if it could protect her should he dismiss her with a pitying smile.

Then she heard a quick light step accompanied by a soft humming. The door was opened by a beautiful suntanned blonde in shorts and a sleeveless T-shirt. She was barefoot and the smile she gave Sarah was friendly and welcoming. She looked as if she belonged and wasn't the least uncomfortable being there.

"I'm—I'm looking for Tyler Lassiter," Sarah said, knowing she had just made the gravest mistake of her life.

If embarrassment and a broken heart could kill, she'd be dead in another moment.

"Yes, he's out back. Is he expecting you?"

"No." Sarah took in a deep breath. "As a matter of fact, perhaps I'll come back later." But it was an empty remark; she was stranded on the Pacific Palisades, a million miles from the airport with no help she could ask for in sight.

"Who is it, Nan?" It was Ty, his voice deep, sexy and achingly familiar.

"Sarah," she called, trying for an insouciance she knew wouldn't fool him for an instant.

Ty came into the entrance hall barefoot, wearing khaki shorts and an open shirt. He had acquired a deep tan and it struck Sarah that his hair had grown a little longer. As she watched him move she wondered how she could ever live without seeing him again. A grin spread slowly across his face when he saw her. She hadn't known she was holding her breath until she let it out in a small puff.

He put out his hand and silently pulled her inside. She heard the door close behind her and was aware of the blonde standing somewhere near.

"You've lost weight." He said the words with a kind of fierceness as though he understood what she had gone through. Then he took her into his arms and kissed her deeply.

"Damn it," he said, "what kept you?"

Her arms were at her sides as she allowed the embrace. "What kept me?" She said the words rather stupidly and then twisted to find the woman he called Nan watching them with a smile on her face and her arms folded across her chest. She didn't appear to be in the least annoyed. What kind of lives did these people lead, Sarah wondered with the tiny part of her brain that was still functioning.

"Nan Ralston, I'd like you to meet Sarah Crewes. She's the archivist from Merriman." He gave Sarah a sly grin. "Nan and I were up most of the night and had to have something to talk about."

Sarah's throat went dry and she wondered how she'd get through the next few moments. All she wanted to do was grab her overnight case and rush back to the airport.

"Oh, incidentally, Nan's a landscape designer. The best. She's married to one of our senior partners and she's a hell of an architect. We've been up all night on that project that brought me back from the East. The one that's already overdue, thanks to certain enticements in Merriman County. Nan's husband just went home to relieve the baby-sitter."

"Glad to meet you," Nan said, thrusting her hand out to Sarah and winking. "Watch him, he's tricky. Look, Ty, I'm bushed," she added. "I need to get some sleep."

"You always had a great sensibility, Nan." He planted a chaste kiss on her cheek. "See you Monday at the office."

Once she was gone, Ty turned to Sarah and broke into a broad grin. "Gotcha, didn't I? And you know what? You deserved it."

"Ty, that was cruel and inhuman treatment."

"Serves you right. God, I'm glad to see you."

A long moment passed while they stood apart and watched each other with a kind of wary happiness. Then he gathered her into his arms and held her tight. "I thought of those eyes," he told her, "that blue, that incredible luminous blue. I almost came running back to you."

"But there was always the project. And Nan. And her husband. And even the baby."

"No, it was your blasted stubbornness."

She pulled away from him. "What blasted stubbornness? I came to you without calling, without even knowing what I'd get into."

"And all you found was Nan." He pointed to her overnight bag. "I hope that doesn't indicate how long you're staying."

"I'm only here for four days, Ty, a long weekend—that is, if you're going to be around."

"I know how to use the telephone," he told her gruffly, "but why in hell four days?"

"Four days, Ty, the weekend plus two I wrested from Alec. I took you up on your invitation. You said people stay together and then they see."

"I believe I mentioned a somewhat longer time than four days."

"No," she replied, "you didn't."

"Ah, of course. You're a very specific lady."

"And you're . . . oh damn," she said. "Why can't we be together for five minutes without arguing?"

He took her in his arms. "Beautiful Sarah, if you remember, we began with an argument over a Confederate soldier. Why should anything change between us?"

Yes, she thought, as his lips came down on hers, nothing's changed. There was still a confederate soldier to be disposed of between them.

The power of his touch swept through her, and when he drew her up into his arms and carried her into his bedroom, everything faded but raw emotion. They were on the bed, wrapped around each other, and it wasn't a dream. Everything she had experienced when he last made love to her was real. She held on to him, caressed his skin, breathed in his scent, felt his weight crush mightily against her.

Afterward, bathed in a love-scented dampness, they lay entwined, unable to let go of the fierce desire and powerful passion that had just flooded through them.

"Four days and four nights," he said, his voice husky and his breath still hot. "We're not moving from this bed." He raised his head and gazed down at her, his eyes half-closed yet clearly touched with wonder that she should be there at all. "God, how I've wanted you these past few weeks, wanted to make love to you till the cows came home."

She drew her hand softly along his cheeks. "But you kept your silence."

"I couldn't see battering myself against a brick wall." He waited a moment and placed his lips briefly against hers. "All right, I concede I made a mistake or two. In my infinite wisdom I decided we should live together and test this profound joy we give each other."

"Bad move," she said.

"Bad move."

"I'm completely exonerated from my foolish stubbornness."

He smiled but shook his head. "No, because your stubbornness was mixed with distrust, Sarah. We made incredible love and you still couldn't distinguish between trust and your own feelings. "But," he said, drawing his body over hers once again, "you're here and that's all that matters. Discussion closed forever while I make a pass at you, lady."

"Ty, wait," she began, but his mouth was drawn over hers, and in the fresh heat of their passion, her words were lost.

Later as Ty lay asleep in her arms, Sarah watched the afternoon light edge through the diaphanous curtains to shiver on the ceiling. His breathing was even, she could feel the soft brush of his breath against her skin.

No, the subject of Riveredge was not closed forever, and wouldn't be until she told Ty all she knew. Oh, not about Emma Forrester Crewes, she decided. The manila envelope she had brought would go back with her to Merriman. She wanted him to live with his dream about his ancestor. It was

Riveredge that was still wedged between them, Riveredge and her careful lies and deceit.

He stirred, came awake slowly and then stretched luxuriously. "Have I slept long?"

"We both did. That's an afternoon sun out there."

"Too bad. Three and a half days left."

Sarah disentangled herself from his arms as he drew them around her. "Ty, we have to talk."

"No we don't."

"About—"

"Riveredge," he finished for her. "You have that glint in your eyes. Forget it, I'm not interested."

She exhaled a deep breath and began speaking in a quick earnest manner that told him not to interrupt. "I did a very selfish thing, Ty. I dissembled in order to save Riveredge for my uncle, in order to save three hundred acres of land for me, since I'd inherit them sooner or later, and to save dozens of landowners from a court battle."

A frown creased his brow. "And who's the villain from whom you were saving all these people and yourself?"

"You."

He sat up in bed and regarded her with open-mouthed curiosity. "I'm a villain in a scenario you've written. Splendid. Mind explaining yourself?"

"Ty, do you have any documents that give you claim to Riveredge?"

"No, of course not. If I had, I'd have trotted them out and staked my claim." His eyes narrowed. "What have you done, Sarah?"

"Took a carton of documents from square A and put it somewhere between square P and square Q, where I figured nobody would look for the next ten years."

"To protect your uncle and you and other unnamed constituents of Merriman township."

"You catch on fast," Sarah said. "I came across...all right, I went out of my way to locate a carton of documents labeled Forrester-Riveredge. In it I discovered the literal history of the house and its land up until the approximate time that your ancestor Emma left for Australia."

"It was in the Forrester family," he told her. "In the general's hands. I've always known that. Tell me something I don't know."

"The record drops away after that."

He waited a moment. "And."

"And, I took the carton and carefully placed it where it wouldn't come to light for some time. At least until you left Merriman for good. I didn't destroy anything, I just stacked it away in all that mess in the basement, knowing you'd never have the patience to sift through the stuff down there...."

"If I'd had the patience?" he inquired.

She flushed. "I suppose I'd have been two steps ahead of you."

"You were hiding something I already knew."

"No, you couldn't know that the rest of the record should have logically been in the carton."

"Ah, meaning that nefarious Crewes crew from which you're obviously a proper descendant, destroyed the record of the true ownership of Riveredge. Meaning when the old general died, Crewes paid off county officials to attest that the relatives of the late Greg Crewes, husband of Emma, were the proper claimants to the throne of Riveredge. Well, well, well," Ty said with a broad grin, "when do you suppose I can take possession, throw Wave off the land?"

She pummeled him with her fists. "You bastard, he's turning the place into a home for seniors."

He grabbed her wrists. "Is he now? Clever man. I once hinted I could show him how to put that showplace to good use. I'll have to break out the old drawing pen and send him some blueprints."

"Oh," she groaned, "I hate it when you're smug."

"So you're a dissembler. Good God, you're human after all." Sliding down in bed, he pulled her into his arms. "But then, I know that, don't I?"

"I said I hate it when you're smug. I think you deserve knowing about Emma, your sainted great-great-great-*great*, not-so-great grandmother."

"Three greats please, I couldn't stand any more than that. And I don't like your using her name in vain. After all, you're no relation of hers."

"Thank goodness, and I brought with me a little article I'd like to show you, Ty."

"I never read in bed, only make love."

"And a marriage certificate." At his surprised smile, she amended, "An old one, going back to the end of the Civil War."

"Well, you have been a busy little dissembler, haven't you?" He said the words with no rancor, just curiosity.

"Emma married a Confederate soldier named Kurt Hoving. It's quite obvious she never divorced him. It was his child who was her first-born son."

Ty whistled. "Ah, you're a far better detective than I could ever be. How'd you find out?"

"Footwork. There's more. Your sainted Emma was a bigamist, I'm afraid."

"Wait a minute, hold on. I'll hear no disparaging words about my great-great-great-grandmother."

"Do you want the truth?"

"I'm not so sure, Sarah."

"I think you're going to get it anyway. You see Emma married Greg Crewes when she was pregnant with Kurt Hoving's child. Now Hoving *did* come back for her, but she was already on her way to Australia. It's all in the records in Herkimer County, at the town hall and in the newspaper files. I came across their marriage license in a serendipitous way. I brought it for you, Ty.''

"Don't sweet talk me, you Crewes, you. Bigamist, Emma Forrester *Hoving* Crewes? Where in hell did you get that notion?''

"It's in the record, unless you have proof otherwise. She married him and there's no evidence of a divorce or annulment. Would you like to learn about the real Emma or do you want to wallow in your notion of ancient injustices?''

"Given your bloodline and your own admission to being a first-rate liar, why should I believe anything you say?''

"You didn't do much of a job of raking through the *Times Herald*'s files,'' Sarah told him, ''but Adriana did. She found Emma's story, I didn't. I never came across it, incidentally, because Adriana had the microfiche in her possession and I wasn't even aware it was missing. Adriana wrote the article, I didn't.''

"Go ahead,'' he said resignedly. ''Tell me about Emma.''

Sarah drew up her knees and hugged them. ''She was a little bit of a thing, barely five feet tall. According to the one picture still on file at the newspaper, she had a sweet smile, charming dark eyes and a pretty figure.'' Sarah leaned back and examined Ty. ''Your eyes, I think. Not the color, but something about the slant.''

"Get on with it.''

"Right, of course. The sainted Emma, struggling to bring up a family a million miles from home, with no husband—whoops—husbands to help her.''

"Sarah.'' Ty grabbed her shoulders. ''I'm about to throttle you if you don't get on with it.''

"Emma was barely literate since she had been kicked out of every school her family sent her to. They finally engaged a private tutor for her, but she seduced him and his wife came after Emma with a hatchet. Is a picture beginning to form?''

''Nothing at all wrong with a youngster's high spirits,'' he told her. ''It helped her eventually to survive in a new and rugged country.''

''Spirits, of course,'' Sarah said. ''She was also fond of the bottle.'' She drew her arms around Ty's shoulders, her eyes dancing with humor. ''More?''

''I don't believe a word of it, but keep talking.''

''Being fond of the bottle propelled her into lots of trouble. She was rather insolent toward her fellow citizens and generally a cutup. The police, in fact, picked her up for pinching the watch of a gentleman she had invited up to her room. I think it's the corner bedroom at Riveredge, right wing, or is it the left wing, the one we used? I think that point requires a little research. Incidentally, the gentleman in question wasn't the first she had invited home. Of course that was when the general was away fighting the war, leading his troops to victory. He arrived back in time, however, to save her from a prison term, but that's what happens when you pay off county officials, isn't it?''

''I hate it when you're smug,'' he told her.

''Really.'' She regarded him with delight. ''More?''

''I'm sure I couldn't stop you if I wanted to.''

''As I said, she was a pretty little thing, and men adored her. I think it must have been the number of tattoos on her upper arm.''

Ty reached up and unlocked her arms from around his neck. ''Okay, that's enough. Out, woman, out of bed and out of my life.''

''Scout's honor, Ty.'' Sarah drew the sheet around her naked body. ''It's in the newspaper files.''

"Remind me to cancel my subscription to the *Times Herald.*"

"You don't have a subscription."

"Well then, this day won't end up all bad, will it?"

"More, dear Lassiter. Let's lay Emma to rest once and for all. After all, we won't want to bring up the subject again of that robbery in the mayor's house. Someone fingered Emma. Once again she was threatened with jail, and once again the general came to her rescue. The trouble was, Emma was pregnant at the time. The general clearly didn't know about the Confederate soldier who was his son-in-law. He married her off to my ne'er-do-well ancestor Greg Crewes, a drunk and a gambler, and shipped them off to Australia, where she promptly became the sainted Emma of history. Oh, one other thing. Apparently she also stole the family silver and some gold coins just before she left Riveredge forever. Undoubtedly used it to buy that spread you grew up on," she added with a smile. "And that, Tyler, is the end of the story."

"I'll be damned. So Emma never came back to America—"

"Because there was an outstanding warrant for her arrest. Darling Ty, Riveredge never belonged to my family. My ancestors, thinking she was the widow of Greg, and knowing she couldn't come back, decided to look after her property for her."

"For one hundred and twenty years?"

"We're nice people."

"Evidently. But why the confession now? Because I'm buying the Franklin place and might have stumbled on the truth?"

"Because I don't want you to stumble on the truth. I want you to know from my lips what I did and what my forebears did."

"And about Emma."

She reached for him and drew her arms around his neck once more. "No," she told him, her lips close to his. "I threw Emma in to make up for Nan. I was going to keep the peccadillos of that shady lady all to myself."

Their shared kiss had something chaste to it, as though the air had been cleared and they were starting afresh.

A LONG TIME LATER Sarah moved from the circle of his arms and left the bed. The sun was beginning its descent and the sky had a reddish cast that was reflected in the waters beneath. She watched a bird swoop low over the ocean and then glide up before swooping low again. She wrapped herself in Ty's terry robe and made her way into the kitchen.

She'd have to give him space and time for second thoughts about his claim to the big old house on the Hudson River. She had taken a chance with her confession but had done it willingly for love of the man. A small thrill chased through her. She hadn't run away for love of Ty Lassiter, she had run toward him.

The kitchen was large and airy with a white tile floor and wide screen doors that led out to the terrace. She could see another house in the distance and a ship on the horizon.

"Think you could live here?" Ty was in the doorway, a towel wrapped around his waist. His hair was mussed and sleep still seemed to edge his eyes.

"The offer still open?"

"Sure, but I want the terms changed."

"What now? I haven't asked anything of you."

"I'm doing the asking," he said.

"Are you reconsidering Riveredge?" she asked, taking in a deep breath.

"Among other things," he said.

"Okay, Lassiter, let's have it."

"I love you, you little fool, and I want you to marry me today or in the next five minutes, whichever comes first."

Her heart began to race and she felt a terrible panic well up. "You can't mean it."

"You don't think I'd trust you without a legal paper to tie you down, do you? Considering the larcenous line you descend from, that is."

"Your ancestor wasn't exactly the darling of the age, you know."

He came over to her with a quick stride. "Dare we have children? Well, perhaps it isn't a bad idea after all. We could raise our own little James gang, or we might even outdo the Daltons. Or have a girl and name her Bonnie—"

"Emma."

"And the boy Clyde."

"Yes," she said.

"Yes what?"

"Yes, I'll marry you. But where will we live?"

"Ever hear of a bicoastal arrangement?" He took her into his arms. "I've so much *pro bono* work in Merriman, I'll probably spend half my life there, anyway."

"And I was thinking of leaving the county records to someone else," Sarah said. "An archivist should act in a completely impersonal manner, and I let my imagination and my emotions run away with me."

"My little crook with a conscience. How admirable. Ah," he said, his face suddenly lighting up. "I almost forgot. Wait right there, don't move." He disappeared and returned almost at once bearing a flat box that he held out to her.

"For me?"

"For you."

"Wait a minute." She held the box up uncertainly and shook it. "How'd you know—?"

"Came express from Australia. Open it."

The box was tied with ribbon in a makeshift manner, as though Tyler had examined the contents and then impatiently tried to put it all back together. Still, Sarah was careful about undoing the ribbon. Inside she found a faded blue silk net shawl embroidered with silver threads. "Emma's," she whispered, drawing the shawl around her shoulders. "But, Ty, I don't understand."

"I told my mother it was time to deliver Emma's heirlooms to the next generation. Oh, and this." He held out a small blue velvet ring case.

"But."

"Just open it, Sarah, but no buts."

With trembling fingers she lifted the lid and discovered within a small yellow-gold and diamond cluster ring. Her eyes shone as she held it up. "Emma's, too."

"Of course."

"Passed on from one generation to the other, how wonderful." Holding the ring to the light, she squinted to see the inscription inside. "A.R.V. to O.L." She looked at Ty. "Emma's ring?"

He gave her an abashed smile, took the ring and slipped it on her finger. "Emma's. We always wondered about those initials."

"Oh darling, wonderful Ty, I love you so," she said, throwing her arms around him and offering her lips for a kiss.

"Ah, at last, the words." He kissed the tip of her nose. "And God help me, I believe them."

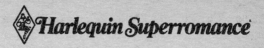

Harlequin Superromance

The elemental passions of *Spring Thunder*
come alive once again in the sequel....

SUMMER LIGHTNING

by

SANDRA JAMES

You enjoyed Maggie Howard's strong fiery nature
in *Spring Thunder*. Now she's back in *Summer
Lightning*, determined to fight against the resump-
tion of logging in her small Oregon town. McBride
Lumber has caused nothing but grief for her in the
past. But when Jared McBride returns to head the
operation, Maggie finds that her greatest struggle is
with her heart.

Summer Lightning is Maggie Howard's story of
love. Coming in April.

SR335-1

COMING IN MARCH FROM

Harlequin
Superromance

Book Two of the
Merriman County Trilogy
AFTER ALL THESE YEARS
the sizzle of Eve Gladstone's
One Hot Summer continues!

Sarah Crewes is at it again, throwing Merriman County
into a tailspin with her archival diggings. In *One Hot
Summer* (September 1988) she discovered that the town
of Ramsey Falls was celebrating its tricentennial one
year too early.

Now she's found that Riveredge, the Creweses'
ancestral home and property, does not rightfully belong
to her family. Worse, the legitimate heir to Riveredge
may be none other than the disquieting Australian,
Tyler Lassiter.

Sarah's not sure why Tyler's in town, but she suspects
he is out to right some old wrongs—and some new
ones!

The unforgettable characters of *One Hot Summer* and
After All These Years will continue to delight you in
book three of the trilogy. Watch for *Wouldn't It Be
Lovely* in November 1989.

SR349-1

You'll flip . . . your pages won't!
Read paperbacks *hands-free* with

Book Mate • I

The perfect "mate" for all your romance paperbacks

Traveling • Vacationing • At Work • In Bed • Studying • Cooking • Eating

Perfect size for all standard paperbacks, this wonderful invention makes reading a pure pleasure! Ingenious design holds paperback books OPEN and FLAT so even wind can't ruffle pages — leaves your hands free to do other things. Reinforced, wipe-clean vinyl-covered holder flexes to let you turn pages without undoing the strap . . . supports paperbacks so well, they have the strength of hardcovers!

Pages turn WITHOUT opening the strap.

SEE-THROUGH STRAP

Reinforced back stays flat.

Built in bookmark

BOOK MARK

BACK COVER HOLDING STRIP

10˝ x 7¼˝ opened.
Snaps closed for easy carrying, too.

Available now. Send your name, address, and zip code, along with a check or money order for just $5.95 + .75¢ for postage & handling (for a total of $6.70) payable to Reader Service to:

Reader Service
Bookmate Offer
901 Fuhrmann Blvd.
P.O. Box 1396
Buffalo, N.Y. 14269-1396

Offer not available in Canada
*New York and Iowa residents add appropriate sales tax.

BM-G

Harlequin
Superromance

COMING NEXT MONTH

#350 EDEN • Penny Richards
Eden Calloway was too much of a woman not to
crave a man, and too proudly female not to wait a
lifetime for the right one. When Nick Logan pulled
into her driveway on a motorcycle, he seemed the
least likely mate possible for Eden. But the heart has
reasons that are inexplicable, and love has a magic
that casts an unbreakable spell....

#351 ECHOES ON THE WIND • Tina Vasilos
In Greece to negotiate a deal, Joanna Paradises was
surprised to run into legal eagle Alex Gregory. As
teens in Vancouver, they'd shared adolescent kisses.
Now, years later, the possibilities were endless ... if
Joanna would allow Alex to breach her defenses.

#352 SUMMER LIGHTNING • Sandra James
Maggie Howard was furious when she discovered
that Jared McBride was back in Silver Creek,
preparing to reopen his family's logging business.
McBride Lumber had caused Maggie nothing but
grief in the past, and she was determined to stop
him. But when it came to fighting Jared, Maggie's
greatest struggle was with her heart....

#353 SPECIAL TREASURES • Sharon Brondos
When Colorado-based jeweler Maggie Wellington
teamed up with Aussie opal miner Mick O'Shay to
track down a killer, she wondered if she could get
along with a man whose ideas about justice were so
different from her own. But once in the outback she
began to understand the elemental passions that
drove Nick....

Harlequin Regency Romance™

Romance the way it was *always* meant to be!

The time is 1811, when a Regent Prince rules the empire. The place is London, the glittering capital where rakish dukes and dazzling debutantes scheme and flirt in a dangerously exciting game. Where marriage is the passport to wealth and power, yet every girl hopes secretly for love....

Welcome to Harlequin Regency Romance where reading is an adventure and romance is *not* just a thing of the past! Two delightful books a month, beginning May '89.

Available wherever Harlequin Books are sold.

REG-1